A Book Of

BUSINESS PLANNING

AND

PROJECT MANAGEMENT

For

BBA Semester - VI

As Per New Syllabus w.e.f. 2015

Vidya Bhagwat
B.E., M.B.A. (H.R.)
PMP Certified

NIRALI PRAKASHAN
ADVANCEMENT OF KNOWLEDGE

N3462

Business Planning and Project Management (BBA - VI) | **ISBN 978-93-5164-836-9**

Second Edition : January 2017

© : Author

Published By :

NIRALI PRAKASHAN

Abhyudaya Pragati, 1312, Shivaji Nagar,
Off J.M. Road, PUNE – 411005
Tel - (020) 25512336/37/39, Fax - (020) 25511379
Email : niralipune@pragationline.com

➤ DISTRIBUTION CENTRES

PUNE

Nirali Prakashan : 119, Budhwar Peth, Jogeshwari Mandir Lane, Pune 411002, Maharashtra
Tel : (020) 2445 2044, 66022708, Fax : (020) 2445 1538
Email : bookorder@pragationline.com, niralilocal@pragationline.com

Nirali Prakashan : S. No. 28/27, Dhyari, Near Pari Company, Pune 411041
Tel : (020) 24690204 Fax : (020) 24690316
Email : dhyari@pragationline.com, bookorder@pragationline.com

MUMBAI

Nirali Prakashan : 385, S.V.P. Road, Rasdhara Co-op. Hsg. Society Ltd.,
Girgaum, Mumbai 400004, Maharashtra
Tel : (022) 2385 6339 / 2386 9976, Fax : (022) 2386 9976
Email : niralimumbai@pragationline.com

➤ DISTRIBUTION BRANCHES

JALGAON

Nirali Prakashan : 34, V. V. Golani Market, Navi Peth, Jalgaon 425001,
Maharashtra, Tel : (0257) 222 0395, Mob : 94234 91860

KOLHAPUR

Nirali Prakashan : New Mahadvar Road, Kedar Plaza, 1st Floor Opp. IDBI Bank
Kolhapur 416 012, Maharashtra. Mob : 9850046155

NAGPUR

Pratibha Book Distributors : Above Maratha Mandir, Shop No. 3, First Floor,
Rani Jhanshi Square, Sitabuldi, Nagpur 440012, Maharashtra
Tel : (0712) 254 7129

DELHI

Nirali Prakashan : 4593/21, Basement, Aggarwal Lane 15, Ansari Road, Daryaganj
Near Times of India Building, New Delhi 110002 Mob : 08505972553

BENGALURU

Pragati Book House : House No. 1, Sanjeevappa Lane, Avenue Road Cross,
Opp. Rice Church, Bengaluru – 560002.
Tel : (080) 64513344, 64513355,Mob : 9880582331, 9845021552
Email:bharatsavla@yahoo.com

CHENNAI

Pragati Books : 9/1, Montieth Road, Behind Taas Mahal, Egmore,
Chennai 600008 Tamil Nadu, Tel : (044) 6518 3535,
Mob : 94440 01782 / 98450 21552 / 98805 82331,
Email : bharatsavla@yahoo.com

niralipune@pragationline.com | www.pragationline.com

Also find us on [f] www.facebook.com/niralibooks

Acknowledgements

A million thanks to my parents, specially my mother, who has been my inspiration and support, to my teachers whose guidance and blessings have made this task possible. I thank all people who have uploaded project management information on the internet and made it freely available and in easy to use formats. My special thanks to Prof. Abhijeet Kulkarni for his support. I am grateful to my publishers, Shri. Dinesh Furia and Shri. Jignesh Furia for giving me the opportunity to write this book. I acknowledge Ms. Narjis, for her persistence without which the completion of this book would have not been possible. I am also thankful to Mr. Akbar Shaikh and Ms. Chaitali for all their assistance. Last but not the least, I thank all those who have directly or indirectly facilitated the publishing of this book.

Preface ...

After conducting several trainings on project management and also gaining hands-on experience while working on several projects for the past 15 years, every effort has been made to correlate my experience with the syllabus prescribed by the university.

Project management techniques that are practically used in day to day functions has been the major focus along with keeping the students in mind. The book has been oriented to provide information in notes format, in a sequence prescribed by the syllabus that will serve as a ready reckoner in very simple language. Most of the references are taken from PMBOK® and have been extensively used to give a clear understanding on the subject matter as recognised internationally. The glossary of the terms used in project management (nationally and internationally) specified by PMBOK® are provided at the end of this book to give more clarity.

I am very grateful to Shri. Dinesh bhai Furia, Shri. Jigneshbhai Furia, our publishers, for providing us with this opportunity and the entire staff of Nirali Prakashan for their support. A special word of appreciation for Supriya Singh and Ms. Narjis, who has been instrumental in getting this book to the stands. We would also like to express our thanks to Mr. Akbar Shaikh for his co-operation.

I shall consider our hard work amply rewarded if this book is appreciated by those for whom it is meant. We extend all our good wishes to the students, teachers, and readers whose valuable and constructive suggestions would be welcome to improve this book.

Vidya Bhagwat

Syllabus ...

1. Planning

1.1 Introduction, Meaning, Definition, Characteristics, Objective, Nature of Planning.

1.2 Advantages and Limitations of Planning.

1.3 Steps in Planning Process.

1.4 Methods of Planning.

1.5 Essentials of a Good Planning.

1.6 Obstacles in Planning, Planning Premises and Classification of Planning Premises.

1.7 Plan and Planning, Business Planning.

Planning and Forecasting

1.8 Introduction, Meaning, Definition, Characteristics, Process.

1.9 Importance of Forecasting.

1.10 Areas of Forecasting.

1.11 Forecasting Techniques : Types, Methods.

1.12 Advantages of Forecasting, Limitations of Forecasting.

1.13 Difference between Forecasting and Planning.

2. Project Management

2.1 Definition of a "Project".

2.2 Why Project Management, The Project Life-Cycle, Project Management Maturity.

2.3 Project Selection and Criteria of Choice.

2.4 The Nature of Project Selection Models, Types of Project Selection Models.

2.5 Project Portfolio Process, Project Proposals.

2.6 The Project Manager: Qualities, Project Management and the Project Manager, Special Demands on the Project Manager.

2.7 Problems of Cultural Differences, Impact of Institutional Environments, Project Organisation.

2.8 The Project as Part of Functional Organisation, Pure Project Organisation, The Matrix organisation.

2.9 Choosing an Organisational form.

2.10 The Project Team.

3. Initial Project Co-ordination

3.1 The Nature of Negotiation, Partnering, Chartering and Change, Conflict and the Project life Cycle.

3.2 Estimating Project Budgets, Improving the Process of Cost Estimation.

4. Network Techniques

4.1 PERT and CPM.

4.2 Risk Analysis Using Simulation with Crystal Ball 2000.

4.3 Critical Path Method: Crashing a Project, The Resource Allocation Problem, Resource Loading, Resource Leveling, Constrained Resource Allocation.

4.4 The Planning –Monitoring – Controlling Cycle, Information Needs and the Reporting Process, Earned Value Analysis.

4.5 The Fundamental Purposes of Control, Three Types of Control Processes, Comments on the Design of Control Systems, Control as a Function of Management.

5. Purposes of Evaluation

5.1 Goals of the System.

5.2 The Project Audit, Construction and use of Audit Report, The Project Audit Life Cycle, Some essentials of an Audit / Evolution.

5.3 The Varieties of Project Termination, When to Terminate a Project, The Termination Process.

Contents ...

Chapter 1 ...

Planning

Contents ...

Learning Objectives ...

- To Understand the Meaning, Advantages and Limitations of Planning
- To Explain the Methods of Planning
- To Discuss the Essentials of Good Planning
- To Describe the Meaning of Forecasting
- To Learn the Forecasting Types and Methods
- To Elaborate Advantages and Limitations of Forecasting
- To Differentiate between Forecasting and Planning

1.1 Planning

1.1.1 Introduction

For completion of tasks or to achieve an objective, one can start working randomly in a haphazard manner. However, when tasks are completed in such a manner, there is no assurance that it would be completed on time, within budget, and with expected qualitative outcome. Also, there is no clarity on how many people should be working on the tasks and if there exists any dependencies. There is no preparation of contingencies or alternatives. Such methods of working generally result in high stress and substandard outcome.

Planning is, when we systematically decide the procedure to accomplish best outcomes prior to working on a specific task. It includes factors like what needs to be done, how it needs to be done, what is the quality standard that needs to be maintained, when and in what duration it should be achieved, the costs (direct or indirect cost) involved for the completion of a specific task, how many people would be involved, what are the dependencies, what are the limitations and alternative method to be adapted, etc.

Let's take an example, say, you decide to go on a tour and just set out. In this situation you do not know where to go, how to go, what you will do when you reach your destination and how and when you will return. Instead, if you decide and plan an outing considering factors like date, location, stay, sightseeing, expenditure, etc. then it would be known as a planned approach to achieve a goal.

To a better understanding of planning we have some quotes from great people –

Dr. Steven Covey, *one of the management gurus has stated in his book "7 Habits of Highly Effective People", he quotes one of the habits as "Begin with end in mind".*

"We must plan for the future, because people who stay in the present will remain in the past."

Abraham Lincoln – *"Failing to plan is planning to fail. You can always change your plan, but only after you have one!"*

1.1.2 Meaning

Planning is the primary function of management. It is an intellectual process of thinking resorted to decide a course of action that helps achieve a predetermined objective/s. F. W. Taylor had pointed out in his report on Scientific Management, that planning is separated from execution. Separate plans are prepared for various business units and then the top executive combines them at various department levels. Planning is deciding beforehand what has to be done, when, where, how, and by whom it has to be executed. It serves as a link from where we are to where we want to go. Planning consists of selecting objectives, policies, procedures, and programmes from chosen alternatives. It is a course of action for achieving a specific goal. It is an intellectual process characterised by thinking before doing.

In short, planning is a process for determining if the task has to be attempted, for working out the most effective way of reaching goals, and preparing to overcome unexpected complications with sufficient resources. Planning serves as a beginning process of a business by which ideas are turned into achievements. It helps you to avoid the trap of working extremely hard but achieving little or nothing.

1.1.3 Definition

There are multiple definitions for planning:

- "Bridging the gap from where we are to where we want to go"
- **Terry** states "Planning is selecting and relating of facts and making and using assumptions regarding the future in the visualisation and formulation of proposed activities believed necessary to achieve desired results."
- **H. Fayol** states "Planning is deciding best alternatives among others to perform different managerial operations in order to achieve the pre-determined goals."
- **Peter F. Drucker** defines planning as "Planning is a continues process of making present entrepreneurial (risk taking) decisions systematically and with best possible knowledge of their futurity, organising systematically the efforts needed to carry out these decisions and measuring the results of these decisions against the expectations through organised, systematic feedback."
- According to **Koontz and O'Donnell**, "Planning is deciding in advance what to do, how to do it, when to do it, and who is to do it".
- According to **Haimann**, "Planning is deciding in advance what is to be done".
- According to **M. E. Harley**, "Planning is deciding in advance what is to be done. It involves the selection of objectives, policies, procedures and programmes from among alternatives".
- According to **Billy E. Goetz**, "Planning is fundamentally choosing and a planning problem arises only when alternative course of action is discovered".

The above mentioned definitions tell us that planning involves choosing and its chief objective is to anticipate the future course of events and give it a desired direction. In reality planning becomes necessary when there are many alternatives to choose from.

1.1.4 Objectives of Planning

Planning in any organisation serves to realise the following objectives:

1. **Create a vision or a roadmap:** Planning gives a clear understanding of what is to be achieved and how it is to be achieved. It caters to all aspects involved for completing a specific task.

2. **Reduces ambiguity:** A complex task generally entails multiple resources, both, human as well as material and a huge amount of communication is needed for co-ordinating the resources. As a result, there is a probability of misunderstandings or gaps in expected results. Planning provides an awareness of such vagueness or ambiguity and facilitates the overcoming of such uncertainties.

3. **Builds better interpersonal relations:** Planning can bring co-operation and co-ordination among various sections of the organisation. The conflicts among different departments can be avoided by providing greater clarity and through proper planning. It also helps avoid duplication of work.

4. **Cost effective:** Since planning aids selecting the best alternative among the various available alternatives, it leads to best utilisation of resources. Thus, planning can prevent unnecessary expenditure that might incur proving better utilisation of resources to be cost effective.

5. **Anticipates unpredictable contingencies:** Some events could not be predicted. Such events are termed as contingencies. These events may affect the smooth functioning of an enterprise. Planning provides provision to meet such contingencies and tackle them successfully.

6. **Achieving the pre-determined goal:** Planning activities are aimed at achieving the objectives of the enterprise. Timely and qualitative achievement of objectives is possible only through effective planning.

7. **Reduce competition:** The existence of competition enables an enterprise to grow. Since it is highly impossible to avoid competition, planning could provide a better awareness and preparedness to face such competitions.

1.1.5 Nature or Characteristics of Planning

Planning is a logical and realistic act mixed with a little precaution. It is seen all over. In a business, planning is the most important factor of all the managerial functions as it involves deciding of future course of action. Thus, planning logically leads the execution of all managerial functions. Planning is the procedure of deciding in advance what is to be done, where, how, and by whom it is to be done. Planning as a process entails anticipation of future course of events and deciding the best course of action. On the whole, it is a process of 'thinking before doing'. All these elements speak about the futurity of an action. There are a number of ways available to complete a specific task. Planning helps to identify and select the best way. Time, quality, and cost are considered while selecting the best alternative.

The characteristic or nature of planning can be understood with the help of the following points:

1. **Primary Requirement:** The most important function of management like any other functions such as organising, staffing, preparing projections, directing, controlling, etc. is planning, the reason being the manager who wants to achieve pre-determined goals and set an action path.

2. **Planning contributes to objectives:** It provides clear vision for the steps required to be taken, the sequence of the action and the execution of the steps according to its priority/need. For example, while constructing a building, the upper floors cannot be constructed even before the foundation is completed. Hence, such tasks are to be completed in a sequence; however, marketing and sales activities can be started simultaneously. Therefore planning is the key to achieve a goal.

3. **Planning is an intellectual activity:** Planning helps in selecting the best alternatives. It involves the knack to foresee mishaps that might occur in future affecting the smooth functioning. Therefore, planning is an intellectual activity. In real projects, this forms an integral part of quality and risk management.

4. **Planning increases efficiency:** Planning efficiency is measured in terms of input to output ratios. Planning leads to maximum output with minimum expenditure. This relationship is mainly dependent on money, labour hours, and production units. They are also influenced by the degree of satisfaction for an individual or a group. Motivation of different kinds facilitates workers to produce more within the specified time.

5. **Planning is a continuous process:** Planning does not come to an end with establishment of business concern. With new challenges and market competitions, planning is required. Planning is necessary to implement decisions taken during the functioning of business activities. Hence, planning is an integral part of business process and is required continuously.

6. **Planning provides flexibility:** Planning selects the best alternative available based on assumptions; if the assumption is incorrect or tends to go wrong, it directly affects the selected alternative outcomes. This may lead to dead logs in the management functions. Thus, planning process caters to preparation of alternative plans to allow flexibility.

7. **Unity and consistency:** Planning is related to achievement of objectives. In order to achieve organisation's goal, managerial actions of different business unit heads try to bring in unified management process and procedures. Policies and procedures of the organisation provide the basis for the consistency of executive behaviour and action in matters of planning.

8. **Planning is generic:** In order to accomplish the desired outcomes, planning is done at every level. It forms the basis to all professional and business functions.

9. **Planning serves better co-ordination:** Planning co-ordinates various business activities in an orderly and timely manner.

10. **Understanding of limiting factors:** Almost all plans will contain information on the limiting factors. These can be money, skilled labour, quality materials, and machinery.

Apart from the above-mentioned characteristics, the following can be the other characteristics for planning in business management:

1. Planning is looking into the future.

2. Planning involves predetermined line of action.

3. Planning discovers the best alternative out of the many available alternatives.

4. Planning reduces time during implementation.

5. Planning helps to reduce cost.

6. Planning's object is to achieve predetermined objectives in a better way. It helps to be ready for the short comings or changes that might creep in.

7. Planning integrates various activities of organisation.

8. Planning not only selects the objectives but also develops policies, programs and procedures to achieve the objectives.

9. Planning is required at all levels of management.

10. Planning reduces stress and helps achieve quality outcome.

11. Planning directs the members of the organisation.

12. Growth and prosperity of any organisation depends upon planning.

1.1.6 Advantages of Planning

By using the planning process effectively you can get the following advantages –

1. **Achieving goals:** Planning sets goals or objectives. It gives a road map of where to go, when to go and how to reach the goal. It also helps in planning for the alternatives. Planning helps the organisation to accomplish pre-determined goals or objectives.

2. **Reduces efforts:** Large amount of time on activities that are irrelevant to the success of the business can be avoided by proper planning. Alternatively you can miss deadlines by not assessing the order in which dependent jobs should be carried out. Planning helps you to achieve the maximum effect from a given effort.

3. **Focuses on critical issues:** When we plan we can take into account all the pros and cons and focus on critical issues.

4. **Risk identification:** You can identify the amount of risk and prepare for overcoming changes. This also makes you prepared for the consequences in case of failure of the plan and take timely action to ensure that they will be successful.

5. **Resource availability:** This ensures that at the critical stage sufficient and efficient resources are available on time. Planning decides what to produce and how to produce. Then, there is the possibility of utilising the resources effectively.

6. **Carry out the task in the most efficient way,** so that you save on your resources and avoid wasting ecological resources, make a fair profit.

7. **Economy in operations:** Unnecessary production, ineffective utilisation of resources and unnecessary activities of an organisation are eliminated through planning. This results in the economy of operations.

8. **Preparedness for uncertainties:** The uncertain future increases the importance of planning. Planning foresees the changes and uncertainties taking shape in future and devices methods to face them. Some future uncertainties are thus minimised through planning.

9. **Improves competitive strength:** Competitive strength is improved by adding new line of products, changes in quality and size of the product, expansion of plant capacity and changes in methods of work. These are achieved through planning.

10. **Effective control:** Control without planning is an impossible one. Control is used only when there is well chalked out plan. So, planning provides a basis for controlling.

11. **Motivation:** A well prepared plan encourages the employees of an organisation and gives them a sense of effective participation. Planning motivates the employees to achieve organisation's goals and defines a path to achieve it.

12. **Co-operation:** Planning helps management pull individuals to achieve common objectives or goals. Planning provides well defined objectives, unity of direction, well published policies, procedures, and programs. All these aid in co-ordination, which consequently avoids duplication of work and interdepartmental conflicts.

13. **Promote growth and improvement:** Unwanted and aimless activities are avoided through planning. It leads to the growth and improvement of an individual and the organisation.

14. **Develops rationality among management executives:** Disciplined thinking of management executives is geared up through formal planning. Management executives take action only after putting their thoughts in blueprint. In this way, planning brings rational thinking and approach among management executives.

15. **Prevents hasty judgement:** We can analyse the problem through a plan and consider the alternatives before taking a sound decision. It is possible to plan in advance as to what will be done and how it will be done. This process avoids hasty judgement.

16. **Reduces red-tapism:** The junior most executive can act according to pre-planned decisions. There is no need for him to take any fresh permission for his action. It saves time, energy and cost and reduces red-tapism.

17. **Encourages innovative thoughts:** A good plan should provide a basis for new thinking in an individual. It seeks out ways to encourage people to co-ordinate and to achieve common objectives. According to D. E. Hussey, "A good planning process will provide avenues for individual participation, will throw up more ideas about the company and its environment, will encourage an atmosphere of frankness, co-operation, self-criticism and will stimulate managers to achieve more.

18. **Improves ability to handle change:** Planning helps managers improve their ability to cope with changes but it cannot prevent changes from happening. This creates awareness among the managers regarding the incidence of change.

19. **Creates positive attitude in management:** Planning helps a manager create positive working attitude, ensuring stability in management.

20. **Delegation of authority:** A well-prepared plan will always facilitate delegation of authority.

1.1.7 Disadvantages of Planning

The limitations of planning can be stated as below –

1. **Occurrence of change:** Occurrence of change is inevitable and its impact may be at times devastating. However, predicting changes and incorporating its alternatives in the plan is a relatively difficult task and poses limitation to planning.

2. **Inflexibility:** The more detailed and widespread the plans, the greater inflexibility they have.

3. **Limitation of forecast:** Planning is fully based on forecast. If there is any defect in forecast, the planning will lose its value.

4. **Unsuitability:** In planning, objectives, policies, procedures, etc. are set after careful investigation of all the relevant factors. Since business continuously faces new opportunities and challenges, there is a constant need for upgradation of such framed objectives and policies in the light of latest opportunities and challenges.

5. **Time consuming:** The management cannot prepare any plan simply. It collects varied information and holds discussion with others. So, planning is a time-consuming process.

6. **Costly:** Planning is preceded with collection of necessary information, careful analysis and interpretation of various courses of action, selection of the best plan among them. This work cannot be completed without incurring any expenses. So, the process of planning is a costly one.

7. **False sense of security:** Future is uncertain. The management people think that there is security, if planning is properly adhered to. This difficulty makes the management have a false sense of security.

8. **Delay during emergency period:** Planning does not give any benefits to an organisation during the emergency period. Although, provisions can be made for emergency period.

9. **Capital investment:** If sizeable amounts are invested in fixed assets, the ability to change future course of action will be limited and planning will become precise.

10. **Political climate:** Government can change its attitudes according to the changes of the political climate. Taxation policy, regulations of business and finances through financial institutions are generating constraints on the organisational planning process.

11. **Trade unions:** The freedom of planning is restricted through the organisation of trade unions at the national level. Trade unions can interfere in the management activities on work rule, fixation of wages, productivity and associated benefits. Hence, managers are not free to take decisions in this area to some extent.

12. **Technological changes:** When there is a change in technology, the management has to face a number of problems. The problems may be high cost of production, competition in the market etc. Management is not in a position to change its policies according to technological changes. It will affect the planning.

1.1.8 Steps in Planning Process

Planning is best thought of as a cycle, not a straight-through process. Once a plan has been formulated it should be evaluated. This evaluation may be cost or number-based or may use other analytical tools. This analysis may show that the plan specified may cause unwanted consequences, may cost too much or may simply not work. In this case, the planning process will have to cycle back to an earlier stage or the plan may have to be abandoned altogether – the outcome of your planning may simply be that it is best to do nothing. After a plan is ready you need to assess the plan, and check how to improve the execution. The following points help in classifying –

1. **Analysis of external environment:** It is necessary to consider the external environment of an organisation. The term external environment includes socio-economic conditions and the political conditions prevailing in a country. Socio-economic condition refers to classification of society on the basis of income, age, class, living conditions, aspirations, expectations etc. These factors are not controllable. But, every organisation has to prepare the plan according to the changing trends in the external environment.

2. **Analysis of internal environment:** It is also known are resource audit. It gives an analysis of the strengths and weaknesses of the organisation.

3. **Determination of objectives:** The objectives of the organisation are pre-planned. Control process is very easy if the objectives are clearly defined.

4. **Determining planning premises and constraints:** Planning is based on forecasting. Forecasting means the assumption of and the anticipation of certain events. It implies a calculation of how certain factors will behave in future. The planning must consider the likely behaviour of these factors. In this sense, these constitute the planning premises.

   Generally, forecasting is made in the following ways:

   (a) What will be the market force? Market force refers to demand, supply, buying capacity etc.

   (b) The expectation of volume of sales.

   (c) What kind of products are to be sold and at what price?

   (d) What would be their manufacturing cost?

   (e) What would be the tax policy and economic policy of the government?

   (f) The expectation of technology change in production.

   (g) How is the finance raised for expansion and or modernisation of the business?

5. **Examination of alternative course of action:** Management should find alternative ways to examine them in light of planning premises.

6. **Weighing alternative course of action:** All alternatives are not suitable. Each alternative has its own positive or negative point. Hence, it is essential to weigh all the alternatives before selecting a course of action. A course of action is determined according to the prevailing circumstances. No partiality is shown while selecting an alternative.

7. **Establishing a sequence of activities:** In order to follow the determined course of action, the manager needs to draft a final plan in definite terms.

8. **Formulation of action programs:** The term action program includes fixing time limit for performance, allocation of work to individuals and work schedule. These are necessary to achieve the objectives within the specified period.

9. **Determining contingency plans:** The preparation of secondary or contingency plan is essential to expedite the achievement of the basic plan. Secondary plans are also prepared in lieu of the activities to be followed from the main plan.

10. **Securing participation of employees:** The successful execution of any plan depends upon the extent of participation of employees. So, management should involve them through communication, consultation, and participation.

11. **Follow-up and evaluation**: There should be a system of follow-up. The management should keep a check if planning is being executed. The shortcomings of planning can

be identified through a follow-up action and rectified then and there. The continuous evaluation of planning is also necessary. It means that the actual performance is compared with the planning and then corrective action is taken if there is any deviation.

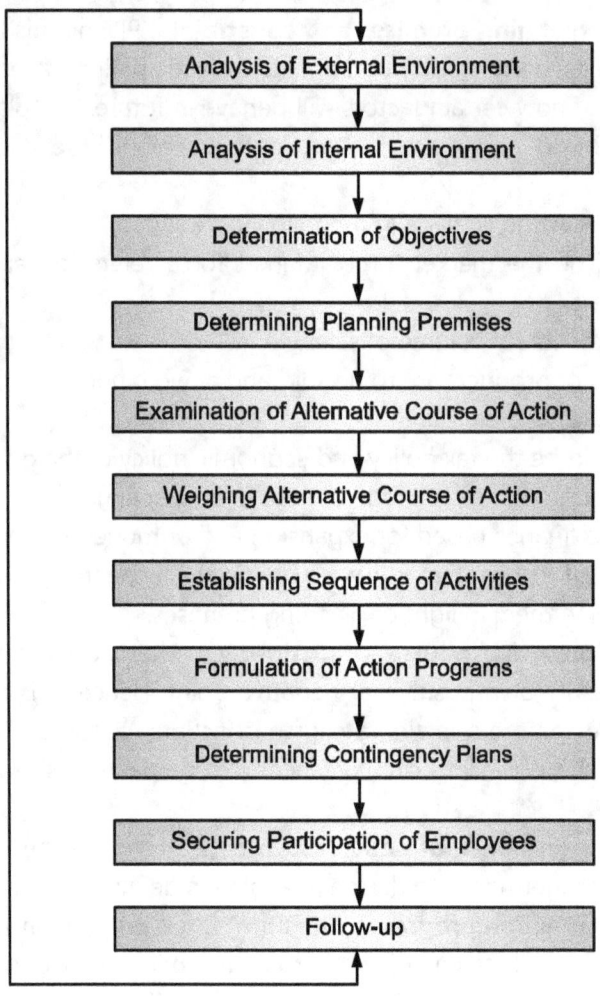

Fig. 1.1

1.1.9 Methods of Planning

According to the usage and nature of planning, the methods of planning are divided into the following categories –

1. **Objective plans:** Objectives are treated as basic plans. These basic plans are necessary for all types of planning operations. Objectives not only dominate the planning activity but also play an important role in the managerial work of organising, directing and controlling.

2. **Standing plans:** Standing plans include policies and procedures and they are liable to repetitive action. An action may be divided into two categories, that is, repetitive and non-repetitive actions. Standing plans provide a ready guideline for solving recurring problems. Special problems are not solved with the help of standing plans, but solved in a different way.

3. **Master plans:** Master plan covers the complete course of action along with the consideration of time and strategy. Small plans are added together in an orderly way to speed-up the course of action. If the plans are prepared function-wise, plans may be concerned with production, sales, purchase etc.

1.1.10 Essentials of Good Planning

Every business begins with an idea, but, a plan is essential to understand the full scope and complexity of managing a business. In addition, most businesses require funding from investors; and to get them, a detailed business plan is needed. An effective business plan is essential to obtain funding and to direct a business start-up. At the same time, one needs to develop an internal business plan to guide the day-to-day operations. Everything from structuring the management team to marketing is an essential mechanism of an effective organisational plan. In order to make an effective plan the following points should be considered –

1. Linked to long-term objectives.
2. Keep consistency as the plan flow progresses.
3. Communicate – to explore new ideas as well as check the clear understanding of the plan.
4. Involve people affected by the plan to gain their support. Take efforts to check everyone participates.
5. Feasibility and purpose - Explain why the plan is being carried out. Sell and resell the benefits to everyone involved. Also allow the changes to be incorporated so that the risks are minimised.
6. Ensure that the required resources are available and remain available.
7. As far as possible keep to existing ways of doing things. This avoids unnecessary disruption.
8. Build in milestones and review progress. This helps in controlling the project and taking timely decisions to avoid failures to the business plan and allows achievement to be rewarded.
9. Use KISS (Keep It Simple and Straightforward).
10. Try to gain support and involve top management in the process.

11. Have a clear aim.

12. Reflect the resources available.

13. Detail the tasks to be carried out, whose responsibility they are, their priorities and deadlines.

14. Explain control mechanisms that will alert the manager to difficulties in achieving the plan.

15. Plan for contingencies, so that a rapid and effective response may be made to crises, perhaps at a time when you are at low ebb or are confused following a set-back.

16. Keep in mind the traditions and cultures to be followed – how will you keep things going while you implement the plan?

1.1.11 Obstacles in Planning

Planning may face difficulties or obstacles during the planning process. Let us first analyse the hindrance in planning –

1. Organisational Problems

- **Poor reward structures:** Lack of motivation or political issues within the organisation result in not showing the management what needs to be done at the micro level.

- **Fire-fighting:** An organisation can be so deeply involved in crisis management and fire-fighting that it simply does not have the time to plan.

- **The 'get stuck in' culture:** An organisation may oppose planning as a waste of time. This may be the case where either the organisation is doing a very simple job, or where managers are so experienced in a job that they do not appreciate planning. The approach cripples inexperienced staff by denying them the benefits of planning, and puts more load on experienced managers.

- **Opposition to time and expense of planning:** Time spent on planning is an investment.

- **Unreliability of forecast:** Future has uncertainty. Therefore, the probable events cannot be ascertained accurately. So, the degree of unreliability is increased correspondingly with the long-term planning.

- **Recurrence of same type of problems:** The nature of problems is changed with the passage of time. Some problems may be postponed and appear after a lapse of time. So, there is a need for maintaining standing plans. It increases the workload of the managerial personnel.

- **Expensive:** Planning involves some expenses. The expenses may be borne by the small business unit. The available planning benefits should be more than the expenses incurred. But this is not possible for a small business unit and expensive to a big business unit if the business unit fails to adhere to the planning after preparing it.

2. **Individual Avoidance of Planning**

- **Laziness:** People may simply not be bothered to devote time on thinking about a plan.
- **Lack of Commitment and Resistance to Change:** The individuals may feel that if they submit their plans they are giving written commitment that may jeopardise their actions or may perceive things are okay as they stand.
- **Fear of Failure:** Whenever something worthwhile is attempted there is some risk of failure.
- **Experience:** As individuals amass experience they may find that they rely less and less on formalised planning. It is easy, however, to be overconfident and overestimate experience that may result in failure of the business or the project.
- **Poor Experience of Planning:** People may have had a previous bad experience with planning, where plans have been long, cumbersome, impractical or inflexible.
- **Loss of Initiative:** Every person has some idea of his own. These ideas cannot be materialised and suppressed due to pre-planned programs. Some firms have suggestion boxes, but the weightage is not given to the suggestions offered because planning sets some standards and the work should be carried accordingly.

1.2 Planning Premises

1.2.1 Meaning

Planning is generally based on premises. Planning premises is the foundation or base of planning. Planning premises are planning conditions in which planning activities can be carried out. Planning premise is also known as planning assumptions. They usually refer to the estimates or projections of the upcoming occurrence of events.

Basically, planning premises are assumptions about the environment. These assumptions are important to make plans more reasonable and operational. Planning premises present a framework within which all plans are made. Many environmental factors influence the plan. Assumptions are made about these factors. These assumptions are called premises. In short, premises are the assumptions of the future environment on which plans are to be carried out. Premises are anticipated environment. It is to predict sales volume, cost, political and legal environment, technological change, availability of labour. Premises are important because they give important information about the future to managers. Establishment of premises is an important step in planning. Premises are the forecast of future expectations about – demographic trend, future economic business condition, forecast about political and legal aspects of the country, technological change and innovations, resource availability, socio-cultural forces.

If planning premises are changed, planning will have to be modified accordingly. Therefore, correct assessment of planning premises is the most significant step in managerial planning. The factors and forces which have material impact on business environment are to be concentrated in much and ignore the process and factors which affect the business environment to a lesser extent. The recognition of affecting forces and factors guides the management executives to select the proper and perfect planning premises upon which they may raise the superstructure of planning. The main purpose of planning premises is to facilitate the planning process by guiding, directing, simplifying and reducing the degree of uncertainties in it. Hence, developing sound premises is very important for successful planning.

1.2.2 Classification of Planning Premises

There are different factors or premises that affect directly or indirectly planning and result in decision-making for the organisation. Some of these factors are –

1. **Internal and External Factors:** Internal factors are the ones that exist within a business unit. Examples are human resources, material resources, machine resources, financial resources and methods which are some of the kinds of internal premises. The most important internal premises are competence of managerial personnel and skill of labour force. The external factors are economic, technological, political, social conditions and market conditions which are some of the kinds of external premises or factors. Economic premise refer to purchasing power of the customers, technological premise refers to application of latest technology, political premise refers to policy of the governments, social conditions refer to culture and market condition refers to demand and supply forces for the product or service.

2. **Tangible and Intangible Factors:** Quantified factors can be termed as tangible premises whereas qualitative factors are termed as intangible premises.

   Money, time and units of production are some types of tangible premises. Money can be quantified as rupees, time can be quantified as seconds, minutes and or hours and units of production can be quantified as kilograms, horse power etc. Examples of intangible factors are goodwill of the company, loyalty of the employees, public relations, employee's morals and motivation etc. Both tangible and intangible planning premises must be taken into account in planning.

3. **Controllable and Uncontrollable Premises:** Factors that are entirely within the control and realm of management are known as controllable premises. For example, policies, methods, procedures, systems, programmers, rules and regulations etc. Whereas, uncontrollable factors, that is, factors that are not within the purview of management are known as uncontrollable premises. Besides, these types of premises cannot be predictable. Uncontrollable factors impact to a very large extent hence should be taken into account and contingency plans to be kept ready for such type of disaster, while framing a plan. War, natural calamities, new discoveries and inventions and human behaviour are some of the kinds of uncontrollable premises.

4. **Semi-controllable Premises:** Some factors can be predicted and are controllable to some extent and are known as semi-controllable premises. In other words, the management has partial control on some factors that are known as semi-controllable premises. For example, trade union and management relations, employer and employee relations, superior and subordinate relations, inter-department relations, supply position in market etc.

5. **Constant and Variable Premises:** Some premises are not changed irrespective of action taken by the management. They are definite, known and well understood. Hence, the management need not consider these types of premises. For example, available skill, machines and finance are some of the kinds of fixed or constant premises. Variable premises may be changed in relation to the course of action taken by the management. These premises have a significant bearing on the success of the plan. Hence, the management should consider these premises with due importance while formulating plans. For example, sales volume and production expenses are some of the kinds of variable premises.

1.3 Plan and Planning, Business Planning

Plan

Plan can be defined as a set of actions that have been thought of as a way to do or achieve something. It can also be defined as something that a person intends to do. Preparing a step by step approach and methodology for initiating, executing and controlling activities is called as plan. The idea behind making a plan is to enable a more defined picture of potential costs and drawbacks to certain business decisions and to help them modify accordingly before implementing these ideas.

Planning

Planning is the process of identifying the steps to create a plan. The process of planning includes the determination of objectives and outlining the future actions that are needed to achieve these objectives. Planning is the function of management that involves setting objectives and determining a course of action for achieving those objectives. Planning requires that managers be aware of environmental conditions facing their organisation and forecast future conditions. It also requires that managers be good decision makers. Planning is a process consisting of several steps.

Business Plan

A business plan is a plan that predetermines what the business proposes to accomplish and how it intends realising its goals. Planning is the starting point of the management process. There are several levels of this plan; however, it always starts from top management and the plan is called strategic plan. It contains a description of the vision to be achieved and the path to be followed, that is, to set the mission and the desired outcomes within the specific time frame. Planning is required at different levels such as –

- Strategic Business Unit (SBU) Level
- Corporate Level
- Functional or Department Level
- Team or Work Group Level
- Individual Level

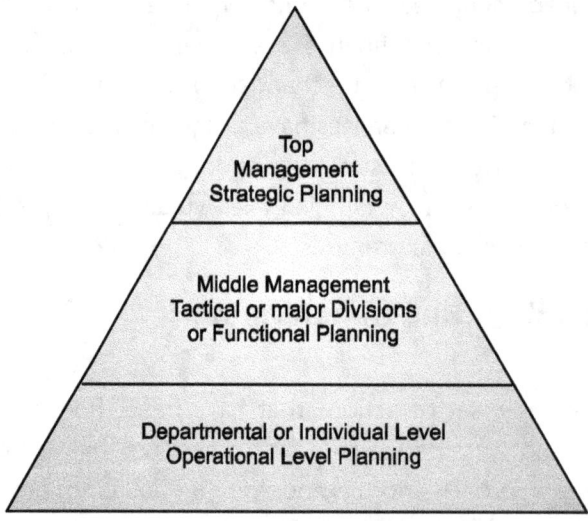

Fig 1.2: Levels of Planning

One must keep in mind the following while making a business plan –

Identify Critical Business Information by using key questions such as:

1. What does your global competitive environment look like?

2. In the last 3 years, what have your competitors done?

3. In the same period, what have you done to them?

4. How might they attack you in the future?

5. What are your plans to leapfrog them?

The next step based on above shall be to –

- **Gather Evidence/Statistical Information:** Combine all the information or the data gathered and put them in a logical order.

- **Prepare Outline:** List the manageable steps required in order of priority along with the details from your obstacles list and help list.

- **Make a List of Keyword Reminders and Conversational Flow:** Get a large sketch pad and play around with the order of things until the plan begins to flow.

- **Flexibility:** Make sure your plan is not too rigid. The plan should have flexibility to accommodate the unexpected changes that may creep in and also if one deadline is missed it should not jeopardise the rest of the plan, that is, prepare contingency plans in advance.

- Keep your customers' need in mind while preparing the entire plan.

A typical business plan normally should contain the following information –

- **Financial Planning:** Looking at sources of finance, forecasts of cash flow, sales, costs and so on.

- **Marketing:** Looking at ways in which the marketing of the venture will be carried out. This requires market analysis, market positioning, market objectives, that is, market share, consumer focus, product focus, brand image, competition, social responsibility etc.

- **Legal Framework:** Ensuring that all the legal requirements of setting up a new venture or existing product or services are adhered to and considered.

- **Operational Planning:** Looking at the nitty-gritty of everyday production issues – securing supplies, hiring staff, deciding on production methods and so on.

- **Self-Development Planning:** Skills required for self development, organisation maturity and processes etc.

- **Networking:** Who do you need to know and how do you get to know them to ensure your business takes off?

For a start-up business a business plan should necessarily contain the following information

A business plan consists of some descriptive financial worksheets. This descriptive template is the main element of the business plan. It includes questions categorised into several sections. Writing *Executive Summary is mandatory*, which should be done last. Skipping questions that do not relate to the business can be done. This forms the first draft of the business plan.

The actual value of creating a business plan is not in having the completed final product in hand; rather, true value lies in the process of researching and thinking about your business in an organised manner. Planning helps you to assume things through study and research if one is unsure of the facts and ideas. It helps in considering the pros and cons. Though it is time consuming initially, avoiding it becomes costly; perhaps leading to disastrous mistakes afterwards.

This business plan is a generic model appropriate for all types of businesses. However, one should modify it to suit their specific requirements of the business. Before beginning, review the section titled "refining the plan", which is at the end. It implies emphasising certain areas depending upon your type of business (manufacturing, retail, service, etc.). It also suggests tips for enhancing the plan for effective presentation. Writing style should be paid more attention to. Along with the idea, the quality and appearance of your work is also judged.

Making a good plan entails several weeks of hard work. Most of that time is spent on researching, considering ideas and assumptions. Finally, it should be made sure that detailed notes on the sources of information and on the assumptions underlying financial data is available.

Format of a Business Plan

OWNERS

Business Name

Address Line 1

Address Line 2

City, State, Zip Code

Telephone

Fax

E-Mail

(I) Executive Summary

Should be written last and should comprise of two or fewer pages, including everything that one would cover up in a five-minute interview. Explaining the fundamentals of the proposed business – What will the product be? Who will the customers be? Who are the owners? What do you think the future holds for the business and the industry?

It should be made enthusiastically, professionally, completely, and concisely. If applying for a loan, terms like how much one needs, precisely how it is going to be used and how the money will make the business more profitable, thereby ensuring repayment.

(II) General Company Description

What business will one be getting into? What and how will one do it? Mission Statement – Many companies have a brief mission statement, usually in 30 words or fewer, explaining their reason for being and their guiding principles. If one wants to draft a mission statement, this is a good place to put it in the plan, followed by –

- **Company Goals and Objectives:** Goals are destinations—where one wants the business to be. Objectives are progress markers along the way to goal achievement. For example, goal can be to have a healthy, successful company that is a leader in customer service and that has a loyal customer following. Objectives might be annual sales targets and some specific measures of customer satisfaction.
- **Business Philosophy or Business/Company Values:** What is important in a business? To whom will one market the products? Describing the industry. Is it a growth industry? What changes does one foresee in the industry, short-term and long-term? How will the company be poised to take advantage of them? Describing important company strengths and core competencies. What factors will make the company succeed? What are the major competitive strengths? What background experience, skills, and strengths can personally be bought to this new venture?
- **Legal Form of Ownership:** Sole proprietor, Partnership, Corporation, Limited Liability Corporation (LLC)? Why is this form selected?

(III) Products and Services

Describing in depth the products or services (technical specifications, drawings, photos, sales brochures, and other bulky items belong in *Appendices*). What factors will boost the competitive advantages or disadvantages? Examples can include level of quality or unique or proprietary features. What are the pricing, fee, or leasing structures of products or services?

(IV) Marketing Plan

Market research: Why market research is required?

Regardless of how good the product and service is, the venture cannot succeed without efficient marketing. This includes careful and systematic research. It can be risky to assume the intended market. Market research is essential to make sure one is on the right track. The business planning process must be used as an opportunity to uncover data and to question the marketing efforts.

Market research – How to do market research?

There are two kinds of market research – **primary and secondary**.

Primary research is information that comes straight from the potential customers. One can assemble this information by themselves or hire someone else to gather it via surveys, focus groups and other methods. It is a research carried out to answer particular issues or questions. It involves questionnaires, surveys, or interviews with individuals or small groups, by direct mail, telephone, etc.

Secondary research is information collected through industry profiles, trade journals, newspapers, magazines, census data, and demographic profiles. This type of information is accessible in public libraries, industry associations, chambers of commerce, from vendors who sell to your industry, and from government agencies. The local library can be a good source. Also, there are online sources than could be possibly used. Even chamber of commerce has good information on local area. Often, trade associations and trade publications have excellent industry-specific data. Marketing plan should be as specific as possible; giving statistics, numbers, and sources.

At a later date, marketing plan will become the basis of the all-important sales projections.

(V) Economics

Facts about the industry –

What is the total size of the market?

- Percent share of the market? (This is important only if the business will be a major factor in the market.)
- Present demand in target market.
- Trends in target market—growth trends, trends in consumer preferences, and trends in product development.
- Growth potential and opportunity for a business.
- Barriers for a new company to enter the market.

Some typical barriers are –

- High production costs
- Consumer acceptance and brand recognition
- Unique technology and patents
- High marketing costs
- High capital costs
- Training and skills
- Unions and labour, skills availability
- Shipping costs
- Tariff barriers and quotas

How to overcome these barriers?

- How could the following affect the company?
- Change in government regulations
- Change in technology
- Change in the economy
- Change in the industry

Product

In the *Products and Services* section, describe them from the customers' point of view.

Features and Benefits

List all of the major products or services.

For each product or service –

- Describe the most important features. Speciality of the product or service?
- Describe the benefits. That is, how will the product benefit the customer?

Make a note of the variation between features and benefits. For example, a house that gives shelter and lasts a long time is made with certain materials and to a certain design; those are its features. Its benefits include pride of ownership, safety for users, financial security providing for the family, and inclusion in a neighbourhood; building features in the products so that benefits are sold.

Describing the after-sales services offered to the customer. Some examples are delivery, warranty, service contracts, support, follow-up, refund policy etc.

Customers

Identify the targeted customers, their characteristics, and their geographic locations, otherwise known as their demographics. The description will be completely different depending on whether one plans to sell to other businesses or directly to consumers. If one sells a consumer product, but through a channel of distributors, wholesalers, and retailers, one must carefully analyse, both, the end consumer and the middleman businesses to which it will be sold.

One may have more than one customer group. Identify the most important groups. Then, for each customer group, construct what is called a demographic profile.

- Age
- Gender
- Location
- Income level
- Social class and occupation
- Education
- Other (specific to your industry)
- Other (products currently liked or used by the customer)

For business customers, the demographic factors might be –

- Industry (or portion of an industry)
- Location
- Size of firm
- Quality, technology, and price preferences
- Packaging specifics
- Other (specific to your industry)

Competition

List the products and companies to compete with.

List the major competitors –

(Names and addresses)

- Will they compete across the board, or just for certain products, certain customers, or in certain locations?
- Will they have important indirect competitors?
- How will the products or services be compared with the competition?
- The competitive analysis table below can be used to compare companies with their competitors. In the first column are key competitive factors. Since these vary from one industry to another, the list of factors can be customised. This table can be utilised to compare the strengths and weaknesses of a specific business.

Table 1.1: Competitive Analysis

Importance To	Strength	Weakness
Customer A		
Customer		
Products		
Price		
Quality		
Selection		
Service		
Reliability		
Stability		
Expertise		
Company		
Reputation		
Location		
Appearance		

contd. ...

Customer B		
Customer		
Products		
Price		
Quality		
Selection		
Service		
Reliability		
Stability		
Expertise		
Company		
Reputation		
Location		
Appearance		
Sales Method		
Credit Policies		
Advertising		
Image		
A short paragraph to be written stating the competitive advantages and disadvantages		

Strategy

Now outline a marketing strategy that is consistent with the niche.

Promotion

- How will one reach customers? Or how will the customer know about the products or services?
- Advertising: What media, why, and how often? Why this mix and not some other?
- Identification of low-cost methods to get the most out of the promotional budget.
- Deciding if methods other than paid advertising, such as trade shows, catalogues, dealer incentives, word of mouth (how to stimulate it) should be used, and network of friends or professionals.
- Image one desires to project.

In addition to advertising, what plans does one have for graphic image support? This includes things like logo design, cards and letterhead, brochures, signage, and interior design (if customers visit the place of business). Having a system to identify repeat customers and then systematically contacting them.

Promotional Budget

- How much will one spend on the items listed above?
- Before start up? (These numbers will go into the start-up budget.)
- Ongoing? (These numbers will go into the operating plan budget.)
- Also, list funds flow and check with the requirements. Often non-synchronisation also results in delays and increases the expenses.

Pricing

Explain method or methods of setting prices. For most small businesses having the lowest price is not a good policy. It robs the needed profit margin; customers may not care as much about price; and large competitors can under price anyway. Usually one does better to have average prices and compete on quality and service.

- Does pricing strategy fit with what was revealed in the competitive analysis?
- Compare prices with those of the competition. Are they higher, lower, the same?
- Why?
- How important is price as a competitive factor? Do intended customers really make their purchase decisions mostly on price?
- What will be the customer service and credit policies?

Proposed Location

Probably a precise location is not yet picked out. This is the time to think about what one wants and needs in a location. Many start-ups run successfully from home for a while. Here, analysing the location criteria is important as they affect the customers.

- Is location important to the customers? If yes, how?
- If customers come to the place of business –
- Is it convenient? Parking? Interior spaces? Not out of the way?
- Is it consistent with the image?
- Is it what customers want and expect?
- Where is the competition located? Is it better to be near them (like car dealers or fast food restaurants) or distant (like convenience food stores)?

Distribution Channels

- How to sell the products or services?
- Retail
- Direct (mail order, Web, catalogue)

- Wholesale
- Your own sales force
- Agents
- Independent representatives
- Bid on contracts

Sales Forecast

Use a sales forecast spreadsheet to prepare a month-by-month projection. The forecast should be based on the historical sales, the marketing strategies that have just identified the market research, and industry data, if available. Two forecasts can be made – 1) a "best guess", which is what is really expected, and 2) a "worst case" scenario estimate that one is confident to reach no matter what happens. Remember to keep notes on research and assumptions, as this sales forecast and all subsequent spreadsheets are built in the plan. This is critical if presenting it to funding sources.

(VI) Operational Plan

Explain the daily operation of the business, its location, equipment, people, processes, and surrounding environment.

Production

How and where are the products or services produced?

Explain the methods of –

- Production techniques and costs
- Quality control
- Customer service
- Inventory control
- Product development

Location

Qualities needed in a location. Describe the type of location.

Physical requirements –

- Amount of space
- Type of building
- Zoning
- Power and other utilities

Access

- Is it important that the location be convenient to both customers as well as the suppliers?
- What are the requirements for parking and proximity to freeway, airports, railroads, and other means of public transport?

Include a drawing or layout of the proposed facility if it is important, as it might be for a manufacturer.

- Construction: Most new companies should not sink capital into construction, but if one is planning to build, costs and specifications will be a big part of the plan.
- Cost: Estimate the occupation expenses, including rent, maintenance, utilities, insurance, and initial re-modelling costs to make the space suit the needs. These numbers will become part of the financial plan.
- What will be the business hours?

Legal Environment

Describe the following –

- Licensing and bonding requirements
- Permits
- Health, workplace, or environmental regulations
- Special regulations covering your industry or profession
- Zoning or building code requirements
- Insurance coverage
- Trademarks, copyrights, or patents (pending, existing, or purchased)

Personnel

- Number of employees
- Type of labour (skilled, unskilled, and professional)
- Where and how will you find the right employees?
- Quality of existing staff
- Pay structure
- Training methods and requirements
- Who does which tasks?
- Do you have schedules and written procedures prepared?
- Have you drafted job descriptions for employees? If not, take time to write some. They really help internal communications with employees.
- For certain functions, will you use contract workers in addition to employees?

Inventory

- What kind of inventory will you keep – raw materials, supplies, finished goods?
- Average value in stock (that is, what is your inventory investment)?
- Rate of turnover and how this compares to the industry averages?
- Seasonal build-ups?
- Lead-time for ordering?

Suppliers

Identify key suppliers –

- Names and addresses
- Type and amount of inventory furnished
- Credit and delivery policies
- History and reliability
- Should one have more than one supplier for critical items (as a backup)?
- Do you expect shortages or short-term delivery problems?
- Are supply costs steady or fluctuating? If fluctuating, how would you deal with changing costs?

Credit Policies

- Does one plan to sell on credit?
- Does one really need to sell on credit? Is it customary in an industry and expected by your clientele?
- If yes, what policies as to who gets credit and how much?
- How will one check the creditworthiness of new applicants?
- What terms will one offer customers, that is, how much credit and when is payment due?
- Offering prompt payment discounts? (Hint: Do this only if it is usual and customary in your industry.)
- Does one know what it will cost you to extend credit? Have you built the costs into prices?

Managing Your Accounts Receivable

For extending credit, one should do an aging, at least monthly, statement to track how much money is tied up in credit given to customers and to alert slow payment problems.

A receivables aging looks like the following table –

	Total	Current	30 Days	60 Days	90 Days	Over 90 Days
Accounts Receivable Aging						

A policy for dealing with slow-paying customers –

- When does one make a phone call?
- When does one send a letter?
- When does one get your attorney to threaten?

Managing Accounts Payable

One should also age accounts payable, which they owe to the suppliers. This helps in planning whom to pay and when. Paying too early depletes cash, but paying late can cost valuable discounts and can damage credit. (Hint: If you know you will be late making a payment, call the creditor before the due date.)

- Do proposed vendors offer prompt payment discounts?

A payables aging looks like the following table –

	Total	Current	30 Days	60 Days	90 Days	Over 90 Days
Accounts Payable Aging						

(VII) Management and Organisation

Who will manage the business on a day-to-day basis? What experience does that person bring to the business? What special or distinctive competencies? Is there a plan for continuation of the business if this person is lost or incapacitated? Creating an organisational chart showing the management hierarchy and who is responsible for key functions can be done, including position descriptions for key employees. While seeking loans or investors, resumes of owners and key employees should also be included.

Professional and Advisory Support

List the following –

- Board of directors
- Management advisory board
- Attorney
- Accountant
- Insurance agent
- Banker
- Consultant or consultants
- Mentors and key advisors

(VIII) Personal Financial Statement

Include personal financial statements for each owner and major stockholder, showing assets and liabilities held outside the business and personal net worth. Owners will often have to draw on personal assets to finance the business, and these statements will show what is available. Bankers and investors usually want this information as well.

(IX) Start up Expenses and Capitalisation

One will have many expenses before even beginning to operate the business. It's important to estimate these expenses accurately and then to plan the source for sufficient capital. Detailed list of expenses shall leave out chance of underestimate them. The best approach is to add a separate line item, called contingencies, to account for the unforeseeable expenses. As a thumb rule contingencies should equal at least 20 percent of the total of all other start-up expenses. Also explain in detail how much will be contributed by each investor and what percent ownership each will have.

(X) Financial Plan

The financial plan consists of a 12-month profit and loss projection, a four-year profit and loss projection (optional), a cash-flow projection, a projected balance sheet, and a break-even calculation. Together they constitute a reasonable estimate of your company's financial future. More important, the process of thinking through the financial plan will improve your insight into the inner financial workings of your company.

12-Month Profit and Loss Projection

Many business owners think of the 12-month profit and loss projection as their plan. This is where it is put all together in numbers and gets an idea of what it will take to make a profit and be successful.

Sales projections come from a sales forecast in which forecast sales, cost of goods sold, expenses, and profit month-by-month for one year. Profit projections should be accompanied by a narrative explaining the major assumptions used to estimate company income and expenses. Research Notes: Keeping careful notes on research and assumptions, can help in explaining them later if necessary, and also so that one can go back to the sources when it's time to revise the plan.

Three or Five-Year Profit Projection (Optional)

The 12-month projection is the heart of the financial plan. This section is for those who want to carry their forecasts beyond the first year. Of course, keep notes of the key assumptions, especially about things that one expects will change dramatically after the first year.

Projected Cash Flow

If the profit projection is the heart of the business plan, cash flow is the blood. Businesses fail because they cannot pay their bills. Every part of the business plan is important, but none of it means a thing if one runs out of cash. The point of this worksheet is to plan how much one needs before start-up, for preliminary expenses, operating expenses, and reserves. One should keep updating it. It will enable us to foresee shortages in time to do something about them—perhaps cut expenses, or perhaps negotiate a loan. But foremost, one shouldn't be taken by surprise. There is no great trick to preparing it. The cash-flow projection is just a forward look at the checking account. For each item, determine when one actually expects to receive cash (for sales) or when one will actually have to write a check (for expense items). One should track essential operating data, which is not necessarily part of cash flow but also allows one to track items that have a heavy impact on cash flow, such as sales and inventory purchases.

The cash flow will show whether the working capital is adequate. Clearly, if the projected cash balance ever goes negative, one will need more start-up capital. This plan will also predict just when and how much will be needed to pump in funds or borrow. Explain major assumptions, especially those that make the cash flow differ from the *Profit and Loss Projection*. For example, a sale in one month –

- When does one actually collect the cash?
- While buying inventory or materials, does one pay in advance, upon delivery, or much later?
- How will this affect cash flow?
- Is it possible to pay expenses in advance or if any credit periods are available? When?
- Are there irregular expenses, such as quarterly tax payments, maintenance and repairs, or seasonal inventory build-up that should be budgeted?
- Loan payments, equipment purchases, and owner's draws usually do not show on profit and loss statements but definitely do take cash out. Be sure to include them.
- Interest payable should also be considered as it drastically reduces the profit.
- Also take depreciation into account as it does not appear in the cash flow statement.

Opening Day Balance Sheet

A balance sheet is one of the fundamental financial reports that any business needs for reporting and financial management. A balance sheet shows what items of value are held by the company (assets), and what its debts are (liabilities). When liabilities are subtracted from assets, the remainder is the owners' equity.

Use start-up expenses and capitalisation spreadsheet as a guide to preparing a balance sheet as of opening day. Then detail how the account balances are calculated on the opening day balance sheet. Optional – Some people want to add a projected balance sheet showing the estimated financial position of the company at the end of the first year. This is especially useful when selling your proposal to investors.

Break-Even Analysis

A break-even analysis predicts the sales volume, at a given price, required to recover total costs. In other words, it's the sales level that is the dividing line between operating at a loss and operating at a profit.

Expressed as a formula, break-even is –

Break-Even Sales = Fixed Costs

1 - Variable Costs

(Where fixed costs are expressed in rupees, but variable costs expressed as a percent of total sales)

Include all assumptions upon which your break-even calculation is based.

(XI) Appendices

Include details and studies used in your business plan, for example –

- Brochures and advertising materials.
- Industry studies.
- Blueprints and plans.
- Maps and photos of location.
- Magazine or other articles.
- Detailed lists of equipment owned or to be purchased.
- Copies of leases and contracts.
- Letters of support from future customers.
- Any other materials needed to support the assumptions in this plan.
- Market research studies.
- List of assets available as collateral for a loan.

(XII) Refining the Plan

The generic business plan presented above should be modified to suit your specific type of business and the audience for which the plan is written.

For Raising Capital

For Bankers

- Bankers want assurance of orderly repayment. If you intend using this plan to present to lenders, include –
- Amount of loan.
- How will the funds be used?
- What this will accomplish—how will it make the business stronger?
- Requested repayment terms (number of years to repay). You will probably not have much negotiating room on interest rate but may be able to negotiate a longer repayment term, which will help cash flow.
- Collateral offered, and a list of all existing liens against collateral.

For Investors

- Investors have a different perspective. They are looking for dramatic growth, and they expect to share in the rewards –
- Funds needed short-term.
- Funds needed in two to five years.
- How the company will use the funds, and what this will accomplish for growth.
- Estimated return on investment.
- Exit strategy for investors (buyback, sale, or IPO).
- Percent of ownership that you will give up to investors.
- Milestones or conditions that you will accept.
- Financial reporting to be provided.
- Involvement of investors on the board or in management.

For Type of Business

Manufacturing

- Planned production levels
- Anticipated levels of direct production costs and indirect (overhead) costs—how do these compare to industry averages (if available)?
- Prices per product line.
- Gross profit margin, overall and for each product line.
- Production/capacity limits of planned physical plant.
- Production/capacity limits of equipment.
- Purchasing and inventory management procedures.
- New products under development or anticipated to come online after start-up.

Service Businesses

- Service businesses sell intangible products. They are usually more flexible than other types of businesses, but they also have higher labour costs and generally very little in fixed assets.
- What are the key competitive factors in this industry?
- Your prices.
- Methods used to set prices.
- System of production management.
- Quality control procedures. Standard or accepted industry quality standards.
- How will one measure labour productivity?
- Percent of work subcontracted to other firms. Will one benefit from profit on subcontracting?
- Credit, payment, and collections policies and procedures.
- Strategy for keeping client base.

High Technology Companies

- Economic outlook for the industry.
- Will the company have information systems in place to manage rapidly changing prices, costs, and markets?
- Will you be on the cutting edge with your products and services?
- What is the status of research and development? And what is required to –
- Bring product/service to market?
- Keep the company competitive?

How does the company –

- Protect intellectual property?
- Avoid technological obsolescence?
- Supply necessary capital?
- Retain key personnel?

High-tech companies sometimes have to operate for a long time without profits and sometimes even without sales. If this fits your situation, a banker probably will not want to lend to you. Venture capitalists may invest, but your story must be very good. You must do longer-term financial forecasts to show when profit take-off is expected to occur, and the assumptions must be well documented and well argued.

Retail Business

- Company image.
- Pricing.
- Explain mark-up policies.
- Prices should be profitable, competitive, and in accordance with company image.
- Inventory.
- Selection and price should be consistent with company image.
- Inventory level – Find industry average numbers for annual inventory turnover rate (available in RMA book). Multiply your initial inventory investment by the average turnover rate. The result should be at least equal to your projected first year's cost of goods sold. If it is not, one may not have enough budgeted for start-up inventory.
- Customer service policies: These should be competitive and in accord with company image.
- Location: Does it give the exposure that one needs? Is it convenient for customers? Is it consistent with company image?
- Promotion: Methods used, cost. Does it project a consistent company image?
- Credit: Is credit to customers extended? If yes, is it really needed and is this factor included into prices?

1.4 Forecasting

1.4.1 Introduction

Forecasting is a method or technique for estimating various future aspects of a business or other operations. It forms the basis for understanding the customer demand or market demand in business operations. In business forecasting, the business plan is assessed for the probabilities of failures and the reasons that could cause such failures. The impact of such cause may upset time, cost and quality of the project performance or on the product itself. By forecasting we try and prepare a list of such events or causes and prevent them from occurring or take corrective actions in time. Past data on similar project helps in accurate forecasting. Many kinds of statistical tools are used. Thus, forecasting involves detailed analysis of the past and present events to get a clear-cut idea of the probability of similar events that may occur in future. This also forms a base to identify the type of risk, quantum of risk and prepare strategies to avoid, mitigate or accept the risk factors.

Accurate forecasting of economic activities like product demand is almost impossible due to interdependent factors. Regardless of the fact that highly reliable forecasting is unrealistic, the approximate estimation technique forms the basis of planning process. Thus, in other words forecasting is the method of making statements about events whose definite outcomes (typically) have not yet been observed. Any, among the eleven types of forecasting methods, can be used. Usage can vary between areas of application. Risk and uncertainty are essential to forecasting and prediction. It is, in general, considered a good practice to indicate the degree of uncertainty attached to forecasts. Forecasting is used in the practice of Customer Demand Planning in everyday business forecasting for manufacturing companies. The discipline of demand planning, also sometimes referred to as supply chain forecasting, includes both statistical forecasting and a consensus process. An essential aspect of forecasting is the relationship it holds with planning. Forecasting can be described as predicting what the future will look like, whereas planning predicts what the future should look like. There is no single right forecasting method. Selection of a method should be based on objectives and conditions (data etc.).

1.4.2 Meaning of Forecasting

Forecasting is speculating or assuming future course of events based on information or data collected from the past or present events. Forecasting is the first major activity while planning involves careful study of past data and present scenario. The main purpose of forecasting is to estimate the occurrence, timing, or magnitude of future events. For example, the trend of the past ten years in the demand for cars and corresponding purchasing power of the consumers may form a basis of forecasting the demand for cars during the next year. Once the reliable forecast for the demand is available, a good planning of activities is needed to meet the future demand. Forecasting thus provides the input to the planning and scheduling process.

1.4.3 Definition

Neter and Wasserman state that *"Business forecasting refers to the statistical analysis of the past and current movement in the given time series so as to obtain clues about the future pattern of those movements."*

Webster's Collegiate Dictionary defines that *"A forecast is a prediction and its purpose is to calculate and predict some future event or condition."*

1.4.4 Characteristics of Forecasting

There are various characteristics compiled under the concept of forecasting. They can be enumerated as follows –

1. Forecasting is concerned with future events.
2. Forecasting is necessary for planning process. Planning is not possible without forecasting.
3. The impact of future events has to be considered in the planning process.
4. Forecasting is predicting of future events. Therefore, it is only an assumption and not the real facts of the future events that might happen.
5. Inferences or conclusions are drawn from past and present relevant events.
6. Forecasting considers all the factors which affect organisational functions.
7. The analysis of various factors may require the use of scientific, mathematical and statistical techniques. Personal observation also helps forecasting.
8. The application of scientific, mathematical and statistical techniques is more reliable than the use of ordinary tools for obtaining conclusions.

1.4.5 Forecasting Process

Forecasting period may be a short-term or long-term. In either of the cases, certain steps have to be passed through while making the forecast. These steps have been briefly discussed below –

1. **Detailed study is required:** It is important to collect detailed information and analysis of the company for forecasting. It is based on the organisational structure of the company and its past performance. The growth of a company or a business is accessed over a period of time and the factors responsible for such are identified. It is also essential to identify the extent of the dependence of all the dependant factors that impact growth of a company.

   Organise for forecasting –
   - Pinpoint responsibility
   - Only one corporate forecast
   - Separate forecasting and planning

2. **Estimation of future: Future business success can be estimated by collecting information of past,** company performance and experience and expertise of the leaders in the company. This type of information helps the management to identify the key personnel and fix the responsibility for fulfilling the promises of these forecast and accountability for any deviations from this forecast.

Estimate confidence limits –
- What is the range of forecast errors in past?

3. **Collection of results**: All the relevant information of the past performance and experiences needs to be collected and stored in a structured format that is available for analysis. Nothing can be omitted. However, irrelevant information can be avoided while collecting the results.

Scrub the data –
- Adjust outliers
- Throw out unique data

4. **Comparison of results:** The actual results are compared with estimated results to know amount of deviation. If the deviation is significant between the estimated and actual results, the reason for such deviations can also be found. This will also help management to identify the amount of risk associated in future.

Compare alternative forecasts –
- Top-down vs. Bottom-up
- Monthly vs. quarterly data
- Depersonalised vs. raw data
- Percent change data
- Time series forecasts
- Regression forecasts

5. **Accuracy of forecast:** It is almost impossible to obtain the accurate forecast every time. This is due to many factors, which affect the trend in data. It is difficult to capture the exact interrelation of these influencing factors. Therefore, some error in forecasted value and actual value is quite common. Sometimes, it is important to know if the forecasting technique is unbiased or not. An unbiased model should overestimate or underestimate the forecast in almost equal ratio.

Monitor accuracy –
- Choose a standard measure
- Keep a track record
- Benchmark
- Hold performance reviews

Simulate forecasting –
- One-step-ahead
- Long-range

1.4.6 Importance of Forecasting

In planning process, the planning is done based on the forecasting. Forecasting helps the management in the following ways –

1. **Pivotal role in an organisation:** Many organisations have failed due to lack of forecasting or defective forecasting. The reason is that planning is based on accurate forecasting. According to Louis A. Allen, *"A systematic attempt to probe the future by inference from known facts helps integrate all management planning so that unified overall plans can be developed into which divisional and departmental plans can be merged."*

2. **Development of a business:** Business is set up to achieve a particular objective. This can be achieved by performing certain activities. The performance of these activities depends upon the proper forecasting. So, the development of a business or an organisation is fully based on the forecasting.

3. **In project implementation:** When an entrepreneur plans to start up a new project, the decisions are based on experience and data available on the project. The information on criticality and risk factors involved and controlling factors at different stages of the project ensures the success of the project.

4. **Co-ordination:** Forecasting gives clarity on the resource requirements in advance and therefore the management executives can effectively co-ordinate to make the resources available on time. Thus, forecasting helps to collect the information about the internal and external factors and such information provides a basis for co-ordination. In project management forecasting forms the base for planning of activity scheduling.

5. **Effective control:** Management executive can discover the strengths and weaknesses of subordinates or employees during forecasting. Then, the executive can take appropriate action on the subordinates. So, forecasting can provide adequate information for exercising effective control.

6. **Key to success:** All business organisations are confronting risks. Success is the reward for confronting risk and functioning under uncertainties. Risks and uncertainties could be condensed with the help of forecasting. Forecasting provides clues about risks and uncertainties. The management executives can save the business and get success by taking appropriate timely action.

1.4.7 Areas of forecasting

The decision of today affects the business environment of tomorrow. So, the decision should be a sound one. A sound decision can be taken with the help of systematic and rational forecasting. Accurate forecasting is therefore necessary for efficient management. So, making accurate forecast is of utmost necessity in the following areas –

1. **Competition:** It is necessary to predict the strategies followed by the competitors. The strategies may be low cost, granting credit facility, allowing discount, long guarantee period, free articles, etc. When a new business unit enters an industry, the market share of each of the competitors has to be taken into consideration for forecasting. This would enable the management to identify the action needed to outperform competitors. Forecasting helps the management to enhance their market share of the company.

2. **Labour Availability:** Availability of human resource for the specific task play a crucial role in success of the project. The labour can be divided into three categories –

    (A) Skilled worker

    (B) Semi-skilled worker

    (C) Unskilled worker

    Skilled workers are highly in demand. Specialised or skilled workers are required for effective performance of a job; the management can, therefore forecast availability of labour force. If the management has a plan for expansion or modernisation, the prime forecast of management will pertain to the supply of such labour. No industry can be expanded or modernised without adequate labour force.

3. **Economic Condition:** The economic condition of a business unit forms the basis of its strength. Here, the term economic condition includes cash position, working capital requirement, and repaying capacity etc; the operating efficiency of any unit could be improved by the sound economic condition. In other words, good economic condition accelerates the growth of the company.

4. **The Growth Trend:** A detailed analysis of growth trend of a business is also necessary. A forecast on the growth trend helps the management decide the operating level. The upward growth trend is always preferred. This could be achieved through forecasting. Failure to make accurate forecasting on growth trend may put the company out of business.

5. **Study of Environment:** The customer tastes, demands and attitudes may change. The change can be identified with the help of proper forecasting. Convenience and comforts are responsible for changes. Here the forecasting could predict the convenience and comforts that would be enjoyed by the customers in future.

6. **Political Change:** Forecasting in the field of politics is also an important one. Any political change may impact smooth running of any business unit. Frequent changes in politics bring about frequent changes in government policies towards business.

7. **Technology:** The invention of the new technology may change the operations of an organisation. So, forecast predicts the new technological developments. An active organisation keeps updated to the new technological developments and adopts new technology to enhance performance. Failure to forecast on technology may ruin the company. It will find itself difficult to survive in business world.

8. **New laws and regulations:** A meticulous adaption of new laws and regulations is necessary for effective functioning of an organisation. Laws relating to consumer protection assume much importance these days. Consumer is the king to any business. The operational style of any business is affected by new laws and regulations.

1.4.8 Techniques or Types of Forecasting

There are major three types of forecasting methods –

1. **Qualitative or judgmental methods:** It relies on experts or senior managers' opinion while predicting the future. It is also useful for small or long duration forecasting task. This method provides a base during making some decisions. Three important qualitative methods are –
    *   Delphi technique – Develop forecast through group consensus.
    *   Market Surveys – Involves the use of questionnaires, consumer panels and test of new products and services.
    *   Scenario writing – process of analysing possible future events by considering alternative possible outcomes.

2. **Extrapolative or time series methods:** This method uses past history information for demand. It comprises of four separate components – trend component, cyclical component, seasonal component and irregular component. The objective of this method is to identify the pattern in historic data and extrapolate it for the future.
    Types of extrapolative methods
    *   **Moving average method:** It considers the average of demands occurring in several of the most recent periods.
    *   **Weighted moving average:** This method allows for varying the weights of old demands.
    *   **Exponential smoothing:** It exponentially decreases the weights of old demands.

3. **Causal or explanatory methods:** A statistical forecasting model based on historical demand data as well as on variables believed to influence the demand. There are two types of causal forecasting methods –
    *   **Regression analysis:** A functional relationship is established between variables from the historical data and then used to forecast dependent variable values.
    *   **Econometric method:** An extension of regression analysis and includes system of simultaneous regression equations.

1.4.9 Methods of Forecasting

Various types of forecasting are used in the field of business because future of any business can never be predicted with certainty. An accurate forecasting may reduce the degree of uncertainty. However, no technique can be considered as correct, the one which is universally applicable. In practice, more than one technique may be used to make forecasting more effective.

Some techniques can be described as –

1. **Human Judgement**
   - Subject to bias and inconsistency: Predictability of human judgement is dependent on how the judgement was done, that is, adherence to the policies and processes of the organisation.
   - Models usually beat humans: Models are idealistic versions and human interference or adaptations definitely vary from the idealistic conditions.

2. **Jury of Executive Option**
   - The opinion of experts is sought under this method and a meritorious one is accepted. For example, an opinion on profitability of starting a new unit is received from various experts and decision is made on the basis of experts' opinion. The opinion may be on the area of sales, finance, purchase etc. Some ideas are generated which can be evaluated for their feasibility and profitability. Experts may be requested to comment on the opinion of the others in order to arrive at consensus of opinion. The reason for favouring a particular opinion by an expert is known to the management.

3. **Similarity Events Method**
   - It is otherwise called historical analogy method. In this method, forecasts are made on the basis of the events happened in the past which are most similar to the current events. For example, in analysing the changes in the attitude of employee regarding in equality, the management can find out prudential attitude of employee in the days to come by considering past attitude. The similarity of events of past and present is properly analysed in order to make an effective forecast.

4. **Sales Forecasting**
   - The sales forecasting of the existing product can be done with the help of opinions of salespersons. Salespersons are very close to the consumers. So, the opinions expressed by the salesperson are of great value. A reasonable sales trend can be predicted based on the opinions of the salespersons.

5. **Time Series Forecasting**
   - Based on analysis of past history
   - Cheap and easy
   - On average, most accurate method
   - Should always be attempted

6. Time Series Analysis

- In time series analysis, the future is forecasted on the assumption that the past activities are good indicators of future activities. In other words, future activities are the extension of the past. This method is quite accurate where future is expected to be similar to the past. For example in construction of a building, majority of activities are repeated from past. Time series analysis can be applied only when the data is available for a long period of time. In a nutshell, forecasts are based on the assumption that the business conditions affecting its steady growth or decline are reasonably expected to remain unchanged in future.

7. Regression Modelling

- Based on causal relationships
- Expensive and difficult
- Must forecast independent variables

8. Regression Analysis

- Regression analysis is used to find out the effects of changes of the relative movements of two or more inter-related variables. In other words, a change in one variable has an effect on the other inter-related variables. In modern business conditions and situations, the number of factors is responsible for the changes made in the variables. Here, regression analysis helps in isolating the effects of such factors to a great extent. For example, if we take two inter-related variables, for example, cost of production and profit there will be a direct relationship prevailing between these two variables. It is possible to have an estimate of profit on the basis of cost of production, provided other things remain the same. In this way, forecasting can be made.

9. Growth or Market Development Models

- Based on assumed growth patterns: The forecast is based on previous growth patterns observed.
- Cheap and easy: Since the data gives clear indications of the market growth, it is easy to use this method for forecasting.
- Difficult to validate: It is possible that the data used for this type of forecasting is accumulated from various known and unknown sources; therefore, it becomes difficult to verify the accuracy of such data.

10. Survey Method

- Field survey can be conducted to collect information regarding the attitude of people. For example, information may be collected through surveys about the savings habits of the public. Both quantitative and qualitative information may be collected. Such information is useful for proper forecasting. The demand for both new and existing products can be forecasted through the survey method.

11. Indexing Method

- Index numbers are used to measure the state of condition of business between two or more periods. Business trend, seasonal fluctuations of a business and cyclical movements are studied with the help of index numbers. Index numbers indicate the direction in which the business is going on. Besides these, index numbers give some advance signals for likely changes in the future. For example, a pay rise to the government employees, industrial and agricultural employees may reflect higher sales volume and higher income after some time. Thus, it is very easy to forecast the future trend of a business with the help of business activity index number. However, index numbers do not give an assurance for success. The reason is that all types of business do not follow the general trend. For example, sales of umbrellas might be associated with weather conditions. If the causes are understood, projections of the influencing variables can be made and used in the forecast.

12. Input and Output Analysis

- The method is based on the known relationship between the input and output. At the same time, input requirements can be forecasted based on the output. For example, drinking water requirements of an area can be forecasted on the basis of the present usage rate in various sectors such as industry, transport, household etc. and how the water requirements of these various sectors will increase in future.

13. Econometric Models

- It is otherwise called as casual models. The complex relationships of various variables are responsible for the future behaviours of one variable. For example, availability of suitable products in the market, changes in preferences, credit availability, changes in lifestyle. All these variables produce some effects on present sales in addition to past sales. This forecasting technique is applied in projecting gross national product. Here the past data has been used to know the degree of relationship prevailing among these variables.

14. Expectations of Consumer

- Under this method, a survey is conducted in order to know the future needs of consumers. An overall forecast can be made on the basis of the expectation of consumers. An organisation can find out the consumer preferences, impact of advertisement on buying behaviour and lacuna prevailing in the existing product. This is also known as "Market Research Method."

15. Delphi Method

- Rand Corporation had developed the Delphi method initially in 1969, to forecast the military events. Then, it has been applied in other areas also. A panel of experts is prepared. These experts are requested to give their opinions in writing for a prescribed questionnaire. Their opinions are analysed, summarised and submitted once again to the same experts for future considerations and evaluations. The authors of these opinions are not disclosed, so that no expert is influenced by others' opinions. This process is continued up to the stage at which a consensus opinion is obtained. Delphi method is useful when past data are not available and where the past data do not give an indication for the future events. Delphi is used for long-range forecast. It is useful in forecasting problems like future petroleum and diesel needs, likely or probable after effects of a price expected social changes and the like. It is generally used for new product demand, technological forecast for new technology, effect of scientific advances, changes in society, changes in competitive environment, etc. For example, the effect of internet/intranet or information-highway in the educational system of India in next 25 years may be forecasted through this approach.

Advantages of Delphi Method
o   It is effective, when past data is absent.
o   It does not require experts to meet in person.
o   It is extremely useful for the forecast of new technology or new product.

Limitations of Delphi Method
It is a time-consuming process, which may be around one year. During this period, the experts may change their perception. Sometimes, the very need of forecasting loses its significance due to the delay. Accuracy or reliability of forecast is relatively poor in Delphi. Therefore, it should only be used when past trend is absent and quantitative models are difficult to use.
o   As experts are not accountable, their response may be less meaningful.
o   If the questionnaires are poorly designed, Delphi would be ineffective.

16. Mean Absolute Deviation Method
*   This is calculated as the average of absolute value of difference between actual and forecasted value. The negative sign in this difference is ignored as over-estimate as well as under-estimate are both off-target and thus undesirable.

17. Statistical Forecasting
*   Statistical forecasting is based on the past data. We evaluate the expected errors that might occur. There are number of tools such as Pareto, Fish-bone, PFMEA etc. that facilitate the forecasting as well as controlling of errors.

18. Weighted Average Method
*   This approach is based on the principle that more weight should be applied to a relatively newer data. The forecast is the weighted average of data. It may be noted that when more weight is given to the recent values, the forecast gives clarity on likely trends.

19. Technology Forecasting

- Primarily, a technological forecast deals with the characteristics of technology, such as levels of technical performance, like speed of a military aircraft, the power in watts of a particular future engine, the accuracy or precision of a measuring instrument, the number of transistors in a chip in the year 2015, etc. The forecast does not have to state how these characteristics will be achieved.

- Secondly, technological forecasting usually deals with only useful machines, procedures or techniques. This is to exclude from the domain of technological forecasting those commodities, services or techniques intended for luxury or amusement.

- Normative methods of technology forecasting—like the relevance trees, morphological models, and mission flow diagrams—are also commonly used.

20. Extrapolation

- Extrapolation means estimation of future behaviour from the known data, that is, past behaviour. Factors that are responsible for the behaviour change and the effects of such various factors are taken into consideration. The reason is that it assumes that the effect of these factors is of a constant and stable pattern and would continue as such in future. It is necessary that the future behaviour is to be decided only after a very careful study of past behaviour.

- Extrapolation is one of the easiest ways to forecast. For example, based on the past few values of a production capacity, next value may be extrapolated on a graph paper. This may be done by extending the curve (or line) joining the already known values. For example, if the production capacity of a firm has been 445, 545 and 645, then in the next year one may expect a production capacity requirement of 745 units. The limitation with the extrapolation method is its inability to deal with non-linear and swing in the pattern of past data.

1.4.10 Advantages of Forecasting

Forecasting helps the business in a number of ways. The anticipation of future problems and events will make it imperative to accelerate an early achievement of objectives. Some of the advantages or merits of the forecasting are briefly discussed below –

1. **Facilitates Planning:** Forecasting precedes the planning function of management. Forecasting provides a basis for preparing a business plan. Planning requires the estimation of probable changes likely to take place in the future. Forecasting helps the management to guard against the weakness of the management. This will minimise the business risk.

2. **Ensures Co-ordination:** Forecasting of an organisation cannot be done by an individual. It involves group effort. This group consists of all department members of the organisation. This creates team spirit and ensures co-ordination. According to **Henry Fayol**, *"The act of forecasting is a great benefit to all who take part in the process and is the best means of ensuring adaptability to changing circumstances. The collaboration of all concerned leads to a unified front, and understanding of the reasons and a broader outlook."*

3. **Easy Controlling:** Forecasting helps the management to exercise control. Control is necessary if there is any deviation, the actual from the predicted result. The result can be predicted on the basis of forecasting. Control is not possible in the absence of forecasting. So, control will be an easy function in the presence of forecasting.

4. **Helps to Predict The Future:** Forecasting does not provide you with a crystal ball to see exactly what will happen to the market and your company over the coming years, but it will help give you a general idea. This will provide you with a sense of direction which will allow your company to get the most out of the marketplace.

5. **Keep Your Customers Happy:** In order to keep your customers satisfied you need to provide them with the product they want when they want it. This advantage of forecasting in business will help predict product demand so that enough products are available to meet customer orders.

6. **Keeps Companies Looking Ahead:** By forecasting on a regular basis, it forces companies to continually think about their future and where their company is headed. This will allow them to foresee changing market trends and keep up with the competition.

1.4.11 Limitations of Forecasting

Forecasting has several limitations:

1. It has lot of dependencies such as
   (i) Dependency on human judgement.
   (ii) Data validity on which the forecasting is done.

2. Forecasting can be considered as a method for guessing events as it does not specify any concrete relationship between past and future events.

3. Detailed and high degree of accuracy in forecasting requires human beings with lots of experience. Even then the dependencies such as mentioned above generate variance in the forecasted outcomes.

4. Certainty of events occurring as per forecasted plan also defuses the use of forecasting methods.

5. The more number of days constituting the period of forecasting higher will be the degree of error. Forecasting cannot be applied to a long period.

6.   Heavy cost and time is involved in forecasting but the benefits derived from them will not be worthy. The collection of information and conversion of qualitative data into quantitative one involves a lot of time and money. So, smaller organisations, cannot afford the cost and time required for forecasting.

1.4.12 Difference between Forecasting and Planning

Both forecasting and planning deal with future events. Despite of differences between them, they are briefly explained below –

Forecasting is an integral part of the planning process. Forecasting provides scope for guessing future happenings. According the Henry Albers, *"A successful forecast is something of a miracle and often occurs for the wrong reasons. A part of the problem is that too much is expected from forecasting people want more precise answers than are possible in an environment characterised by uncertainty".*

Sr. No.	Forecasting	Planning
1.	Forecasting is the basis for planning. Forecasting is attempting to predict the future through empirical means.	Planning is the attempt to create the future by building a path that leads to the future you desire.
2.	No decision can be taken without the help of forecasting.	Planning helps to arrive at certain decisions. The decisions regarding what is to be done, how is to be done and when it's to be done.
3.	Forecasting is done at the middle or lower level of management.	Planning is done at the top level of management.
4.	A forecast is what you think will happen to something which you can't influence yourself, like the weather or exchange rates.	A plan is something in which you can influence the outcome, like "we'll try to get a 10% increase in younger customers by advertising outside schools".
5.	A few members are involved in forecasting process.	A large number of persons are involved in planning process.
6.	Forecasting does not stimulate activity among employees.	Planning stimulates some activity to achieve the objective of the organisation.
7.	Forecasting is a tool of planning.	Planning is not a tool of forecasting.
8.	Forecasting is done by experts.	Planning can be done by any person.

Points to Remember

- Planning is an intellectual process of thinking to decide a course of action that helps achieve a predetermined objective/s.
- Forecasting is speculating or assuming future course of events based on information or data collected from the past or present events.
- In Similarity Events Method forecasts are made on the basis of the events happened in the past which are most similar to the current events.
- The sales forecasting of the existing product can be done with the help of opinions of salespersons.
- In time series analysis, the future is forecasted on the assumption that the past activities are good indicators of future activities.
- Regression Analysis is used to find out the effects of changes of the relative movements of two or more inter-related variables.
- Field survey can be conducted to collect information regarding the attitude of people.
- Index numbers are used to measure the state of condition of business between two or more periods.
- Under Expectations of Consumer, a survey is conducted in order to know the future needs of consumers. An overall forecast can be made on the basis of the expectation of consumers.
- Under Delphi Method a panel of experts is prepared. These experts are requested to give their opinions in writing for a prescribed questionnaire. Their opinions are analysed, summarised and submitted once again to the same experts for future considerations and evaluations.
- Mean Absolute Deviation Method is calculated as the average of absolute value of difference between actual and forecasted value.
- Extrapolation means estimation of future behaviour from the known data, that is, past behaviour.

Questions for Discussion

1. What are the contents of a business plan for a start-up?
2. Briefly describe importance and advantages of planning.
3. What are the essentials of a good planning?
4. What is business forecasting? Explain its need and limitations.
5. What are the various techniques of forecasting?
6. What is the difference between forecasting and planning?

■■■

Chapter 2...

Project Management

Contents ...

Learning Objectives ...

- To understand project management
- To describe project life-cycle
- To study project management maturity
- To apply the nature of project selection models
- To discuss the types of project selection models
- To know the project portfolio process
- To explain project management and the project manager
- To identify the steps of selecting the project manager
- To demonstrate the problems of cultural differences
- To study the impact of institutional environments
- To understand project organisation
- To define matrix organisation

2.1 Project

2.1.1 Definition of Project

Project is a great opportunity for organisations and individuals to achieve their business and non-business objectives more efficiently through implementing change. Projects help us make desired changes in an organised manner and with reduced probability of failure. Projects differ from other types of work (e.g. process, task, procedure). Meanwhile, in the broadest sense a project is defined as a specific, finite activity that produces an observable and measurable result under certain preset requirements. It usually includes a series of interrelated tasks that are planned for execution over a fixed period of time and within certain requirements and limitations such as cost, quality, performance, others.

A project is temporary in the sense that it has a clear beginning and end in time, hence defining scope and resources. A project is unique in the sense that it is not a regular operation, but a definite set of operations intended to achieve a singular goal. So, a project team often includes people who generally don't work together – at times from different organisations and across multiple geographies.

The PMBOK® (Project Management Body of Knowledge) is a standard that has been internationally accepted, this body has defined "Project" as –"*A project is a temporary endeavour undertaken to create a unique product or service*".

Examples of Project

- Engineering projects: construction, software development.
- Industrial projects: factory expansion, new business.

- Infrastructure projects: toll way, sky train.
- Organisational projects: ISO9000, Six Sigma, CMM.
- Development projects: drug eradication, administrative reform.
- Small and personal projects: MBA study, wedding party.

2.1.2 Characteristics of Project

1. A unique, one-time effort which requires the completion of a large number of interrelated activities. It can be divided into sub-tasks that must be accomplished in order to achieve the project goal.
2. A project has a *well-defined purpose*: goal, main objective
3. It's a *non-repetitive activity. Projects have life cycle that is, a finite start and end date.*
4. Requires dedicated *resources*.
5. The team is responsible for planning, scheduling and controlling the project to its completion.
6. Projects are (typically) under-specified.
7. Requirements and solutions are refined as work progresses.
8. Changes are to be expected.
9. It is temporary – temporary means that every project has a definite beginning and a definite end. Project always has a definitive time frame.
10. A project creates unique deliverables, which are products, services, or results.
11. A project creates a capability to perform a service.
12. Project is always developed in steps and continuing by increments – Progressive Elaboration.

2.2 Project Management

Project management is the process of planning and controlling the development of a system within a specified timeframe at a minimum cost with the right functionality. It provides an organisation with powerful tools that improve its ability to plan, implement and control its activities to utilise its resources and people in the most efficient way. It also facilitates co-ordination of resources and labour activities in a meaningful way, such as to meet the requirements of quality, time and money. Project management techniques were mostly used by Military, however nowadays it is commonly used in construction firms, automotive companies; it's also been used in shoes and ship manufacturing companies. It finds its use also in service industry such as advertising companies, etc.

PMBOK® defines project management as *"The application of knowledge, skills, tools, and techniques to project activities in order to meet stake holder's needs and expectations from a project.* 'Its importance is felt when a change occurs in a project that may lead to conflicts and upset the project. So in other words we can say that project management helps preparedness for change. The change can be due to:

1. Requirements change that impact on time, cost, team configuration.
2. Budget changes.
3. Team changes: unexpected departures; realigning work; additions or dismissals.

2.2.1 Why Project Management?

The Need for Project Management therefore is based on following factors

1. Today's Business Environment:
   o Global competitiveness
   o Strong focus on time and on reduced project costs
   o Integration of technology
2. Complexity of project and their needs for coordination:
   o Multiple people
   o Multiple resources (labs, equipment, etc.)
   o Multiple tasks – some must precede others
   o Multiple decision points – approvals
   o Phased expenditure of funds
   o Matching of people/resources to tasks
3. Accelerating Trend:
   o Corporate globalisation
   o Massive mergers and reorganisations
   o Flatter organisations
   o Drive for faster results
   o Multinational projects
4. We can therefore say that "Project Management" provides :
   o Disciplined framework of methods, processes, monitoring and change control
   o A focal point for effective communications, coordination, and control
   o Emphasis on time and cost performance
   o A plan to assess progress

2.2.2 Project Life Cycle

With reference to PMBOK® any project will require following aspects of business, they are:

1. Scope of the project
2. Time required for completion of project

3. Cost involved in a project
4. Human resource – requirements of human resource for the project
5. Procurement of materials
6. Quality standards for the project
7. Risk involved
8. Communication plan

Once the above are considered, the entire plan needs to be integrated as one plan

Each of these business aspects are further broadly classified in to five processes. They are:

1. **Initiating Process Group:** Concept development and feasibility. Processes performed to define a new project or a new phase of an existing project by obtaining authorisation to start the project or phase. The key benefit of this process group is to define the strategy and tactics as well as the course of action or path for successful completion of the project or phase.

2. **Planning Process Group - Design and Development:** Those processes required to establish the scope of the project, refine the objectives, and define the course of action required to attain the objectives that the project was undertaken to achieve.

3. **Execution Process Group - Implementation Phase:** Those processes performed to complete the work defined in the project management plan to satisfy the project specifications.

4. **Controlling Process Group:** Monitoring, Reviewing and Control.

5. **Closing Process Group:** Compiling project assets.

Fig. 2.1: Project Life Cycle

During the **initiation** phase, the activities that are carried out are:

1. Concept development.
2. Creation of designs, drawings etc.
3. Creation of test plans.
4. Creation of training plans – especially if there are technological changes and the team does not possess compatible skills.
5. Creation of deployment plans.
6. Creation of draft operations and maintenance plan.
7. Creating feasibility reports on knowledge availability and risk.
8. Schedule the tasks, account for known vacations, holidays and "busy" times.
9. Update risks.

10. Get approvals.
11. Cost analysis – ROI (return on investment).
12. Estimate time and cost.
13. Project end result - Impact to organisation.
14. Stakeholders are identified.
15. Check for resource over allocation.
16. Communication channels and processes are defined.

During the Project start-up phase these actions are rigorously performed:

1. Plan review and adjustments.
2. Establish a document repository.
3. Kickoff meetings.
4. Include everyone impacted.
5. Use a start-up checklist.
6. Set expectations.
7. All communication channels are used.

The second stage is planning, in this stage the main activity is identification of:

1. Who (project organisation, resources and stakeholders).
2. What (statement of work that is, what work is needed for completion of project, objectives and scope that is, to what extent).
3. What if (contingency plans – alternative plans are also planned just in case earlier plan fails or needs to be ceased).
4. When (schedule and milestones, date and time for each activity of the project is identified).
5. Where (facilities required).
6. How (development approach, work breakdown structures, processes and procedures).

After the above points are carried out it results in creation of project charter that describes:

1. Organisational structure and describes the identified project manager.
2. Methodology, scope and assumptions.
3. Schedule for management for procuring required resources as well as in execution.
4. Communication management.
5. Change and risk management.
6. Cost management.
7. Provisioning and quality benchmarks.
8. Security.

During Project execution phase the following activities are carried out:

1. Work on the plan is carried out.

2. Status updates are recorded.

3. Issue identification and mitigation.

4. Change control is enabled.

5. Quality control is most effective at this stage.

6. Risk mitigation may be required in event of unanticipated change occurs.

7. Always be on the lookout for "scope creep that is, changes in schedule".

8. Keep the plan in front of the team.

9. Regular feedback from all stakeholders and use the feedback provided.

10. Don't "make it up".

In order to effectively execute the projects, the project manager, requires to undertake the following steps:

1. Status Updates

- He/she should conduct regular meetings
- Discuss issues with all team members and stakeholders
- Make required adjustments
- Update the plans based on approved changes

2. Issue Resolution, project manager has to

- Be proactive
- Keep focus on the plan
- Involve management

3. Risk Mitigation

- Conduct regular risk review
- Update "top" risks
- Re-allocate risk reserves
- If you haven't planned for it, this can be painful

During the Project controlling phase the actions of following types are observed:

1. Corrective actions

2. Review and revise project plan

3. Review and revise estimates

4. Communication

Project Conclusion phase:

1. Post implementation evaluation
2. Lessons learned and documentation is completed
3. Measuring success
4. Recognition
5. Celebration

The project life cycle can thus be concluded with the following diagram.

There are 8 areas of project management and each area has five stages that are:

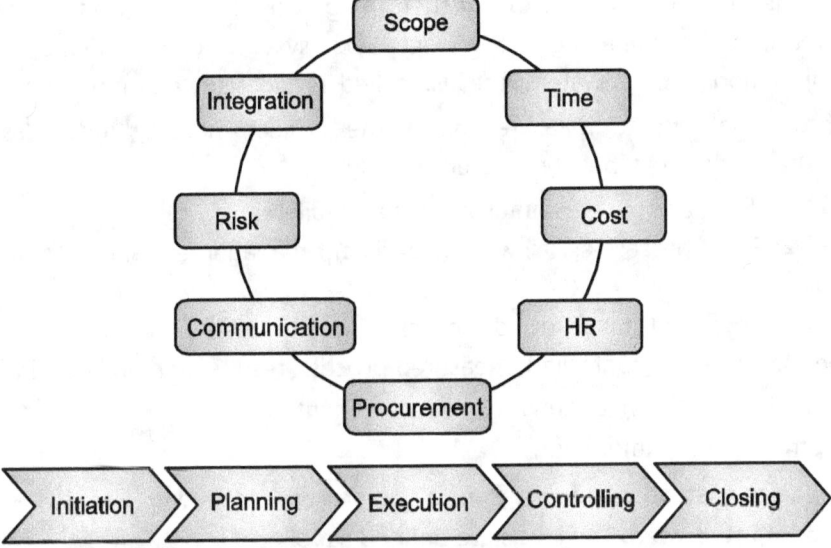

Fig. 2.2 Project Management

Advantages and Benefits of Project Management:

1. Increase stakeholder trust and confidence.
2. Balance competing demands and Identify problem areas.
3. Improve monitoring and control (providing a consistent method for tracking tasks and milestones).
4. Expand communication among participants.
5. Clarify project goals and project scope.
6. Refine projections of resource requirements.
7. Quantify project risk.

Project Management Benefits to Individual

1. Creates high visibility of project results.
2. Enhances both professional and personal growth opportunities.

3. Builds one's reputation and network.

4. Develops portable skills and experience.

5. Provide a mechanism for performance measurement.

6. Future source of company leadership.

2.2.3 Project Maturity Model

Organisations that deal in multiple projects in order to achieve their objectives, it becomes natural for the senior managers to understand if the organisations have the competency for managing multiple projects. For managing the large complex projects the organisations develop process and follow them religiously. Such projects are said to have developed maturity for managing the project. Such systems of operations are called as project maturity models. Such systems are also called as capability maturity models.

One of the methods to measure this is the project maturity model as described by **R Remy**. The model describes the 5 levels namely:

1. **Level 1:** Disorganised, accidental success and failures.
2. **Level 2:** Some process exists, with inconsistent management and with unpredictable results.
3. **Level 3:** Organised standardised processes, more predictable results.
4. **Level 4:** Managed (controlled) measured process, results more in line with plans.
5. **Level 5:** Adaptive, continuous improvement in process, success is normal, performance keep improving.

Another industry standard for measuring the process maturity is **CMMI® – Capability Maturity Model Integrated.** The levels are defined as follows

1. **Level 1 - Initial**

   o Processes are usually ad hoc and the organisation usually does not provide a stable environment. In spite of this ad hoc, chaotic environment, maturity level 1 organisations often produce products and services that work; however, they frequently exceed the budget and schedule of their projects. Such organisations are characterised by a tendency to over commit, abandon processes in the time of crisis, and not be able to repeat their past successes again.

2. **Level 2 - Repeatable**

   o Process discipline helps ensure that existing practices are retained during times of stress. When these practices are in place, projects are performed and managed according to their documented plans.

   o Project status and the delivery of services are visible to management at defined points (for example, at major milestones and at the completion of major tasks).

3. **Level 3 - Defined**

   o The organisation's set of standard processes, which is the basis for level 3, is established and improved over time. These standard processes are used to establish consistency across the organisation.

   o The organisation's management establishes process objectives based on the organisation's set of standard processes and ensures that these objectives are appropriately addressed.

   o A critical distinction between level 2 and level 3 is the scope of standards, process descriptions, and procedures. At level 2, the standards, process descriptions, and procedures may be quite different in each specific instance of the process (for example, on a particular project). At level 3, the standards, process descriptions, and procedures for a project are tailored from the organisation's set of standard processes to suit a particular project or organisational unit.

4. **Level 4 - Managed**

   o Using precise measurements, management can effectively control the project development effort. In particular, management can identify ways to adjust and adapt the process to particular projects without measurable losses of quality or deviations from specifications.

   o Sub-processes are selected that significantly contribute to overall process performance. These selected sub-processes are controlled using statistical and other quantitative techniques.

   o A critical distinction between maturity level 3 and maturity level 4 is the predictability of process performance. At maturity level 4, the performance of processes is controlled using statistical and other quantitative techniques, and is quantitatively predictable. At maturity level 3, processes are only qualitatively predictable.

5. **Level 5 - Optimising**

   o Focusing on continually improving process performance through both incremental and innovative technological improvements.

2.2.4 Project Selection and Criteria of Choice

When the organisations have multiple projects in hand and have shortage of resources or need to go through planning for scheduling the available resources to get maximum benefit. Organisations use a method called project selection criteria matrix. The matrix is prepared by considering total benefits from the projects, value of risks involved, completion time, considerations for funds requirements etc. Each such criterion is than measured against a scale or a grade. The project with maximum grade is then given priority for start.

Example of project selection matrix is given below:

Project selection criteria template is shown below as an example

Criteria's	Weighting	Project 1	Project 2	Project 3	Project 4	Project 5
Benefits (Higher is better)						
Positive financial impact (ROI)	5					
Alignment with strategic direction	5					
Increases standardisation/improves quality	5					
Subtotals						
Risks (Higher is better)						
Appropriate backup plans are in place	5					
Likelihood of project success	5					
Well understood project scope and objectives	5					
Likely willingness of organisation to adopt project	5					
Understanding of project's impact on organisation	5					
Use of standard well understood technologies	5					
Availability of expert resources for assistance	5					
Low time to realise benefits	5					
Low cost to completion	5					
Other prominent aspect	5					
Subtotals						
Total Weighted Score						
Cost Estimate						

2.2.5 The Nature of Project Selection Models

Basically there are two types of project selection models, they are:
1. Numeric
2. Non numeric

A model of some kind is implied by any conscious decision. The choice among two or more alternative courses of action needs reference to some objective(s), and the choice is thus made in accordance with some, perhaps subjective model. Project selection decisions are mainly on the degree to which the financial objectives of the organisation are met.

When the list of objectives has been developed, an extra refinement is suggested. The elements in the list should be subjective. Each item is added to the list since it represents a contribution to the achievement of the organisation. The weights reveal different degrees of contribution, each element makes in achieving a set of goals. Once the list of goals has been developed the probable contribution of each project to each of the goals should be estimated. In general, the kind of information required to calculate a project can be listed under production, marketing, financial, personnel, administrative, etc.

Factors for project selection

1. **Financial Factors:**
    - Profitability, net present value of the investment
    - Impact on cash flows
    - Payout period
    - Cash requirements
    - Time until break even
    - Size of investment required
    - Impact on seasonal and cyclical fluctuations

2. **Marketing Factors:**
    - Size of potential market for the product
    - Probable market share for the product
    - Time until market share is acquired
    - Impact on current product line
    - Consumer acceptance
    - Impact on consumer safety
    - Estimated life of the product
    - Spin-off project possibilities

3. **Production Factors:**
    - Time until ready to install
    - Length of disruption during installation
    - Learning's till full functionality is achieved
    - Effects on waste and rejects
    - Energy requirements
    - Facility and other equipment requirements
    - Safety of processes
    - Other applications of technology
    - Change in cost of production
    - Change in raw material usage

- Availability of raw materials
- Required development time and cost
- Impact on current suppliers
- Change in quality of product

4. **Human Resource Factors:**

- Training requirements
- Labour skill requirements
- Availability of required labour skills
- Level of resistance from current work force
- Change in size of labour force
- Inter and intra group communication requirements
- Impact on working conditions

5. **Administrative and miscellaneous factors:**

- Meet statutory safety and environmental standards
- Impact on information system
- Reaction of stock holders and securities markets
- Patent and trade secret protection
- Impact on image with customers, suppliers and competitors
- Level of acceptance for new technology
- Project handling capabilities

2.2.6 Types of Project Selection Models

1. **Non Numeric Models:**

- **Influential Decision:** In this case the project is suggested by a senior and powerful official in the organisation. The immediate result of this ordinary statement is the creation of the "project" to be investigated. The project is "sacred" in the sense that it will be maintained until successfully concluded or terminated by the boss.

- **The operating Necessity:** If a flood is threatening the plant, the project to build a protective barrier does not require much formal evaluation. The system worth saving at the estimated cost of the project... if the answer is "yes" the project cost will be examined to make sure they are kept as low as is consistent with project success. But the project will be funded.

- **The Competitive Necessity:** A business unit may have started a project some years ago, it becomes apparent that the business may require modernisation if the firm wanted to maintain the competitive position in the market. Such desire to maintain the market position is the competitive necessity for the firm.

- **The Product Line Extension:** In this case, a project to develop and distribute new products would be judged on the degree to which it fits the firms existing product line, fills a gap, strengthens a weak link, or extends the line in a new, desirable direction. Sometimes careful calculations of profitability are not required. Decision makers can act on their beliefs about what will be the likely impact on the total system performance if the new product is added to the line.

- **Comparative Benefit Model:** When the organisation has multiple projects to fulfil the goals, a comparative model is considered for selection of the project. The difficulty may be encountered as the projects base for measurements may not be same. However, generally financial benefit of the organisation is kept as basic priority.

2. **Numeric Models: Profit/Profitability**

A large majority of all firms using project evaluation and selection models use profitability as the sole measure of acceptability.

Following are the models used:

- **Payback Period:** The payback period for a project is the initial fixed investment in the project divided by the estimated annual net cash inflows from the project.

- **Average Rate of Return:** The average rate of return is the ration of the average annual profit to the initial or average investment in the project.

- **Discounted Cash Flow:** The discounted cash flow method determines the next present value of all cash flows by discounting them by the required rate of return known as the hurdle rate, cut off rate.

- **Profitability Index:** Also known as the benefit – cost ratio, the profitability index is the net present value of all future expected cash flows divided by the initial cash investment.

Both the model should have:

- **Realism:** The actual information and not just hypothetical considerations.

- **Capability:** It should be practical and implementable.

- **Flexibility:** It should have inbuilt flexibility so that when changes occur they can be easily accommodated.

- **Ease of use:** They should be simple to use. Complex model tends to defuse the accuracy of results.

- **Cost Effectiveness:** The implementation of such models should be economically viable.

- **Comparability:** The expected results should be compatible for comparison. If they are comparable they will ease decision-making for use of such models.

Advantages of using Models:

1. The undiscounted models are simple to use and understand.
2. All use readily available accounting data to determine the cash flows.
3. With a few exceptions, model output is on an "absolute" profit/profitability scale and allows go ahead or stop decisions.
4. Model output is in terms familiar to business decision makers.
5. Some profit models account for project risk.

Disadvantages of these Models are:

1. These models ignore all non monetary factors except risk.
2. Models that do not include discounting ignore the timing of the cash flows and the time value of money.
3. Models that reduce cash flows to their present value are strongly biased towards the short run.
4. Pay back type models ignore cash flows beyond the payback period.
5. The internal rate of return model can result in multiple solutions.
6. All are sensitive to errors in the input data for the earlier period of the project.
7. All discounting models are non linear and the effects of changes in the variable parameters are generally not obvious to most decision makers.
8. All these models depend for input on the determination of cash flows, but it is not clear exactly of the concept of cash flow is properly defined for the purpose of evaluating projects.

2.2.7 Project Portfolio Process

A portfolio refers to projects, programs, sub-portfolios, and operations managed as a group to achieve strategic objectives. The projects or programs of the portfolio may not necessarily be interdependent or directly related. For example, an infrastructure firm that has the strategic objective of "maximising the return on its investments" may put together a portfolio that includes a mix of projects in oil and gas, power, water, roads, rail, and airports. From this mix, the firm may choose to manage related projects as one program. All of the power projects may be grouped together as a power program. Similarly, all of the water projects may be grouped together as a water program. Thus, the power program and the water program become integral components of the enterprise portfolio of the infrastructure firm.

Project Portfolio management process, is the centralised management of the processes, methods, and technologies used by project managers and project management offices (PMOs) to analyse and jointly handle current or proposed projects based on several key characteristics.

It is used for the following purposes:

- To identify profitable projects and prioritise the list of such projects.
- To intentionally limit the number of overall projects being managed so the important projects get the resources and attention they need.
- To identify project's that are best suited to achieve multiple organisations goals and objectives.
- To eliminate projects that incur excessive risk or cost.
- To keep from overloading organisations resource availability.
- To balance short, medium and long term returns.

Project portfolio process attempts to link the organisations projects directly to the goals and strategies. This occurs not only in the initiation and planning phases, but also throughout the life cycle of the projects. Project portfolio process is also a means for monitoring and controlling the organisation's strategic projects.

2.2.8 Project Proposals

The project proposal is the document prepared before the execution of the project. The project proposal mainly forms the outline of the project and depicts the results of the project. It describes the identified work to be done, explain why this work needs to be done, inform that the team is qualified for the work, have a plausible management plan and technical approach, and have the resources needed to complete the task within the stated time and cost constraints.

It is generally used for giving clarity to the investors and project owners. It is also mainly used for getting funding from financial institution. In short, the set of documents being evaluated is called a project proposal, whether it is brief or extensive, and regardless of the formats used for presentation. The project proposals generally include the following

1. **The Technical Approach:** The proposal commences with a basic description of the problem to be addressed or project to be taken on. If the problem is difficult, the major sub-systems of the problem or project are noted collectively with an organisations approach to each. The presentation is insufficient detail that a familiar reader can understand what the proposer aims to do. Additionally, any special client requirements are listed along with proposed ways of meeting them. All tests and inspection procedures to guarantee performance, value, reliability, and compliance with specifications are noted.

2. **Implementation Plan:** The implementation plan for the project contains estimates of the time required, the cost, and the material used. Every major subsystem of the project is planned along with estimates of its cost. These costs are calculated collectively for the entire project and totals are shown for each cost category. Hours

of work and quantities of material utilised are shown (along with the wage rate and unit material costs). A record of all equipment costs are added as is a list of all overhead and administrative costs.

3. **The Plan for Logistic Support and Administration:** The proposal contains a description of the knack of the proposed to acquire facilities, equipment, and skills required during any project. A crucial issue that needs to be addressed is a reasonably detailed description of how alteration will be handled and how their costs will be estimated.

Components of project proposal:

1. Cover Page
2. Introduction
   o Antecedents
   o History and definition of the problem
   o Justification and intervention
3. Objectives
4. Intervention design and strategy
5. Activities and timeline
6. Budget
7. Evaluation indicators
8. Bibliography
9. Annex

2.3 The Project Manager

The project manager is the person assigned by the performing organisation to lead the team that is responsible for achieving the project objectives. They are the people who have overall responsibility for the successful initiation, planning, design, execution, monitoring, controlling and closure of a project. They are organised, passionate and goal-oriented who understand what projects have in common, and their strategic role in how organisations succeed, learn and change.

Project managers are change agents: they make project goals their own and use their skills and expertise to inspire a sense of shared purpose within the project team. They enjoy the organised adrenaline of new challenges and the responsibility of driving business results. They work well under pressure and are comfortable with change and complexity in dynamic environments. They can shift readily between the "big picture" and the small-but-crucial details, knowing when to concentrate on each. Project managers cultivate the people skills needed to develop trust and communication among all of a project's stakeholders: its sponsors, those who will make use of the project's results, those who command the resources needed, and the project team members. They have a broad and flexible toolkit of techniques, resolving complex, interdependent activities into tasks and sub-tasks that are documented, monitored and controlled. They adapt their approach to the context and constraints of each project, knowing that no "one size" can fit all the variety of projects. And they are always improving their own and their teams' skills through lessons-learned reviews at project completion. Project managers are found in every kind of organisation - as employees, managers, contractors and independent consultants.

2.3.1 Qualities of a Project Manager

1. **Personal Effectiveness**: Personal effectiveness encompasses attitudes, core personality characteristics, and leadership, which provides the ability to guide the project team while achieving project objectives and balancing the project constraints.

2. **Knowledge and Performance**: Domain expertise and project management knowledge is one of the key factor, whereas performance indicates how the project manager applies the knowledge during the process

3. **Ethical, Interpersonal and Conceptual Skills**: Effective project managers require a balance of ethical, interpersonal, and conceptual skills that help them analyse situations and interact appropriately. Interpersonal Skills describes important interpersonal skills, such as:

    o   Leadership

    o   Analytical skills and decision-making

    o   Communication management: A project manager needs to plan the communication channels to facilitate communication between the project manager and top management, the functional areas and the client. The project manager holds meetings and briefings and at times chalks out the agenda's for the meetings, identify the stakeholders and their demands that will have to be met while the project is being implemented.

    o   Team and trust building

    o   Conflict management

    o   Motivating and influencing

    o   Coaching

    o   Negotiation

    o   Political and cultural awareness

2.3.2 Project Manager's Role

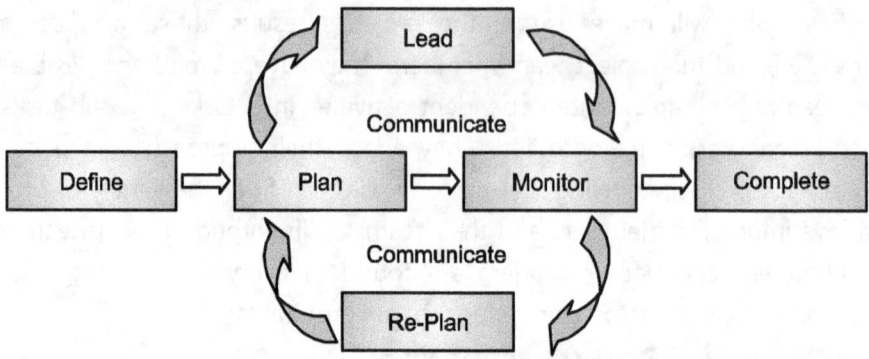

Fig. 2.3: The Project Manager's Role

Project Managers role and responsibilities can be defined as:

1. The project manager is required to manage shared resources across all projects administered by the PMO;
2. Identifying and developing project management methodology, best practices, and standards;
3. Coaching, mentoring, training, and oversight;
4. Monitoring compliance with project management standards, policies, procedures, and templates by means of project audits;
5. Developing and managing project policies, procedures, templates, and other shared documentation (organisational process assets);
6. Co-ordinating communication across projects,
7. Taking timely actions and revising the project plans in accordance with real time implications;
8. The project manager also works closely and in collaboration with other roles, such as a business analyst, quality assurance manager, and subject matter experts;
9. The details of managing the project through its entire life cycle are spread out, even to the point of planning for project termination when the project is finally completed.

2.3.3 Project Management and Project Manager

The unique role of a project manager is in contrast with the functional managers who are in charge of functional departments such as marketing, sales, finance etc. These functional heads are the specialists in the areas they manage. Being specialist they are aware of the details of each operation for which they are responsible. They are decision makers for how a task is to be carried out, whom the task is to be assigned and what are the resources that might be required to accomplish that task. The project manager must see each of the functional areas each with its own specialist. The project manager should therefore be skilled at synthesis whereas the functional managers should be skilled at analysis. The functional manager uses analytical approach whereas the project manager uses systems approach.

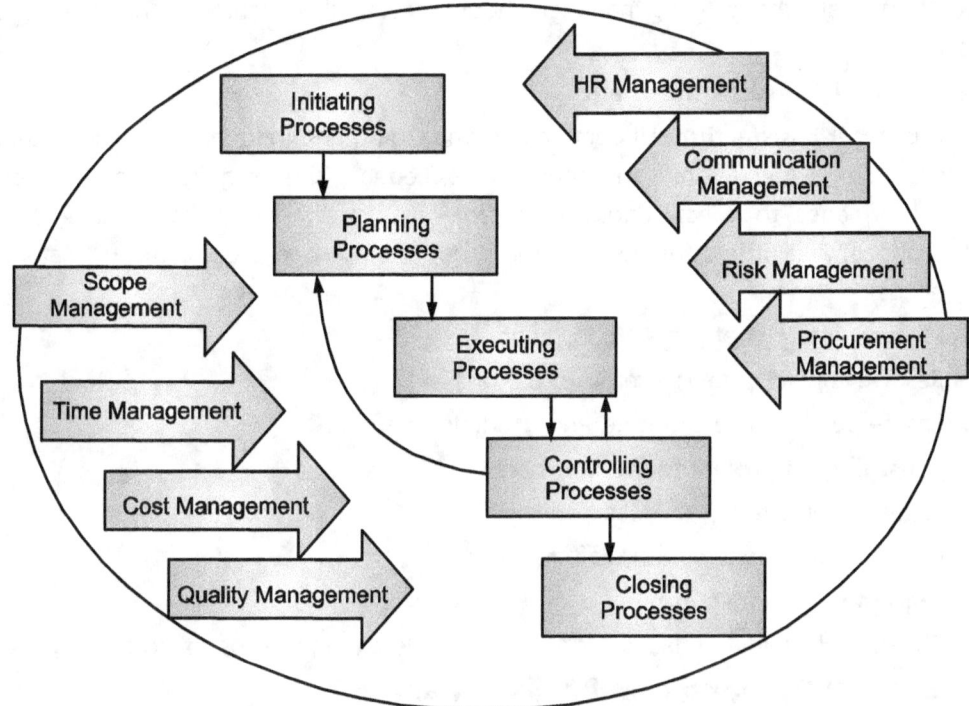

Fig. 2.4: Responsibility areas for a Project Manager

The above figure shows the five stages of project life cycle namely initiation, planning, executing, controlling and closing. These are the responsibility areas for a project manager. However, he also is required to communicate and co-ordinate with other functional areas at different times in the whole project life cycle. The project manager should be identified and assigned as early as possible in the project.

As stated earlier, the project manager is responsible for organising, staffing, budgeting, directing, planning and controlling the project, but the functional managers may affect the choice of technology to be used by the project and the specific individuals who will do the work.

1. Responsibilities towards the Parent Organisation:

Responsibilities to the firm itself include proper conservation of resources, timely and accurate project communications and the careful, competent management of the project. It is very important to keep senior management of the parent organisation informed about the project's status, cost, timing, prospects and outcomes. Senior managers should be warned about likely future problems. The project manager should note the chances of running over budget or being late, as well as methods available to reduce the likelihood of these dread events. Reports must be accurate and timely if the project manager is to maintain credibility, protect the organisation from high risk and allow the senior management to intercede where needed. Above all, the project manager should never allow senior management to be surprised.

2. **Responsibility towards the Client**

   - **Customer Satisfaction:** Understanding, managing and influencing needs so that the customer expectations are met or exceeded. This requires combination of conformance to specifications (the project must produce what it said it would produce) and fitness for the use (the product or service produced must satisfy real needs).
   - Preserve integrity of project and client.
   - Resolve conflict among interested parties.
   - Ensure performance, budgets, and deadlines are met.

3. **Responsibility to project team members**

   - Fairness, consistency, respect, honesty
   - Concern for members' future after project

4. **Prevention over Inspection:**

   - The cost of avoiding mistakes is always much less than the cost of correcting them.

2.3.4 Special Demands on Project Manager

A lot of demands are exclusive to the management of projects and the success of the PM to a huge extent depends on how skilfully they are handled. These special demands can be categorised under the following headings:

   o Acquiring sufficient resources
   o Acquiring and inspiring personnel
   o Finding sources of internal motivation
   o Dealing with obstacles
   o Making project goal trade-offs
   o Dealing with risk and failure (perceived or otherwise)
   o Maintaining multiple channels of communication
   o Negotiation

   1. **Acquiring Sufficient Resources:** Project manager needs to do planning for getting necessary resources for the project. In case of human resource, the project manager needs to identify how many people will be needed, when would they be required in the project, what type of skills set would be required, what cost would they be

available. In case of material requirements, the project manager needs to plan for procurement such as identification of suppliers, quality and quantity requirements, payment terms and conditions etc.

2. **Acquiring and Inspiring Personnel:** Project manager functions as the leader and has to keep his team motivated to perform and deliver results. Not all motivation comes from financial offerings. Project manager needs to identify different sources of motivation for his team

3. **Finding Sources of Internal Motivation:** Changes and conflicts are an integral part of projects. They do occur and at times the frustration level of the project manager crosses the stress limits. Therefore the first motivator is project manager himself and needs to find sources of internal motivation or motivation from his near and dear ones.

4. **Dealing with Obstacles:** The project manager should work on processes to avoid occurrence of problems in the projects.

5. **Making Project Goal Trade-offs:** Project manager needs to constantly work to keep check on the implementation/execution. He needs to constantly make adjustments that is, trade-offs and keep the process in line with the project management plans.

6. **Dealing with Risk and Failure (Perceived or otherwise):** Project manager works on three levels

    o   He keeps vigilance on risks that might occur and avoid them at early stage.

    o   He tries to mitigate the risk in case it occurs.

    o   He accepts the risk and moves ahead with the project. Here many times if the risk is not identified in the beginning and is of a large value it may result in total project failure.

7. **Maintaining Multiple Channels of Communication:** He works on communication plan and keeps track to understand that the team and the stakeholders are using the multiple communication channels for clarity and avoid problems arising from miscommunication.

8. **Negotiation:** The project manager has to negotiate at different levels. For funding and other approvals the project manager needs to negotiate with project owners, financial institution or major stakeholders. The project manager has to negotiate for costs and terms with material suppliers and vendors. The project manager also strongly needs to negotiate with human resource for their unplanned demands and the consequences that may impact the project.

2.4 Problems of Cultural Differences

Major complication for project managers is in managing projects that are being carried out in a multicultural environment. It is not merely the differences in cultures that matter but it is the differences between the environment within which the projects are conducted such as economic, political, legal and socio-technical environments that require understanding of specific cultural requirements of the region.

While the impacts of these dissimilarities are greatest and most visible in the case of international projects, they exist to some extent in all organisations (including the different parts of the same organisation).

The salient features of the term culture in context of project management are as follows:

1. The term "culture" refers to the entire way of life for a group of people. It encompasses every aspect of living and has four elements that are common to all cultures, technology, institutions, language and arts.

2. The technology of a culture includes such things as the tools used by people, the material things they produce and use, the way they prepare food, their skills and their attitude towards work. It considers all aspects of their material lives.

3. Institutions of a culture make up the structure of the society. This category contains the organisation of the government, the nature of the family, the way in which the religion is organised as well as the content of the religious doctrine, the division of labour, the kind of economic system adopted, the system of education and the way in which voluntary associations are formed and maintained.

2.4.1 Dimensions of Culture

The most Popular Dimensions of culture are:

1. **Language:** The languages of the world such as English and Chinese are spoken by millions and others such as Maltase are spoken by only few. Some countries have one official language whereas countries like India, Canada and Switzerland have more than one official language.

2. **Time orientation:** Concept of time is treated differently in different countries.

3. **Use of space:** This concept is different in different countries. Space where the person sits and a distance of 2 feet should be avoided as it is considered as intimate space. 2 to 4 feet is considered ideal for business negotiations. This space is termed as personal space. 4 to 12 feet is a social arena and beyond 12 feet is considered as space for public.

4. **Religion:** A major element of culture. The influence of religion often prescribed as rituals, holy days, and foods that can be eaten. Codes of ethics and moral behaviour often have their roots in religious beliefs. In Malaysia, business dinners are scheduled about 8 pm so that Muslim guests can first attend to their evening prayers

2.4.2 Cultural Influences

Culture is the "totality of socially transmitted behaviour patterns, arts, beliefs, institutions and all other products of human work and thought". Every project must operate within a context of one or more cultural norms. This area of influence includes political, economic, demographic, educational, ethical, ethnic, religious and other areas of practice, belief and attitudes that affect the way people and organisations interact.

2.4.3 Organisational Cultures and Style

1. Most organisations have developed unique and described cultures. These cultures are reflected in their shared values, norms, beliefs and expectations. They are also reflected in their policies and procedures, in their view of authority relationships and in numerous other factors. Organisational cultures often have direct influence on the project. For example:-

2. A team proposing an unusual or high risk approach is more likely to secure approval in an aggressive or entrepreneur organisation.

3. A project manager with a highly participative style is apt to encounter problems in a rigidly hierarchical organisation, while a project manager with an authoritarian style will be equally challenged in a participative organisation.

4. Finally, the arts or aesthetic values of culture are as important to communication as the culture's language. If communication is the glue that binds a culture together, art is the most efficient means of communicating.

2.5 Impact of Institutional Environments

In a general systems theory, the environment of a system is defined as everything external to the system that receives system outputs from it or delivers inputs to it. This is also called as "Business or Work Climate". The project management team should understand that present existing conditions and trends in this area may have an important effect on their projects. A minute change can translate, usually with a pause, in to disruption in the project itself. Apart from the many potential socioeconomic influences, some major categories that regularly affect projects are described below:

1. **Socio-economic Environment:** The need to interact with government and representatives of governments is one of the primary concerns for the project manager. The project managers or the senior management can expect to deal with bureaucracy at several different levels (that is, local, regional, and national government functionaries). Any project manager should include responsibility for acquiring working knowledge of the culture of any country in which to conduct a project. An unwelcome truth is that the cultures of many countries will not offer a female project manager the same level of respect shown to a male project manager. There are antisocial elements that are to be dealt with by the project manager and they often are the cause of delays and unsafe environment.

2. **Legal Environment:** The impact that different cultures have on the process of negotiation, with special attention paid to the society's institutional structure and patterns of communication. Failure to understand the culture of a nation in which negotiations are taking place puts ignorant party at a severe disadvantage. Law results from the attempt to reduce conflict by regularised process, because the conflicts in a country are in part, a reflection of its unique culture; it follows that the laws of a nation will also be unique. The project manger and senior management should, if proprietary knowledge is valuable, make adequate provision for its protection by using the country's law.

3. **Business Cycle as an Environment:** The project manager should be aware of the general level of business conditions in the nation hosting the project. In times of relatively high unemployment, most nations will erect institutional barriers in order to slow or prevent projects that might negatively affect their balances of trade. These barriers may take the form of mandated delays, failure to approve investments, unwillingness to allow repatriation of earnings, "inability" to locate necessary rare resources, local officials to grant required permissions, lack of needed capital and equipment and great many other forms. The project managers can earn valuable goodwill by purchasing goods and services from vendors in the host country and by employing qualified nationals. Project managers should be sensitive to economic problems in the host country and be willing to adapt, as far as possible to local commercial customs.

2.6 Project Organisation

Most organisations when they grow generally are found to add resources and people. Managing the communication and reporting an organisational structure is created and is pictorially depicted; such diagram is called as organisation structure diagram.

Whether the organisation is conducting a few occasional projects or is fully project-oriented and carries on scores of projects, any time a project is initiated, three organisational issues immediately arise.

1. A decision must be made about how to tie the project to the parent firm.
2. A decision must be made about how to organise the project itself.
3. A decision must be made about how to organise activities that are common to other projects. This is also called as resource pooling.

Organisational Systems

Project-based organisations are those whose operations consist primarily of projects. These organisations fall in to following categories

1. Organisations that derive their revenue primarily from performing projects for others– architectural firms, engineering firms, consultants, construction contractors, government contractors etc.

2. Organisations that have adopted management by project. These organisations tend to have management systems in place to facilitate project management. For example, their financial systems are often specifically designed for accounting, tracking and reporting on multiple simultaneous projects.

Non-project based organisations: Manufacturing companies, financial service firms, etc, seldom have management systems designed to support project needs efficiently and effectively. The absence of the project – oriented systems usually make project management more difficult. In some cases, non – project - based organisations will have departments or other sub units that operate as project based organisation with systems to match.

2.6.1 The Project as a Part of the Functional Organisation

For functionally organised projects, the project is assigned to the functional unit that has the utmost interest in ensuring its successes or can be most helpful in implementing it.

Organisational Structure Influences on Project:

Organisation Type / Project Characteristics	Functional	Matrix			Project based
		Weak Matrix	**Balanced Matrix**	**Strong Matrix**	
Project Manager's Authority	Little or none	Limited	Low to Moderate	Moderate to High	High to Almost Total
Percent of Performing Organisations Personnel Assigned Full-time to Project Work	Virtually None	0-25%	15-60%	50-95%	85-100%
Project Manager's Role	Part-time	Part-time	Full-time	Full-time	Full-time
Common Titles for Project Manager's Role	Project Co-ordinator / Project Leader	Project Co-ordinator / Project Leader	Project Manager / Project Officer	Project Manager / Program Manager	Project Manager / Program Manager
Project Management Administrative Staffing	Part-time	Part-time	Part-time	Full-time	Full-time

The table is taken as reference from PMBOK®.

The project management team should be acutely aware of how the organisation's systems affect the project. For example, if the organisation rewards it functional managers for charging staff time to projects, the project management team may need to implement controls to ensure that assigned staff are being used effectively on the project.

2.6.2 Organisation Structures

The classic functional organisation as shown in figure below is a hierarchy where each employee has one clear superior. Staffs are grouped by speciality, such as production, marketing, engineering and accounting at the top level, with engineering further subdivided into mechanical and electrical. Functional organisations still have projects, but the perceived scope of the project is limited to the boundaries of the function. The engineering department in a functional organisation will do its work independent of the manufacturing or marketing departments. For example, when a new product development is undertaken in a purely functional organisation, the design phase is often called a "design project" and includes only engineering department staff. If questions about manufacturing arise, they are passed up the hierarchy to the department head who consults with the head of the manufacturing departments. The engineering department head then passes the answer back down the hierarchy to the engineering project manager.

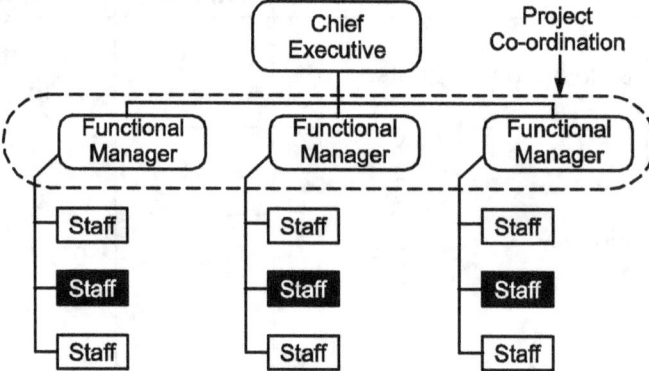

Fig. 2.5: Organisation Structures

The above information and figure has been taken as reference from PMBOK®

2.6.3 Pure Project-based Organisation

Any organisational structure in which the project manager has full authority to assign priorities and to direct the work of individuals assigned to the project. In a project-based organisation, team members are often collocated. Most of the organisation's resources are involved in project work and project managers have a great deal of independence and authority. Project-based organisations often have organisational units called departments, but these groups either report directly to the project manager or provide support services to the various projects.

With pure project-based organisation, the project team is established as a new self-sufficient organisational unit. The project manager and the project team members work full-time on the project. The project manager has the responsibility of the complete management and complete decision-making authority with the exemption of the milestone decisions, the outcome of which is an efficient and independent task force. This structure can be significantly more costly as new recruits have to be hired into the existing posts. In case the project does not make use of everyone's time, there can be a loss of unused staff time. This structure is apt for complex projects, for time-critical activities or for projects that will create results, crucial and decisive for the company.

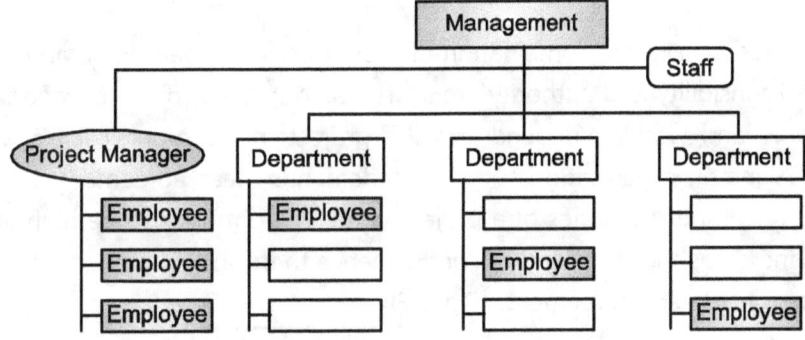

Fig. 2.6: Pure Project-Based Organisation

The advantages are:

- Easy and quick, as the project manager has complete authority over the project and all members of the project team report directly to the project manager.
- Less of communication and more of work; the ability to make a swift decision is improved - A cross-functional integration is supported as a pure project organisation can sustain a permanent cadre of experts who develop skills in specific technologies.
- A project team that has a strong and unique identity and develops a high level of commitment from its members.
- The organisational structure tends to support a holistic approach to the project.

The disadvantages are:

- Each project has to be entirely staffed which can lead to duplication of staff numbers.
- Project managers tend to store equipment and technical assistance as this represents the value of their project in the organisation.
- Pure project groups seem to promote inconsistency in the way in which policies and procedures are carried out.
- In a pure project organisation, the project takes on a life of its own, with own rules and processes - The post-project evolution is difficult as it tends to concern the team members about their careers after the project ends.

2.6.4 Matrix Organisation

Matrix organisations are blend of functional and project-based characteristics. Weak matrices maintain many of the characteristics of a functional organisation and project manager role is more that of a co-ordinator or expeditor than that of a manager. In similar manner, strong matrices have many of the characteristics of the project-based organisation, full-time project managers with considerable authority and full-time project administrative staff. Any organisational structure in which the project manager shares responsibility with the functional managers for assigning priorities and for directing the work of individuals assigned to the project.

Matrix organisations are a combination of a pure project organisation and a project co-ordination. Responsibility and authority are shared among the project manager and the line bodies. Dividing and working depends on the project in question which again can vary significantly. A matrix organisational structure demands clear agreement concerning the duties of line team and the duties of a project team. There must also be high awareness of roles. All this increases the likelihood of conflict hence there should be good communication to resolve issues and reach agreements (Fig. 2.7).

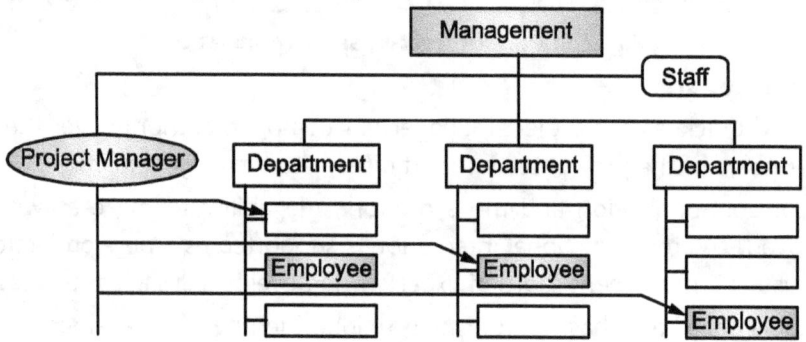

Fig. 2.7: Matrix Organisational Structure

A matrix organisation can take on a wider form:

"Project" or "strong" matrix organisations most closely resemble the pure project organisation. The project manager chooses work and personnel-progress, the line manager offers resources and consults the project manager as an expert.

The "co-ordination" or "functional" or "weak" matrix most directly resembles the functional form. The project manager only co-ordinates the assistance of different departments, the authority stays with the department-directors.

The "balanced" matrix lies in between the others. Project and line managers roughly have equal competence and agree upon a common decision.

The advantages are:

- The advantages of a functional organisation and project team structure are reserved.
- Resources can be co-ordinated in a way that applies to them efficiently to different projects.
- Team members can be in touch with project teams plus their functional department colleagues, they can be chosen in-time, as per the needs of the project.
- The project team will be more responsive and be able to analyse problems in a different way as specialists have been brought together mutually in a new environment.
- Project managers are directly accountable for completing the project by a specific deadline and budget.
- Team members can return to their old line responsibility after completing the project.

The disadvantages are:

- Possiblility of conflict among functional v/s project groups due to unclear responsibilities as the principle of unity of command is violated with a matrix organisation.
- If more (project) managers are produced through the use of project teams, a conflict of loyalty between line managers and project managers over the allocation of resources costs increases. The balance of power involving the project and functional areas is very delicate.
- The division of authority and responsibility in a matrix organisation is complex and uncomfortable for the project manager.
- Project workers have at least two bosses, their functional heads and the project manager.

2.6.5 Choosing the Organisational Form

The first and most important key to success for project management is choosing the right project organisation. As a result, consideration should be given to the decision about formation, preparation, and initiation of the project organisation.

Even experienced practitioners find it difficult to explain how one should proceed when choosing the organisational interface between project and firm. There are few accepted principles of design, and no step-by-step procedures that give detailed instructions for determining what kind of structure is needed and how it can be built. All we can do is consider the nature of the potential project, the characteristics of the various organisational options, the advantages and disadvantages of each, the cultural preferences of the parent organisation, and take the best compromise.

A firm that handles large number of similar projects simultaneously for example, construction project, the pure project form of organisation is preferred. The same form would generally be used for one time, highly specific unique task that require careful control and are not appropriate for a single functional area.

Additional matters to be considered are the individuals (or small groups) who will do the work, their personalities, the technology to be employed, the clients to be served, the political relationships of the functional units involved and the culture of the parent organisation. Environmental factors inside and outside the parent organisation must also be taken into account, by understanding various structures, their advantages and disadvantages, a firm can select the organisational structure that seems to offer the most effective and efficient choice.

In order to define the goals and implications of the project in the current organisational structure a step-wise approach is advisable:

Step 1: Definition of the project, with a statement that reveals the major outcomes from all different points of view (top management, shareholder, stakeholder etc.) Standardised decision matrixes are accessible in a wide range with experienced project managers. However, the following points already will give a hint of what should be considered:

- Size of project
- Strategic importance, how important is the project to the firm's successes?
- Novelty and need for innovation
- Integration requirements (departments involved)
- Complexity (number of external interfaces)
- Budget and time constraints
- What level of resources (human and physical) is available?
- Stability of resource requirements

Step 2: Determination of the key tasks related to sub-goal or objective and identification of the specialist / individuals in the parent organisation and their "home- departments.

Step 3: Breaking down the project into tasks and deciding which organisational units are necessary to carry out the work packages and which units will work closely with one another.

Step 4: List of any special characteristic or obstructing factor associated with the project.

Step 5: With the findings gained from steps 1-4 and the knowledge of all advantages and disadvantages choice of structural organisation form.

Recent developments show that today companies tend to change the project organisation more during the project, as shown in figure 2.8.

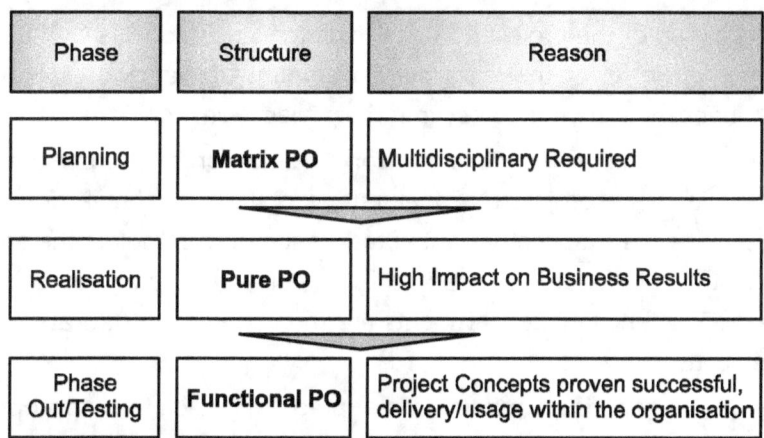

Phase	Structure	Reason
Planning	**Matrix PO**	Multidisciplinary Required
Realisation	**Pure PO**	High Impact on Business Results
Phase Out/Testing	**Functional PO**	Project Concepts proven successful, delivery/usage within the organisation

Fig. 2.8: Organisational Structures in the Project Life Cycle

The advantages of different project organisations are utilised by such an approach. All through the planning period, maximum knowledge of different departments can be given to the project, while not all team members have to be involved completely in the project. In the realisation phase, a pure project organisation assists the project team to concentrate only on the completion of the project goals and in the last stage, team members can more simply reintegrate into their line function by selecting a functional project organisation and can facilitate the integration of the newly found knowledge into their "home" departments.

The organisational set-up determines the way a project is delivered. Therefore, an effective organisation is vital to the successful delivery of projects on time, to budget and for specification. Consequently, a great deal of time and attention must be given to project organisations while initiating new projects.

An effective project organisation identifies the key positions across the wider organisation, including the advisory team, the steering committee and the sponsor, if possible. On deciding upon these key roles, clear terms of reference and accountabilities for all roles and bodies; for example, project manager, steering committee have to be established and also communicated (in writing) to the project team. The position and the role of the organisation framework, like supplier, partner or customer interfaces has to be defined at all levels, along with their definite responsibilities towards the project. The operational structure also has to contain the ways of working for the team, featuring the execution of the work with key partners, supplier, and the customer. Lastly, a governance structure for the project has to be developed.

2.7 The Project Team

A project team is a team whose members usually belong to different groups, functions and are assigned to activities for the same project. A team can be divided into sub-teams according to need. Usually project teams are only used for a defined period of time. They are disbanded after the project is deemed complete.

From the beginning of the project, to its termination, crisis appears without warning. The better the planning, the fewer the crisis but no amount of planning can take account of innumerable changes that can and do occur in the project's environment.

To staff the project, the project manager works from a forecast of personnel needs over the projects life cycle. The project manager refers to the work break down structures is prepared to determine the exact nature of the task required to complete the project. The skill requirements for these tasks are assessed and like skills are aggregated to determine the work force needs. The functional departments are then contacted to locate individuals who can meet these needs.

Sometimes, subcontracting option is adopted because the appropriately skilled personnel are unavailable or cannot be located, or even because some special equipments required for the project is not available in house. There are some people who are more critical to the project's success than others such as

1. Senior project team members who will have long-term relationship with the project.
2. Those with which the project manager will require continuous or close communication.
3. Those with rare skills necessary for project's success.

Although the project manager has to bargain for fewer individuals then in the case of stronger matrix organisations, the project managers negotiation skills are just as critical. It is typical for the success of weak matrix organisation projects to be dependent on the skills of the few technical specialists who are assigned directly to the project. The ability of the project manager to negotiate for skilled technicians as well as for the timely delivery of services from functional departments is a key determinant of success.

2.7.1 Project Team Members

Let us use the example of an engineering project to determine how to form a project team.

1. **Project engineers:** The project engineer is in charge of the product design and development and is responsible for functional analysis, specifications, drawings, cost estimates, quality/reliability, engineering changes and documentation.
2. **Manufacturing engineers:** This engineer's task is the efficient production of the product or process the project that the engineer has designed, including the responsibility for manufacturing, engineering, design and production of tooling, jigs/fixtures, production scheduling and other production tasks.
3. **Field Manager:** This person is responsible for the installation, testing and support of the product or process once it is delivered to the customer.

4. **Contract Administrator:** The administrator is in charge of all official paper work, keeping track of customer changes, billings, questions, complaints, legal aspects, cost and other matters related to the contract authorising the project. Not uncommonly, the contract administrator also serves project historians and activists.

5. **Project controller:** The controller keeps daily account of budgets, cost variance, labour charges, project supplies, capital equipment status etc. The controller also makes regular reports and keeps in close touch with both the project manager and the company controller. If the administrator does not serve as historian, the controller can do so.

6. **Support services manager:** The person in charge of a product support, subcontractors, data processing and general management support function.

2.7.2 Criteria for Selection of Project Team Members

Selection of project team members is based on the following criteria:

1. **High Quality Technical Skills:** Team members should be able to solve most of the technical problems of a project without any outside assistance. Even if the relevant functional department has furnished technical specialist to the project, the exact way technology that is applied, usually requires adaptation by the project team. In addition, a great many minor technical difficulties occur, always at inconvenient times and need to be handled rapidly. In such cases, project schedules will suffer, and therefore these difficulties must be referred back to the functional departments where they will have to stand in line for a solution along with the departments own problem.

2. **Political Sensitivity:** It is obvious that the project manger requires political skills of a high order. Although it is less obvious, senior project members also need to be politically skilled and sensitive to organisational politics.

3. **Strong Problem Orientation:** Chances for successful completion of a multidisciplinary project are greatly increased if project team members are problem-oriented rather than discipline-oriented.

4. **Strong Goal Orientation:** Projects do not provide a comfortable work environment for individuals whose focus is on activity rather than on results.

5. **High self esteem:** As we noted earlier, a prime law for projects is: never surprise the boss! Projects can get rapidly into deep trouble if the team members hide their failures, or even a significant risk of failure, from the project manager. Individual's in the team should have sufficient self esteem that they are not threatened by acknowledgement of their own errors, or by pointing out possible problems caused by the work of others.

6. **Current Practices in organisations:** Nowadays many organisations especially for large and long term projects are selecting project team members based on soft skills such as attitude and behaviour and interpersonal skills. For this purpose, many psychometric tests are used that can help project managers to identify the right person with right skills, knowledge and attitude.

Points to Remember

- A project is a great opportunity for organisations and individuals to achieve their business and non-business objectives more efficiently through implementing change.

- Project management is the process of planning and controlling the development of a system within a specified time frame at a minimum cost with the right functionality. It provides an organisation with powerful tools that improve its ability to plan, implement and control its activities to utilise its resources and people in most efficient way.

- Managing the large complex projects, developing processes and following them religiously, is a system of operations called as project maturity models.

- There are two types of project selection models, they are:
  1. Numeric
  2. Non numeric

- A portfolio refers to projects, programs, sub-portfolios, and operations managed as a group to achieve strategic objectives. The projects or programs of the portfolio may not necessarily be interdependent or directly related.

- The project proposal is the document prepared before the execution of the project. The project proposal mainly forms the outline of the project and depicts the results of the project.

- The project manager is the person assigned by the performing organisation to lead the team that is responsible for achieving the project objectives. They are the people who have overall responsibility for the successful initiation, planning, design, execution, monitoring, controlling and closure of a project.

- Most organisations when they grow generally are found to add resources and people. Managing the communication and reporting an organisational structure is created and is pictorially depicted; such diagram is called as organisation structure diagram.

- Matrix organisations are blend of functional and project-based characteristics. Weak matrices maintain many of the characteristics of a functional organisation and a project manager's role is more that of a co-ordinator or expeditor than that of a manager.

- Any organisational structure in which the project manager has full authority to assign priorities and to direct the work of individuals assigned to the project is pure project-based Organisation.

Questions for Discussion

1. What are the areas that are required to be managed in any project?
2. What are the groups of project management process?
3. What is project maturity model?
4. What are project selection critieria?
5. Write briefly the importance and benefits of project management?
6. What are the functions and responsibilities of a project manager?
7. What are the components of project proposal?

■■■

Chapter 3...

Initial Project

Contents ...

Learning Objectives ...

- To Understand the Nature of Negotiation
- To Discuss Partnering
- To Explain Chartering and Change
- To Highlight Conflict and the Project Life Cycle
- To Elaborate on Estimating Project Budgets
- To Explain the improved Process of Cost Estimation

3.1 Initial Project Co-ordination

Project co-ordination generally refers to planning and managing multiple tasks simultaneously. We have seen that planning is essential for successful outcome of a project. However, in real life, as a first step to start working on the project, basic information gathering and feasibility is taken into consideration. For example, construction of building may initially require understanding of the land acquisition, soil testing, funds availability, market survey, etc. This gives the investor or the project owner an understanding of the feasibility and return on investments from the project. In case of information technology product, one needs to co-ordinate activities of requirements gathering from the customer, identifying availability of the resources within the organisation and financial outcome of the project. The above examples indicate that when several tasks are to be performed simultaneously, co-ordination becomes critical.

Projects vary, based on business objectives but may include launching a new product or expanding services into new areas.

1. **Project scope:** Project scope basically consists of an understanding of the following aspects areas within the project

    (a) **Time required:** A block idea of the estimation of the time required to complete all activities of the project. Milestones are also set during this stage to monitor the progress of the project during execution phase.

    (b) **Cost Estimation:** Total cost that may be incurred for completion of the project, availability of funds and ROI from the project is done during the scope of the project.

    (c) **Human Resource Requirement:** This resource information is also mapped to get the first level understanding of how many people would be required and with what skill sets, when would they be required in the project and at what cost would be incurred to acquire such resources. In case of multinational projects, another important factor that needs to be considered is the cultural differences and facilities to be provided in order to reduce the imbalance and conflicts.

    (d) **Quality:** A basic benchmarking for the procurement of resources as well as confirmation to the government regulatory obligations as well as promises to the customer with sales perspective is considered during the scope of the project.

    (e) **Procurement:** Setting guidelines for procuring different material/resources from vendors, their terms and condition for the contract, quality benchmarks and schedule of procurement is prepared during the scope of the project.

    (f) **Risks:** Basic risk list is prepared based on historical information that is, from prior project experiences, estimation of risks and budgets for risk are identified during the scope of the project.

    (g) **Communication:** An understanding of communication plan is prepared which describes who should be given what information, by which medium the information should be communicated and who shall be responsible to take action on the communication.

2. **Software:** Incorporate software programmes to increase efficiency, such as to maintain project files and manage key information. Some commonly available softwares are Microsoft project, Primavera etc. For consistency and better understanding, most of the organisations use standard templates for work flows. For certain projects, spreadsheets, graphs or wall charts work effectively. You also utilise programs like Microsoft Excel or Project, or even develop proprietary software. Make sure that project information remains easily accessible to key participants.

3. **Considerations:** Assumptions and constraints for the project are listed and alternative identification is done during the scope of the project. This also facilitates in cost benefit analysis of the materials with respect to earlier projects. The identification of inclusions and exclusions in the project are also listed while preparing the scope of the project.

4. **Management:** At the end of the scope process, the project charter is prepared which is duly signed by all the stakeholders and the formal authority is given to the project manager to start the project execution process.

3.2 Nature of Negotiation

In business, we negotiate every day. Negotiation is an invaluable skill for any project manager. Not only do you negotiate agreements with vendors and contractors, but one effectively negotiates with stakeholders, customers, and team members throughout the life of a project. Project managers, for example, negotiate for resources, scope changes, costs, contracts and a myriad of other critical items. Functional managers and programme managers negotiate budgets and resources and sometimes hiring and firing. Auditors negotiate with their customers regarding timing of audit, findings, action dates, and report wording. To move up in an organisation, management demands excellent negotiation skills. At the top, the power of negotiation is well-recognised. CEOs sometime use "super lawyers" to negotiate better employment contracts for themselves. Improving your understanding of the negotiation process and your comfort level are keys to improve your skills.

The favoured technique for resolving conflict is negotiation. What is negotiation? Wall in 1985, prefaced defines negotiation as "the process through which two or more parties seek an acceptable rate of exchange for items they own or control.

"Negotiation is a field of knowledge and endeavour that focuses on gaining the favour of people from whom we want things".

Organisations consist of interdependent units that have their own values, interest, perceptions and goals. Each unit seeks to fulfil its particular goal and the effectiveness of the organisation depends on the success of each unit's fulfilment of its specialised task. Important task is the integration of the unit's activities such that each unit's activities aid or at least do not conflict with those of others. Approaching intra project conflicts with a desire to win a victory over other parties is inappropriate.

'Persuasion' and 'Compromise' are the two central features of negotiating. In a typical encounter where we are trying to influence the other person, we will first try to persuade them to adopt our point of view. They will similarly try to persuade us that we cannot maintain our original position. There comes a crucial point in any discussion when you realise that in order to break the impasse, one of you need to compromise and change position. What distinguishes negotiation from other types of persuasion is that both parties are prepared to move from the status quo. If you are truly negotiating, both parties must be prepared to move from their original position, conceding issues to the other person. For a negotiation to be successful, the negotiators must freely reach a viable agreement or compromise. There are many kinds of negotiations conducted during a project, including initial contract negotiations with consultants, change negotiations during planning and design, and construction changes. All parties should recognise that negotiations of scope, price, terms, schedule and other factors are key steps in determining the ultimate project quality as well as customer satisfaction.

In many cases, negotiations establish working relationships for the project. The negotiation process can be used to develop mutual respect and to learn the most effective way to communicate, as well as how best to work together. Additionally, experience has shown dramatically that project contracts which have been effectively negotiated result in far fewer incidences of misunderstanding leading to claims and resultant litigation, which in itself is time consuming, frustrating and expensive. As a result, the process of negotiation must be treated with the same level of respect as the preparation and execution of the project.

During the negotiation process, an ethical situation often arises. The ethics of the situation requires that each party in the negotiation be honest with the other.

3.3 Partnering, Chartering and Change

Projects offer ample opportunities to the project manager to utilise his/her negotiation skills.

1. Partnering

Due to project complexities the project manager is burdened by multiple tasks to be carried out simultaneously. This results in losing out control on certain project areas resulting in losses. To avoid such situations and get timely and qualitative outcomes within the budgeted cost, nowaday's the part of the projects are outsourced. The outsourced vendors act as partners for that particular process or part of the project. This is called partnering. At times for funding purpose, investors are called in the project on profit sharing basis they can also be treated as financing partners for the project.

Partnering, through better teamwork, improves performance. A project mutually draws together, a mix of people and organisations that contribute to and have a stake in the project's achievement. Through partnering, the customer, community, consultants, prime contractor, major subcontractors, and suppliers structure one project team to mutually develop commitments to teamwork, collective goals, open communications, and quick issue resolution. Since, the contributors prioritise their individual interests, creating guarded or adversarial relationships, projects fail to meet their potential. Partnering proposes an alternative approach of management by promoting trust and respect to complete the project meeting shared stakeholders' expectations – in a successful manner for everyone.

Definitions:

"Partnering is the premier team-building tool available to the project manager: Aligning the team to pull together for a smooth running project that meets its potential."

"Project partnering is a method of transforming contractual relationships into a cohesive, co-operative project team with a single set of goals and established procedures for resolving disputes in a timely and effective manner."- *Cowen, Gray and Larson.*

Essentials of a successful sponsor/Project Manager (PM) Partnership

Together, both the parties must execute the partnering process through joint evaluation of the project's progress, by resolving any problems or disagreements, acceptance of a goal for continuous improvement (TQM) for the joint project, continuous support for the process of partnering from senior management of both parties, parties commitment to a joint review of "project execution" when the project is completed. Each and every step in this process must be accompanied by negotiation, and the negotiations must be non-adversarial. The whole concept is firmly rooted in the assumption of mutual trust among the partners. This assumption too is non-adversarial. The essentials of an efficient and successful sponsor or project manager (PM) partnering are as follows:

1. Good sponsors clearly communicate the root-cause of a problem to be resolved. They make sure the team knows (and remembers) what problem is being solved.
2. A good sponsor guarantees root-cause solution for a specific problem. Good PMs do not let solutions to lose focus.
3. Good sponsors impose a "good enough" attitude. They do not use "good enough" as a defence to cut scope.
4. They ensure that the project has right resources to get the work completed. They articulate clear resource requests.
5. Good sponsors hold the PM and team responsible for results. They accept the responsibility and implement it with the team.
6. They play the role of an advocate, coach, and a mentor for the project. They know how to leverage a sponsor and listen to the sponsor's advice.
7. Great sponsors take tough decisions readily despite inconveniences. They give clear and unbiased alternatives, information, and consequences to support decision-making.
8. They opportunistically do not boost scope if the project is going well. They keep the team focused on delivery and do not assume success too soon.
9. Good sponsors constantly calculate priorities and are willing to pull the plug on a project if it has no logic. They don't get emotionally tied to a project and keep it hanging if it should end.

The sponsor/PM partnership is the most important relationship determinant of a project's success potential. Both the sponsor and the PM need to be acutely aware of the relationship and recognise the necessity of working together to better secure a successful outcome and provide value back to the organisation.

2. Chartering

A project charter helps to create a common vision for the project, which is critical as it sets the stage for successful planning, management, and completion. Explicit project chartering ensures that key stakeholders come to an agreement on the scope, objectives, constraints, and completion criteria for the project. A project charter helps ensure team-wide alignment on project priorities.

Project chartering clarifies the priorities and goals for the project to the project team and all stakeholders. By aligning the team, it sets the stage of detailed planning and successful project execution. A project charter should include the following elements:

- A business case for the project including costs and benefits.
- Measurable goals that identify the desired results the project will bring to the organisation.
- A definition of what is in and out of scope for the project.
- Clear project priorities which allow the project team to make appropriate trade-offs to achieve the goals.
- A list of the assumptions, risks, and constraints that could support or impact the outcome.

Basically, a project charter is a written agreement involving the project manager, senior management and the functional managers who are employing resources and people to the project. It details the expected project deliverables, including the project schedule and budget. It attests to the fact that senior management, functional managers and the project manager have a mutual understanding. There is also an implication that none of the parties can modify the agreement unilaterally or, without prior consultation with the other parties. A project charter therefore is a document created at the beginning of the project. It designates the project manager and assigns authority of the project to the project manager. It also describes in brief of all the other stakeholders and their responsibilities, brief of project time, cost and quality requirements, basic terms to be considered in contract with reference to organisation policies, how communication will occur within the project teams, major risks, assumptions, inclusions, exclusions and constraints involved in the project.

(a) Components of a Good Charter:

A good charter should address the following topics:

1. **Business need for the project:** Without a clear, documented business need, a project is a ship with no compass in uncharted water. The business need must indicate the kind of benefits the project will generate for the organisation such as cost reduction, revenue increase, or increased customer satisfaction.

2. **Business case:** The organisation must have a standard format for presenting business cases to evaluate various projects for selection. For example: The business case must convert business need into dollars (or Yen, Pesos, Euros, Pounds, etc.).

3. **High-level project scope:** This must be developed from information collected largely from the project sponsor. As the sponsor is funding the project, it is essential to understand their vision of the project before suffering the slings and arrows of the other stakeholders. Moreover, while the business need may be huge, the project scope may be restricted to specific areas.

4. **Critical success factors:** Identify and document several aspects of the business project, project team, schedule, deliverables, etc. which, if not achieved, would be unfavourable to project success. Well comprehended and documented CSFs will help in resolving differences over project direction when tough choices are to be made regarding project scope, schedule, cost, or quality alternatives.

5. **Project constraints and assumptions:** Document each of these early and revisit them often. There should be project level constraints and assumptions at this point, such as project funding limits, required completion dates, or quality demands.

6. **Authority of the project manager:** In order to simplify the role of the stakeholders and organisation, the charter must lay out the responsibility of the project manager. Without this authority description, the project is dependent on the individual skill of the PM. It is the role of the project manager that must be crystal clear to ensure successful completion of the project.

7. **Signatures:** Getting signatures on a charter may appear like a formality that if missed out is not a big deal (similar to developing the charter in the first place). Signing the charter signifies a threshold that says, "I have read, understood and agree to the information contained in this project charter." Without a signature constraint of some sort, the charter is just another planning document that may or may not be considered and understood by stakeholders. Without sponsor and management signature, stakeholders will not have clarity and knowledge around the project in the organisation.

The team members commit the following in a charter that:

- Meet design intent
- Complete contract without need for litigation
- Finish product on schedule
  - o Timely resolution issues
  - o Manage joint schedule
  - o Keep cost growth to less than 2 percent

(b) Example of a Template for Project Charter

Project Charter Template

[Project Name]

Date

The date when the project commences should be mentioned.

[Company Name]

Address: The address of the location where the project takes place.

City, State Zip: The city where the project takes place.

Project Description

Explain what the project is, and how it will be accomplished. Explain the ultimate intended outcome of the project. This should serve as a brief introduction. Provide some background about the history of how the project got to this point.

Project Purpose

State the purpose of the project. Tie the purpose to the organisation's strategic goals and objectives if possible. Tell the reader why this project is being started and what need it is fulfilling. Identify if there are any specific mandates, policies or laws that are driving this change.

Goals and Objectives

Explain the specific objectives of the project. For example: What value does this project add to the organisation? How does this project align with the strategic priorities of the organisation? What results are expected? What are the deliverables? What benefits will be realised? What problems will be resolved?

Business Case

Provide information on how the project is going to benefit the organisation. Discuss the alternatives that were considered, if any, and provide information on how the organisation came to the selected approach.

Business Requirements

Identify the high level business requirements that the project is going to fulfil. Remember that this is not a detailed list of system requirements.

Market Survey and related projects information

Market survey being the most effective tool must be used to find facts. A survey should be done to identify the real market value for the project.

Assumptions

Assumptions are conditions at the start of the project that must be considered. For example, when developing the new software system that is going to take 3 years to fully complete, an assumption could be that the project budget is approved each year for three years so that the project scope is not impacted.

Constraints

Constraints are situations or events on the ground that must be considered and accounted, for which the project has no control over. For example, a constraint can be a hard deadline or completion date. Other constraints could be resources, tools or hardware so that if the project has no budget for additional servers, then the project must find a way to develop the new system using the hardware already in place. This could mean juggling servers to fit specific development environment needs while ensuring that the production environment stays up.

Risks

State the known risks. These risks are generally at a high level since not much is known about the details of the project yet. If a benefit-cost analysis was performed, then risks identified during the benefit-cost analysis should be placed here. For example, if the project is going to span 5 years and touch multiple third party systems, then integration and technology change would be risks to consider here.

Inclusions

Inclusions are factors included in the objectives that we need to address. In short, they are factors that you identify that you need and know are available to allocate to the project. Inclusions are usually factors that are under your control and which you have the authority to direct to the project.

Exclusion

Exclusions are items that are not currently available or items we have but do not need. When you look at the things you need, you might find that there are resources that are not available when the project needs them.

Project Deliverables

Document what is going to be delivered at the completion of the project.

Project Milestones

Identify the project milestones.

Milestone Date	Milestone Name	Milestone Description
[Jan. 1]	System Requirements Complete	System requirements version 1.0 is approved and baselined so that the project can begin design and development.
[June. 1]	Development Complete	Software development is complete and ready for integration testing
[Dec. 1]	Deployed to Production	System passes integration and end-user acceptance testing and is deployed to production

Project Manager

Identify the project manager here. It is important to clearly identify the project manager so that the project manager has the authority to complete the project. Provide a quick professional biography if available. Explain as clearly as possible, the roles and responsibilities of the project manager. Explain the project manager's levels of authority with respect to resource allocation, schedule modifications and purchasing authority. Review the nine knowledge areas of the Project Management Body of Knowledge (PMBOK) and think about the role that the project manager will fill in each of the areas.

Project Roles and Responsibilities

Define the other key roles and responsibilities within the project team. For example, if the project team has functional team leads then, document them here. The table below provides a quick way to identify specific people within a role.

Name	Role	Responsibilities
Jane Smith	Risk Management Team Lead	Lead the risk management team to ensure risk identification, analysis and mitigation.
John Smith	Testing Lead	<ul><li>Plan and complete testing in all stages of testing.</li><li>Maintain traceability to requirements to ensure that all requirements are tested.</li><li>Responsible for testing tools.</li></ul>

Project Life Cycle Methodology and Tools

Identify what project management methodology the project will be using. In many instances, organisations have their own proprietary version of a waterfall-type life cycle. They may also have their own preferred tools for managing the project management assets (for example, DOORS for managing requirements; SharePoint for document management and versioning; other risk management and testing tools etc.).

Authorisation

Provide the names of those business sponsors that must sign the project charter. Once the project charter is signed by the project sponsors, the project is authorised to start.

Approved by the Project Sponsor:

Date:

[Project Sponsor]

[Project Sponsor Title], [Project Sponsor Organisation or Division]

3. Change

Change is an event that occurs when something passes from one state or phase to another. A change can be described as an occurrence of the event that modifies the planned process or steps. The change is inevitable and when it takes place it usually modifies the time requirements or cost or quality of the product or service being produced as the outcome of the project. In general, when change occurs it changes the scope of the project.

When change occurs, project managers take the responsibility of corrective actions for the changes. The project manager needs to communicate and get approvals from different authorities. Changes like additional functionality requested by customer or delay due to absenteeism of team members or unavailability of materials or shortage of raw materials or delay due to funds shortage may result in to delay of the entire project duration. In such case the project manager has to make amendments in project plan statement or scope statement and get approvals from the project owners, sponsors/ investors and at time from the client. Such changes are referenced to the scope charter prepared at the beginning of the project.

In many organisations change management procedures are well defined. They maintain issue logs and change registers which have clear definitions of the corrective actions to be taken for the pre-identified changes, also risks that may occur due to such changes and person responsible for taking such action. Lesson learned or documentation from the previous projects of similar type, often are used as references to pre-identify the occurrence of changes. Therefore primary responsibility of the project manager is to keep issue logs and change registers updated. This systematic approach to manage occurrence of change within the process, not only protects the project from failures but also enables the project team to expedite and deliver results. Project managers are required to quantify the amount of change and its impact on the project and produce different reports to the management team.

No matter how carefully a project is planned, it is almost certain it changed before completion. No matter how carefully defined at the start, the scope of most projects are subject to considerable uncertainty. There are three basic causes for change in projects. Some changes result because planners erred in their initial assessment about how to achieve a given end or erred in their choice of the proper goal for the project. Technological uncertainty is the fundamental causal factor for either error. The foundation for a building must be changed because a preliminary geological study did not reveal a weakness in the structure of the ground on which the building will stand. An R & D project must be altered because metallurgical test results indicate another approach should be adopted. The project team becomes aware of a recent innovation that allows a faster, cheaper solution to the conformation of a new computer.

Other changes result because the client/user or project team learns more about the nature of the project deliverable or about the setting in which it is to be used. An increase in user or team knowledge or sophistication is the primary factor leading to change. A computer program must be extended or rewritten because the user thinks of new uses for the software. Physicians request that intensive care units in a hospital be equipped with laminar air-flow control in order to accommodate patients highly subject to infection who might otherwise not be admissible in an ICU. The fledgling audio-addict upgrades the specifications for a system to include very high frequencies so that his dog can enjoy the music, too.

A third source of change is the mandate. This is a change in the environment in which the project is being conducted. As such, it cannot be controlled by the PM, a new law is passed. A government regulatory unit articulates a new policy. A trade association sets a new standard. The patent organisation of the user applies a new criterion for its purchases. In other words, the rules of conduct for the project are altered. A state-approved pollution control system must be adopted for each chemical refinery project. The state government requires all new insurance policies to conform to a revised law specifying that certain information must be given to potential purchasers. At times, mandates of only priorities. The mandate in question might move a very important customer to the "head of the line" for some scarce resource or service.

To some extent, risk management techniques can be applied to scope change. Technological uncertainty can be mitigated by careful analysis of the technologies involved, including the use of technological forecasting. Risk of scope change caused by increased user knowledge can only be managed by improving the up-front communication with the client and then establishing a formal process to handle change. Finally, mandates are, for the most part unpredictable. These can be "managed" only by having some flexibility built into the budget and schedule of the project.

A change manager should have a fine understanding of the nature of sponsorship and carefully assist and handle various sponsors in the project.

(a) Four Types of Sponsor

During managing change, one needs to understand and therefore work with the four different types of sponsor. They are as follows:

1. **Initiating Sponsor:** Being the person who starts the change project he may be the person to be met at the first meeting. They may be the key sponsor or maybe someone lower down the order. They may well be the person who asks you to manage or facilitate the change project.

2. **Key Sponsor:** The key sponsor (often the most senior manager) resolves the stickiest of problems, such as differences among other primary sponsors, who offer final authority for the project, and can have a hand in direction and approval.

    One needs to spend quality time directly with the key sponsor to understand their real needs, to ensure that they are in the loop and remain committed. If they drift away and show inadequate interest, then closing down of the project should be considered.

3. **Primary Sponsors:** Primary sponsors are a small group of managers with critical support, having sufficient power to unblock most problems, including problems with secondary sponsors. They are sometimes also known as 'sustaining sponsors' who often work collectively as a core team.

    Quality time should be spent interacting with them, both individually and collectively, showing how close collaboration is present in their interests to ensure the time and commitment of primary sponsors (if it is not, then one needs to connect with the key sponsor over this). One also needs to put appropriate effort into building this group into a cohesive and an effective team.

4. **Secondary Sponsors:** Secondary sponsors support is needed at a limited level. They are important in a way that they have the ability to block a change. However, if they were all to be members of the core team, then that team would become difficult to manage.

However, not including them in the team can be a bad move as they may refuse to co-operate or otherwise block progress. Therefore, they demand require careful handling and usually need to be communicated with on a very regular basis. If not meeting on a regular basis they should be at least kept up to date with progress.

3.4 Conflict and the Project Life Cycle

3.4.1 Conflict

Discrepancies' or disagreements that result into change within the process are called as conflicts.

All stages of the project life cycle appear to conflict. Following are some of the reasons for the conflicts that arise in project management process:

(a) Team member has personal priorities that may conflict with organisation's demand from that person.

(b) Team members may have different views for performing the tasks assigned to them. Such differences occur between the project team and other support groups, as well as between the team and the clients. The solution is to call for a meeting and explain the project charter and take their commitment in the form of signature on the charter as well as during the kick-off meeting.

Checklist of the kick off meeting is given below:

Sr. No.	Description	Check Status
1.	Contracts – vendors identified or basic terms specified. This clarity is to be given to accounts, purchase as well as quality departments.	
2.	Client Needs and priorities communicated to project team.	
3.	Check if Project Plan in Place and commitments from team are given.	
4.	Clarity to project team members on their roles and responsibilities.	
5.	Scope of work is identified and communicated to all stakeholders.	
6.	Project schedule is clearly understood and accepted by the team.	
7.	Issue log and change control procedures are defined and communicated.	
8.	Sanction of project budget.	
9.	Milestones are set for project reviews.	
10.	Project management process (Change, risk, procurement, admin, accounts, QA and PC) are mapped.	
11.	All stake holders expectations have been accounted and communicated.	

(c) Improper communication or miscommunication regarding the task to be performed. This type of conflict is usually between the team member and the manager. Team members often disagree on the management of project process. Solution: Project manager needs to explain the project organisation chart and reporting responsibilities at the beginning of the project.

(d) Inter-personal relationships and cultural differences may also lead to conflicts within team

(e) Non conformance to the agreed values, mostly for the terms and conditions defined in the agreement with vendors/suppliers. This especially true for the quality of the product or service, quantity of supplied items, unclear requirements from the client, unclear terms for return of materials, terms for transportation etc

(f) The conflicts are also seen between project owner or sponsored when changes upsets the budgets of the project. They are also called as cost overruns.

(g) Delay in payments to the vendors/suppliers.

(h) Rejection from QC department

(i) Disagreements may arise over technical specifications and techniques to achieve the required performance. Solution: Call review meetings to reduce this type of conflict.

(j) Conflicts arise due to uneven workload distribution within team members. Solution: Human resource manager to prepare workload analysis and organisation has to have performance and benefits policies in place.

(k) The major stress factor for the project manager is timely management of the task. Therefore the project manager prepares activity log and prepares a schedule of tasks that need to be completed. In other words, the project manager maps the total task required to be performed for the entire project, breaks down the task by preparing a work breakdown structure or sometimes by using network diagrams, identifies the task that can be done simultaneously, tasks that need to be completed in sequence and tasks that can be outsourced. Then duration is estimated for completion of each activity that finally results in understanding total time required for the project to be completed. The project manager will usually consider the longest time taken and tries to control this duration. This is called as critical path of the project.

- **Example of activity list:**

Project Name		Activity List				
Project Number						
Client				**Date**		
Contractor						
Sub-Contractor				**Checked by**		
ID	**Activity Name**	**Activity Description**	**Predecessor**		**Successor**	**Constraints**
			ID	Duration	ID	Duration	

Although there may be numerous reasons for conflicts, it always creates negative impact on the project. The project manager needs to handle the conflict by four simple steps:

1. Project manager should involve the team in the decision-making process.
2. Constantly communicate with all stakeholders including team members.
3. Plan things properly and keep track of the changes. Take timely corrective actions for the changes.
4. Most important skill for the project manager during the conflict situation is not to relent but be patient and consistently pursue the goal.

Budgeting and Cost Estimation:

Once the activity log is prepared the next step the project manager takes is estimating the cost involved for each activity, be it material or human resource cost. This gives project managers evidential information of the cost involved. The next step is to understand the funds availability and funds flow for the project. Here the project owner, investor or the other stakeholders need to approve and make provisions for the cost estimated for the project. Budgeting is very important factor for controlling all the activities of the project plus getting things done from the team members, contractors and vendors.

Therefore the project manager does the two level calculations:

1. He estimates the total cost and includes the cost for contingencies and risks that may crop while executing the project.
2. He also works with the finance department to understand the funds availability and gets the required approvals from the project owner, investors and other stakeholders.

(a) Cost Estimation Template:

Definition: Cost Management template defines the total budgeted cost of the project. It also forms the baseline for the cost variation while the project is in execution. All the resources have cost involved in it. Therefore, once the activity list is completed it is important to assign cost to each activity to derive the total cost of the project. Sample template used in construction industry for cost estimation is given below

Type	Description	Vendor Sub-contractor/ Contractor	Estimated Cost			Actual Cost	Va-riance	% Comp-lete	Cur-rent Paid	Amt. Due	Notes
			Labour	Materials	Total in INR						
					0.00					0.00	
					0.00					0.00	
					0.00					0.00	
					0.00					0.00	

(b) Basic funds flow template:

The template shown below is generic representation of the calculations for cash flows, however, contents might slightly differ from project to project. Also projections for cash-flow should be considered from the beginning till the project handover process.

	Year 1				Year 2				Year 3	Year 4	Year 5
	Q1	Q2	Q3	Q4	Q1	Q2	Q3	Q4			
Operating Activities											
Earnings after tax deduction (EAT)											
Add depreciation											
Add amortisation											
Add Interest											
Increase/Decrease of Working Capital											
Cash flow from operating activities											
Investing Activities											
Cash flow from investing activities											
Financing Activities											
Equity											
Loan											
Less Interest											
Less Loan repayment											
Cash flow from financing activities											
Net cash flow											
Cumulative Cash Balance											
Free Cash Flows (FCE)											
Project Internal rate of return (IRR)											

** Source NSDC

3.4.2 Project Life Cycle

Several types of conflicts derive directly from the inherent nature of projects, not necessarily from the people involved. Conflicts often take place for multiple reasons. Project leaders report that conflicts usually arise over the following seven points of contention. Note that the first six are related more to the situation than to the people in the situation. People are not the source of conflict; they are the players in the situation.

1. **Priorities of Tasks and Objectives:** Participants quite often have different views on the proper sequencing of tasks and regarding the importance of tasks and objectives. Such differences occur not only in the project team but also among the other support groups, plus between the team and the client. The way out is to call for a kick-off meeting and describe the project charter and take their commitment in the form of signature on the charter as well as during the kick-off meeting. The sample of check list is as follows

Sr. No.	Description	Check Status
1.	Contracts – vendors identified or basic terms specified. This clarity is to be given to accounts, purchase as well as quality departments.	
2.	Client needs and priorities communicated to project team.	
3.	Project plan in place.	Signature:
4.	Project plan explained to team members.	
5.	Project team members roles and responsibilities	Signature:
6.	Scope of work	
7.	Project schedule	
8.	Issue log and change control procedures	Signature:
9.	Project Budget	
10.	Project reviews	
11.	Project management process (Change, risk, procurement, admin, accounts, QA and PC)	
12.	Project manager expectations	

2. **Administrative Procedures:** Disagreements often occur over how a project will be managed, for example, over the definition of the project leader's reporting relationships and responsibilities, operational requirements, interdepartmental work agreements, and levels of administrative support. Solution: Project manager needs to clarify the project organisation chart and reporting responsibilities at the opening of the project.

3. **Technical Opinions:** The less routine a project, the more likely it is that there is disparity in opinion about the "best way" to achieve the task. Disagreements may arise over specifications, technical trade-offs, and techniques to attain the required performance. For example, the director and the film editor on a movie project may have complete different and competing viewpoints on how best to achieve a definite effect. Solution: Call review meetings to reduce this type of conflict.

4. **Staffing and Resource Allocations:** Conflicts also arise over how best to allot people to various projects and in project assignments. Individuals disagree over projects assigned to them, competing demands from their project leader and functional manager. This leads to both interpersonal conflict and personal stress. Solution: human resource manager to prepare workload analysis and organisation has to have performance and benefits policies in place.

5. **Costs and Budgets:** During the project cost planning stage, detailed costs and budgets are measured and are reviewed during the risk and integration stage. Since, the change is a non-controllable factor; it may change the estimated cost and budgets. Due to this, experienced project managers generally add buffer budget right through the scope of the project approval and such additional/buffers are kept away from the team. The conflicts are generally seen among project owners or sponsors or among the suppliers and contractors.

6. **Schedules:** The most important stress factor for the project manager is timely management of the task. Therefore, the project manager arranges activity log and prepares a schedule of tasks that should be completed. In other words, the project manager maps the total task important to be performed for the entire project, breaks down the task by preparing a work breakdown arrangement or sometimes by using network diagrams, identifies the task that can be done at the same time, task that needs to be completed in sequence and tasks that can be outsourced. Then duration is estimated for conclusion of each activity that finally results in understanding total time required for the project to be concluded. However, the project manager will usually consider the longest time taken and try to control this duration. This is called as critical path of the project.

Example of activity list:

Project Name		Activity List					
Project Number							
Client					Date		
Contractor							
Sub-Contractor					Checked by		
ID	Activity Name	Activity Description	Predecessor		Successor		Constraints
			ID	Duration	ID	Duration	

7. **Interpersonal and Personality Clashes:** Conflicts occur not only over technical issues but also over "style" or "ego-centred" issues like status, power, control, self-esteem, and friendships. Such conflicts may surface from real personality and style differences, but quite often they are based on differences that emerge from departmental or organisational factors like varying past experiences and diverse perspectives on time horizons.

3.5 Project Budgets

Organisations don't start to work on projects unless they have clarity on resource requirements such as finance, materials, human resource, technology and return on investments. The funds available are then allocated as per the scheduled requirements. This is called budgets for the project. Usually the total amount required is the key focus during analysis of budget requirements. Budgeting helps the organisation to have control on the process and expenditures within the project. The controls are required in the following areas

(a) In controlling the project time frame that is, schedule of the project.

(b) For controlling the total expenditure in the project.

(c) For checking the final product/service outcomes.

The project manager needs to manage four main factors and keeping one of them as constant depending on the need of the project at that point in time.

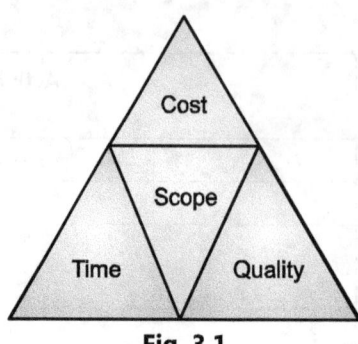

Fig. 3.1

The steps taken for budget management

1. Identifying and defining the budget requirements within the project framework.
2. Executing the budget as per the plan.
3. Taking corrective actions in time for controlling the budget.
4. Constantly updating the budget available and budget used including the reasons for the expenditure made.
5. Maintaining records for future projects.

After the resource planning is done cost estimation process begins.

3.5.1 Cost Budgeting Process

Step 1: The resource requirements list and activity list are taken as inputs for cost estimation or cost budgeting.

Step 2: Cost that would be incurred for each activity and for the materials to be procured is listed and total amount is calculated.

    (a) Top down method: Here the funds available are kept as base and expenses are debited from it. This gives a clear understanding if the total expenditure fits within the available funds.

    (b) Bottom up method: Here the total funds requirement is added and then subtracted from the available funds.

Step 3: This costing is then compared with the cost incurred during the previous similar projects or many times it is verified by getting advance quotes from the vendors and suppliers.

Step 4: Alternatives are identified and defined and costs that would be incurred are re-evaluated.

Step 5: Final decisions for procurement are made based on the cost estimation or budgets are finalised based on the above process.

Input	Process	Output
WBS		
Resource requirements	Plan - Define and estimate the resource requirements and develop budget	Project Budget Baseline
Cost estimates	Do – Obtain approval, and publish budget, authorise expenses	Budget variance report
Schedule	Adapt – Update budget, set corrective	Budget updates are recorded
Historical information		
Market conditions		
Policies		

3.5.2 Estimating Project Budget

The two other major focal points of project management are cost estimation and budgeting. The project budget involves the following steps:

1. It includes the project cost estimate allocated to the various work packages in the project work breakdown structure.
2. The budget for each work package so that it is possible to estimate how much budget should be allotted for that particular package.
3. It also has to cater to the budget requirements for the risk factors analysed during planning.

Developing project budgets is much more difficult than developing budgets for more permanent organisational activities. One aspect of cost estimation and budgeting that is not often discussed has to do with the actual use of resources as opposed to the accounting departments assumptions about how and when the resources will be used. Unless this pattern of expenditure is detailed in the plan, the accounting department, which takes a linear view of the world, will spread the expenditure equally. This may not affect the project's budget but it most certainly affects the project's cash flow.

Another aspect of preparing project budgeting is that every expenditure must be identified with a specific project task and with its associated milestone. Each element in the work breakdown structure (WBS) has a unique account number to which charges are accrued as work is done. These identifiers are needed for the project manager to exercise budgetary control.

There are two fundamentally different strategies for gathering the data:

(a) Top down method
(b) Bottom up method

(a) Top Down Budgeting:

Top down budgeting is based on the strategy of collecting judgements and experiences of the top and middle managers and making them available past data concerning similar activities. These managers estimate overall project costs of major subprojects that it includes. The cost estimates are then handed over to lower-level managers, who are expected to maintain the breakdown into budget estimates for the specific task and work packages that contains the subprojects. The process continues to lowest level. The main advantage of this top down process is that aggregate budgets can often be developed quite perfectly. Not only are budget categories constant as per the percent of the total budget, the statistical distribution of each category is also stable, making for high predictability. One more advantage of the top down process is that small and costly responsibilities should not be individually identified, nor should it be cleared that some small but main aspect has been overlooked. The experience and judgement of the executive is assumed automatically to such elements into the overall estimate.

(b) Bottom up Budgeting

In bottom up budgeting, the elemental task schedules and their individual budgets are constructed once more following the WBS. At first, estimates are made in terms of resources, such as labour hours and materials. These are later converted into currency equivalents. Standard analytical tools like learning curve analysis and work sampling are employed which are apt to improve the estimates. Some templates for this purpose are also offered. The resulting task budgets are combined to give the total direct cost of the project. The project manager adds such indirect cost as general and administrative, possibly a project reserve for contingencies', and then a profit figure to reach the final project budget. Bottom up budgets are more exact in the detailed tasks, but it is critical that all elements are incorporated. The benefits of bottom up process are those usually associated with participative management. Individuals closer to the work are appropriate to have a more perfect idea of the resource requirements than their superiors or others are not personally involved. In addition, the direct involvement of low level managers in budget preparation increases the possibility of accepting the result with a minimum opposition. Bottom up budgets are uncommon. The budget is the most important tool for control of the organisation. They are understandably hesitant to hand over the control to subordinates whose experience and motives are doubtful.

3.5.3 Improving the Process of Cost Estimation

Cost estimates, work breakdown structure and project schedules are interrelated concepts. Once a base line schedule is prepared, it is necessary to develop a base line budget. It is important to note that the cost of a work package cannot be estimated because it is too complex and it must be broken down so that appropriate estimate can be made.

Due to changes incurred while project execution and since the cost estimation and budgeting is done at the beginning of the project, it is possible that the actual costs incurred may vary from the budgets planned. This may become detrimental to the project. If the project cost is over estimated, that is, higher than actual requirement, the project may be lost. It is necessary to put practical constraints on project costs so that realistic budgets can be established.

Company Name							Activity Cost Estimation Sheet			
Project Name							Date:	22/Nov/ 2013		
							Author:			
Sr. No.	Resource:	UOM:	Qty:	Direct cost:	Expe nse:	Reserve (%):	Estimate:	Method:	Remarks:	
1.	Cement	hr.	100	15.00			1,500.00	Bottom-Up		
2.	Labour	bag	30	90.00			2,700.00			

For improvements in the cost estimation process the following steps can be done.

(a) The detailed activity list and requirements list is required to be prepared.

(b) Internal team meeting for brainstorming needs to be done and the gaps if any are to be identified or any perceived changes are taken in to consideration. Accordingly the updates need to be documented.

(c) Meeting with vendors and suppliers is also required to be arranged, to identify the pros and cons in the procurement process. It also helps in updating information on the new products or alternative available in the market.

(d) Final list is to be prepared by the project manager and get the approvals from concerned authorities.

(e) Once this list is approved the project manager should arrange meeting with accounts/finance department of the organisation. Here cost benefit analysis is required to be done. This helps in understanding the previous values and current cost estimates and also forms a baseline for the new cost budgets. This information is then required to be synchronised with the funds flow statement by the account/finance department. This ensures that payments would not be delayed.

(f) Separate budgets should be estimated and managed for
   (i)   Actual requirements
   (ii) Schedule changes
   (iii) Risk buffers

(g) Weekly or monthly meetings to be scheduled and mandatory attendees should be team members, accounts and project manager to understand the expenses and the progress made by the project. Any changes identified should immediately be updated in the cost budgets and approvals for the changes needs to be taken.

The co-operation of several people is required to prepare cost estimates for a project. The major responsibility of a professional estimator is to reduce the level of uncertainty in the cost estimations so that the firm's bid can be made in the light of expert information about its potential costs. In such cases, it is the job of the project manager to generate a description of the work to be done on the project in sufficient detail that the estimator can know what cost the data must be collected.

The simpler and most common way is to make an allowance for contingencies usually 5 to 10 percent of the estimated cost.

Another method in which the forecaster selects, "most likely, optimistic and pessimistic" estimates. For estimating direct cost, project manager often finds it helpful to collect direct cost estimates on a form that not only lists the estimated level of resource needs, but also indicates when each of the resource will be needed and notes if it is available or will be made available at the appropriate time.

The allocation of overhead is arbitrary by its nature. The addition of overhead cost may cause an otherwise attractive project to fail.

Other Factors:

- Scope creep impacts all projects.
- Increase risk by producing errors in cost estimates.
- Changes in resource prices the most commonly used solution to this problem is to increase all cost estimates by some fixed percentage. A more useful approach is to identify each input that accounts for a significant portion of project cost and estimate the direction and rate of price change for each.
- Further improvements can be made by taking into account the fact that the prices of different inputs often change at very different rates and sometimes in different directions.
- A project manager may wish to use different inflators/deflators for each of several different classes of labour or types of commodities. While most PMs are concerned only with price increase, any industry submitting competitive bids on projects must remember that failure to be aware of falling prices will lead to cost overestimation and uncompetitive bids.
- Other elements that need to be factored into the estimated project cost include an allowance and waste and spoilage.
- Human resource cost can be significantly increased by the loss and subsequent replacement of project professionals.

On making better estimates, projects look easier, faster and cheaper to senior managers than to those who must do the work. Estimators tend to overlook details required to do a complete job. Two types of estimation errors are:

(a) There is random error in which overestimates and underestimates are equally likely.

(b) There is bias, which is systematic error.

Points to Remember

- Project co-ordination generally refers to planning and managing multiple tasks simultaneously.
- *"Negotiation is a field of knowledge and endeavour that focuses on gaining the favour of people from whom we want things".*

- Negotiation is an invaluable skill for any project manager. Not only do you negotiate agreements with vendors and contractors, but one effectively negotiates with stakeholders, customers, and team members throughout the life of a project.
- The outsourced vendors who act as partners for a particular process or part of the project is called partnering.
- Partnering, through better teamwork, improves performance. A project mutually draws together, a mix of people and organisations that contribute to and have a stake in the project's achievement.
- A project charter helps to create a common vision for the project, which is critical as it sets the stage for successful planning, management, and completion.
- A project charter is a written agreement involving the project manager, senior management and the functional managers who are employing resources and people to the project. It details the expected project deliverables, including the project schedule and budget.
- Change is an event that occurs when something passes from one state or phase to another. A change can be described as an occurrence of the event that modifies the planned process or steps.
- Discrepancies' or disagreements that result into change within the process are called as conflicts.
- Cost management template defines the total budgeted cost of the project. It also forms the baseline for the cost variation while the project is in execution. All the resources have cost involved in it.
- Top down budgeting is based on the strategy of collecting judgements and experiences of the top and middle managers and making them available past data concerning similar activities.
- In bottom up budgeting, the elemental task schedules and their individual budgets are constructed once more following the WBS.

Questions for Discussion

1. What are the methods and techniques used for estimating project cost?
2. What is required for initial project co-ordinations?
3. How are cash flow requirements identified before the start of the project?
4. What do you understand by terms "Partnering, Chartering and change"?
5. What types of conflicts are observed during different stages of project life cycle?
6. Consider any ten items for a project and identify variance based on the information available on internet.

■■■

Chapter 4...

Network Techniques

Contents ...

Learning Objectives ...

- To describe PERT and CPM
- To understand risk analysis using simulation with crystal ball 2000
- To study the critical path method
- To discuss the planning - monitoring - controlling cycle
- To know the earned value analysis
- To explain the fundamental purposes of control
- To apply the three types of control processes
- To understand control as a function of management

4.1 Programme Evaluation Review Technique [PERT]

4.1.1 Introduction

PERT is a management process of controlling and analysing a system or program using periodic time and money reports, often computergenerated, to determine money and labor status at any given time. It is a graph that represents all of the tasks required for a project's completion, and the order in which they must be completed along with the subsequent time requirements. Some specific tasks are dependent on serial tasks, which must be completed in a specific order. Tasks that are not reliant on the completion of other tasks are called parallel or concurrent tasks and can usually be worked on simultaneously. PERT charts are preferable to Gantt charts as they more clearly identify task dependencies; however, the PERT chart is often more challenging to interpret.

It is a network model that permits uncertainty in activity completion time. PERT was developed in the late 1950's for the U.S. Navy's Polaris project having thousands of contractors. It has the potential to decrease both the time and cost needed to finish a project successfully. Generally, the milestones are numbered as the ending node of an activity having a higher number than the beginning node. Incrementing the numbers by 10 allows for new ones to be included without modifying the numbering of the complete diagram. The activities in the diagram below are labelled with letters along with the expected time required to complete the activity.

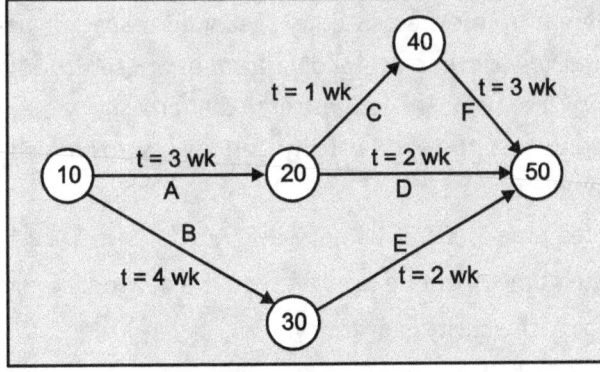

Fig. 4.1: PERT Chart

4.1.2 Steps in the PERT Planning Process

PERT planning comprises of the following steps:

1. Identifying the specific activities and milestones.
2. Determining the proper sequence of the activities.
3. Constructing a network diagram.
4. Estimating the time required for each activity.
5. Determining the critical path.
6. Updating the PERT chart as the project progresses.

1. **Identifying activities and milestones:** The activities are the tasks needed to complete the project. The milestones are events marking the beginning and end of one or more activities.

2. **Determining activity sequence:** This step may be combined collectively with the activity identification step as the activity sequence is known for some tasks. Other tasks may need more analysis to verify the exact order in which they should be performed.

3. **Constructing the Network Diagram:** Using the activity sequence information, a network diagram can be drawn showing the sequence of the serial and parallel activities.

4. **Estimate activity times:** Weeks are a commonly used unit of time for activity completion, but any reliable unit of time can be used.

   One of the distinguishing features of PERT is its ability to deal with uncertainty in activity completion times. For each activity, the model typically includes three time estimates:

   - **Optimistic Time (OT):** Generally the shortest time in which the activity can be finished. (This is what an inexperienced manager believes!)
   - **Most Likely Time (MT):** The completion time having the maximum probability. This is different from expected time. Seasoned managers have a remarkable way of estimating very close to actual data from prior estimation errors.
   - **Pessimistic Time (PT)**: The longest time that an activity may need.
   - The expected time for each activity can be approximated using the following weighted average:

     Expected time = (OT + 4 × MT + PT) / 6

     This expected time might be displayed on the network diagram.

     Variance for each activity is given by:

     $[(PT - OT) / 6]^2$

---

5. **Determining the Critical Path:** The critical path is determined by totalling the time for the activities in each sequence and determining the longest path in the project. The critical path determines the total time needed for the project.

   Here, if activities outside the critical path speed up or slow down (within limits), the total project time does not alter. The amount of time that a non-critical path activity can be postponed without delaying the project is referred to as slack time.

   If the critical path is not immediately obvious, it may be helpful to determine the following four quantities for each activity:

   * ES - Earliest Start time
   * EF - Earliest Finish time
   * LS - Latest Start time
   * LF - Latest Finish time

   (a) **Early Start Date (ES):** In the critical path method, the earliest possible point in time on which the uncompleted portions of an activity (or the project) can begin, based on the network logic and any schedule constraints. Early start dates can alter as the project progresses and changes are made to the project plan.

   (b) **Early Finish Date (EF):** In the critical path method, the earliest possible point in time on which the uncompleted portions of an activity (or project) can end based on the network logic and any schedule restriction. Early finish dates can change as the project progresses and changes are made to the project plan.

   (c) **Late start date (LS):** In the critical path method, the latest possible point in time that an activity may begin without delaying a specified milestone (usually the project finish date).

   (d) **Late Finnish Date (LF):** In the critical path method, the latest possible point in time that an activity may be completed without delaying a particular milestone (usually the project finish date).

   (e) **Lag time:** Lag time is when a modification of a logical relationship which directs a delay in the successor task. For example, in a finish to start dependency with a 10 day lag, the successor activity cannot start until 10 days after the predecessors have finished.

   (f) **Lead Time:** A modification of a logical relationship which permits an acceleration of the successor task. For example, in a finish to start dependency with a 10 day lead, the successor activity can start 10 days before the predecessor has finished. These times are calculated using the expected time for the relevant activities. The ES and EF of each activity are determined by working forward through the network and determining the earliest time at which an activity can start and finish considering its predecessor activities.

6. **Update as project progresses:** Make adjustments in the PERT chart as the project progresses. As the project discloses, the estimated times can be restored with actual times. In cases where there are delays, additional resources may be required to stay on schedule and the PERT chart may be modified to reveal the new situation.

4.1.3 Advantages of PERT

1. It forces managers to plan their projects critically and analyse all factors affecting the development of the plan. The process of the network analysis demands that the project planning be performed on considerable detail from start to finish.

2. It offers the management a tool for forecasting the influence of schedule changes and be prepared to rectify situations, if any. The problem area is recognised at an early stage, so as to apply some corrective actions.

3. A lot of data can be accessible in a highly ordered fashion. The task relationships are graphically represented for easier evaluation. Individuals in various locations can easily determine their role in the total task requirements.

4. The PERT time (Te) is based upon 3-way estimate. It results in greater degree of accuracy in time forecasting.

5. It results in enhanced communication; the network provides a universal ground for various parties such as designers, contractors, project managers etc. and they must all value and appreciate each other's role and contributions.

4.1.4 Disadvantages of PERT

1. Uncertainly about the estimate of time and resources. These must be assumed and the results can only be as good as the assumptions.

2. The costs may be higher than the conventional methods of planning and control. Because of the nature of networking and network analysis, it requires a high degree of planning skill and greater amount of details which would boost the cost in time and manpower resources,

3. It is not appropriate for simple and repetitive processes such as assembly line work which are fixed-sequence jobs.

4.2 Critical Path Method (CPM)

4.2.1 Introduction

DuPont developed a Critical Path Method (CPM) designed to tackle the challenges of closing down of chemical plants for preservation and then resuming the plants once the maintenance had been concluded. This method calculates a single, deterministic early and late start and finish date for every activity based on specified, sequential network logic, and single duration estimate. The main focus of CPM is on calculating float in order to decide which activities have the least scheduling flexibility. The CPM algorithms are often used in other types of mathematical analysis.

In short, CPM is a network analysis technique used to calculate project duration by analysing the sequence of activities (on which path) having the least amount of scheduling flexibility (the least amount of float). Early dates are designed by means of a forward pass using a particular start date of the project. Late dates are calculated by means of backward pass starting from particular completion date (usually the forward pass's calculated project early finish date). This is the most frequently used method for project scheduling and project duration calculation.

In the below example, the numbers marked on top from 1 to 7 are the sequence of activities and below figures represents the minimum number of days/time the tasks would take to complete that particular process.

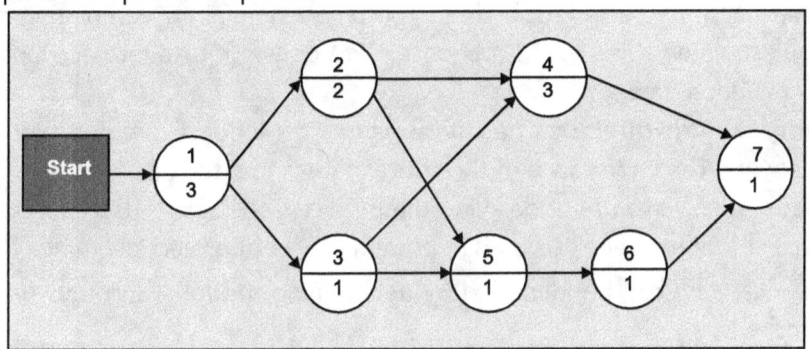

Fig. 4.2: The following figure shows CPM diagram

Therefore the path taken by process A   =   1,2,4,7

     Total duration for completion   =   3 + 2 + 3 + 1 = 9 Months

        Path taken by process B   =   1, 2, 5, 6, 7

     Total duration for completion   =   3 + 2 + 1 + 1 + 1 = 8 Months

        Path taken by process C   =   1,3,4,7

     Total duration for completion   =   3 + 1 + 3 + 1 = 8 Months

        Path taken by process D   =   1,3,5,6,7

     Total duration for completion   =   3 + 1 + 1 + 1 + 1 = 7 Months

The critical path is defined as

- Longest path through a network
- Minimum project completion time

Therefore in the above example the critical path is A;

4.2.2 Steps in CPM Project Planning

1. Specify the individual activities.
2. Determine the sequence of those activities.
3. Draw a network diagram.
4. Estimate the completion time for each activity.
5. Identify the critical path (longest path through the network)
6. Update the CPM diagram as the project progresses.

1. **Specify the individual activities:** All the activities in the project are planned. This list can be used as the foundation for adding sequence and duration information in later steps.

2. **Determine the sequence of the activities:** Various activities rely on the completion of other activities. A list of the direct predecessors of each activity is useful for constructing the CPM network diagram.

3. **Draw the Network Diagram:** Once the activities and their sequences have been defined, the CPM diagram can be drawn. Initially, CPM was developed as an activity on node network.

4. **Estimate activity completion time:** The time essential for completing each activity can be estimated using past experience. CPM does not take into account variation in the completion time.

5. **Identify the Critical Path:** The critical path is the longest-duration path throughout the network. The importance of the critical path is that the activities that depend on it cannot be delayed without delaying the project. Considering its impact on the entire project, critical path analysis is an important aspect of project planning.

    The critical path can be identified by determining the following four parameters for each activity:

    -   ES - Earliest start time: the earliest time at which the activity can begin given that its precedent activities must be finished first.
    -   EF - Earliest finish time, similar to the earliest start time for the activity as well as the time required to complete the activity.
    -   LF - Latest finish time: the latest time at which the activity can be finished with no delay in the project.
    -   LS - Latest start time, equal to the latest finish time minus the time needed to complete the activity.

    Usually, the slack time for an activity is the time between its earliest and latest start time or between its earliest and latest finish time. Slack, is the amount of time that an activity can be delayed past its earliest start or earliest finish without delaying the project.The critical path is the path in the project network where none of the activities have slack, that is, the path for which ES=LS and EF=LF for all activities in the path. A delay in the critical path delays the project. Likewise, to speed up the project it is necessary to decrease the total time required for the activities in the critical path.

6. **Update CPM diagram:** As the project grows, the actual task completion time will be identified and the network diagram can be updated to incorporate this information. If project requirements change, a new critical path may emerge and structural changes may be made in the network. In actual practice this is also called as schedule control.

4.2.3 Advantages of the implementation of CPM

1. CPM makes it simpler for the project managers to create a team and generate human network for efficient handling of a multitasked project.

2. CPM binds the team together mutually and motivates the human resources in timely completion of the tasks in a project.

3. CPM considers the requirements well in advance to complete a project in the most resourceful way possible.

4. CPM helps the project managers determine the duration and estimate the exact time and cost of the project. It helps to supervise human resources, and the direct and indirect costs connected with the project.

5. CPM helps the project managers in planning schedules, monitoring tasks, and also aids control the project expenses.

6. CPM makes it convenient for the project managers to calculate the time needed to complete the tasks of the project. It helps them to forecast completion date of every phase, anticipate problems along the way, if any, and react accordingly.

7. CPM makes it easier to assess parallel activities, handle delays and evaluate the outcome of a task.

8. It facilitates minimising the project length by monitoring the critical path.

9. CPM assists the managers in decision making to deal with the issue promptly. It also enables the project head to decide if the task is on schedule or needs boost to speed up the process.

10. CPM also enables the managers to determine start time, end time, slack time and float time related to every activity of the project.

4.2.4 Disadvantages of the Implementation of CPM

1. CPM can be extremely complex and tricky to comprehend for the new recruits in the project team.

2. CPM demands software to monitor the plan, if the project is far too bulky and lengthy.

3. CPM can become ineffective and complicated to manage if it is not well-defined and stable.

4. It cannot handle sudden changes in the implementation of the plan on ground. It is not easy to redraw the entire CPM chart if the plan of the project suddenly changes halfway.

5. CPM cannot form and control the schedules of people involved in the project.

6. The allotment of resources cannot be properly monitored.

7. The critical path of the CPM is not always clear. A lot of time is needed to calculate it carefully.

8. CPM takes a long time to identity and monitor the critical path.

9. While using CPM, identifying and determining a critical path is complex when there are many other similar duration paths in the project.

10. Designing a CPM is time consuming. Also, it is not easy to estimate the activity completion time in a multidimensional project.

4.2.5 Difference between PERT and CPM

CPM	PERT
• CPM uses activity oriented network.	• PERT uses event oriented network.
• Durations of activity may be estimated with a fair degree of accuracy.	• Estimate of time for activities are not so accurate and definite.
• It is used extensively in construction projects.	• It is used mostly in research and development projects, particularly projects of non-repetitive nature.
• Deterministic concept is used.	• Probabilistic model concept is used.
• CPM can control both time and cost when planning.	• PERT is basically a tool for planning.
• In CPM, cost optimisation is given prime importance. The time for the completion of the project depends upon cost optimization. The cost is not directly proportioned to time. Thus, cost is the controlling factor.	• In PERT, it is assumed that cost varies directly with time. Attention is therefore, given to minimise the time so that minimum cost results. Thus, in PERT, time is the controlling factor.

4.3 Risk Analysis using Critical Simulation with Crystal Ball® 2000

One of the methods for managing uncertainties is to perform risk analysis on such data that has been involved in managerial decisions. This requires us to make assumptions about the probability distributions of the variables and parameters affecting the decisions. The assumptions allow us to assume Monte Carlo simulation modelled mathematically. Individual values for each variable in the model are selected at random from the probability distributions and the outcome of the model is calculated.

Definition of Monte Carlo Analysis: A scheduled risk assessment technique that performs a project simulation several times in order to calculate a distribution of likely results.

4.3.1 Crystal Ball 2000 (CB)

Crystal Ball 2000 (CB) is a software that is used to simulate a decision process that measures whether or not the project was above the organisations hurdle rate of return. Using the same kind of simulation numerous times might be used to manage the uncertainty involved in deciding the level of budgeting a project. We can now examine its use in scheduling projects.

After entering the data XL and CB, we label the columns, first one for such activity and then one for each path through the network and finally one for the "completion time". The most difficult job one faces is identifying all of the paths to be evaluated.

- After the entering the data in appropriate column labels, click on space A3 with the cursor and enter "20" from your earlier solution that assumes a beta distribution. Click on that number to fix the entry in place.
- Click on Cell at the top of the tool bar. Click on the Define assumption in the drop down menu.
- The gallery of distributions will appear, click on triangular and then on OK.
- In the triangular distribution box, enter the pessimistic, most likely and optimistic estimates for activity A and click on OK.
- Note that assumption Cells are coloured green.

Before continuing, there are two things that should be noted. First, the number you originally entered in A3 was "20", the expected duration of the activity a is calculated earlier. These values were calculated previously by the formula (a + 4m + b)/6 rule. When you entered the data on the triangular distribution form for space A3, you entered 10, 22 and 22 in the appropriate spaces. To find the expected duration for an activity with those three estimates, CB applied the correct formula for this distribution. (a + m + b)/3. TE is therefore 18, and not 20. CB properly changes the cell accordingly. You cannot leave the cell A3 blank and click on cell/define assumption because CB won't allow it. Just put any old number in the cell, click on it to fix it and proceed. The CB will change it to the correct number automatically.

Another variance worth mentioning concerned activity b. If you call up the triangular distribution an attempt to enter 20 –20 – 20, the three times given in the problem, CB will not allow it because these numbers will not define a triangle. Do not define cell B3 as an assumption cell. Merely enter 20 in the cell and continue with the next entry. It will be treated by CB as a constant. Activity g is also a cell listing a constant or deterministic time. These cells will not be coloured. Continue entering data until you have completed all activities.

- Continue entering data you have completed entering all activities.
- If observed carefully there will be eight paths in the network. Enter the path identification for each and then enter the formula for path duration for each of the paths. Note that this formula's simply sum the activities for each paths.
- Now enter the formula that calculates the project duration in cell S3, labelled "completion time" Click on cell and then on define forecast. Type in project completion time, as for a title and click ok. The formula will find the longest of the paths for each simulation. That will be the critical path for any given trial.
- Now click on Run and choose run preferences from the drop down menu. Ask for 1000 trials. Click Ok.
- Now click on "Run" and then again on "Run" from the drop down menu. The results will be displayed in the form of statistical distribution.

Before discussing the results of the simulation, it should be noted that altering the assumption about the probability distribution of the activity times from the beta to the triangular distribution has had an interesting effect. Using the new TEs the critical path of the network has been changed from a – d – j under the beta assumption to b – g – i for the triangular assumption. This shift is solely the result of the different formula for calculating activity TEs.

The statistical distribution seen while running a simulation will be similar to the project completion time frequency chart. To the likelihood of completing the project in 52 days, for example, simply enter the number 52 or number of your choice, in the box that reads "+ infinity". Then press enter. The probability you seek will appear in the certainty cell.

If you click on View in the short tool bar at the top of the frequency chart box, you can see other information. For example, click on View and then on statistics in the drop down list. The distribution of 1000 completion times had a mean of 47.8 days and median of 47.6 days. Recall that the expected completion time with the beta distribution was 43 days and the expected time with the triangular assumptions was 44 days. The greater mean time found by simulation is almost certainly due to the impact of merger paths.

The percentiles data show the percent of the trials completed at or below the completion shown. The cumulative chart shows graphically the probability that a project will be completed in 52 days or less. The 52 was simply entered in the cell of either the cumulative chart where shown in the lower right hand frequency chart box.

4.3.2 Critical Path Method – Crashing a Project

Network analysis: Network analysis is the general name given to certain specific techniques which can be used for the planning, management and control of projects.

- **Use of nodes and arrows:**

  Arrows → An arrow leads from tail to head directionally. Indicate Activity, a time consuming effort that is required to perform a part of the work.

  Nodes • A node is represented by a circle.

  Indicate EVENT, a point in time where one or more activities start and/or finish.

- **Activity**
  - A task or a certain amount of work required in the project
  - Requires time to complete
  - Represented by an arrow

- **Dummy Activity**
  - Indicates only precedence relationships
  - Does not require any time or effort

- **Event**
  - Signals the beginning or ending of an activity
  - Designates a point in time
  - Represented by a circle (node)

- **Network**
  - Shows the sequential relationships among activities using nodes and arrows
  - Activity-on-node (AON): Nodes represent activities, and arrows show precedence relationships
  - Activity-on-arrow (AOA): Arrows represent activities and nodes are events for points in time

- **Activity:** An element of work performed during the course of a project. An activity normally has an expected duration, an expected cost and expected resource requirements. Activities are often subdivided into tasks.

- **Event:** It is the result of completing one or more activities. Identifiable end state occurring at a particular time in a project. Events use no resources.

- **Network:** It is the arrangement of all activities (or events) in a project arrayed in their logical sequence and represented by arcs and nodes. This arrangement (network) defines the project and the activity precedence relationship. Networks are usually drawn starting on the left and proceeding to the right. Arrow heads placed on the arcs are used to indicate the direction of flow i.e. to show the proper precedences. Before an event can be realized i.e., achieved all activities that immediately precede it must be completed. These are called its (predecessors). Thus, an event represents an instant in time when each and every predecessor activity has been finished.

- **Path:** A path is a set of sequentially connected activities in a project network diagram. In other words, path is the series of connected activities (intermediate events) between any two events in a network.
- **Critical:** Activities, events or paths which, if delayed will delay the completion of the project. A projects critical path is understood to mean that sequence of critical activities (critical events) that connects the projects start event to its finished event and which cannot be delayed without delaying the project.

    (a) Longest path through a network

    (b) Minimum project completion time

Critical activity: Any activity or task described on a critical path determined by using CPM technique is called "critical activity:

To transform a project plan in to a network, one must know what activities comprise the project and for each activity, what are its predecessors. An activity can be in any of these conditions:

1. It may have successor or successors but no predecessor/s.
2. It may have predecessor(s) but no successor(s).
3. It may have both predecessor(s) and successor(s).

Activities are represented here by rectangles (one form of what in a network are called "nodes") with arrows to show the precedence relationship. This is called as activity – on – node (AON).

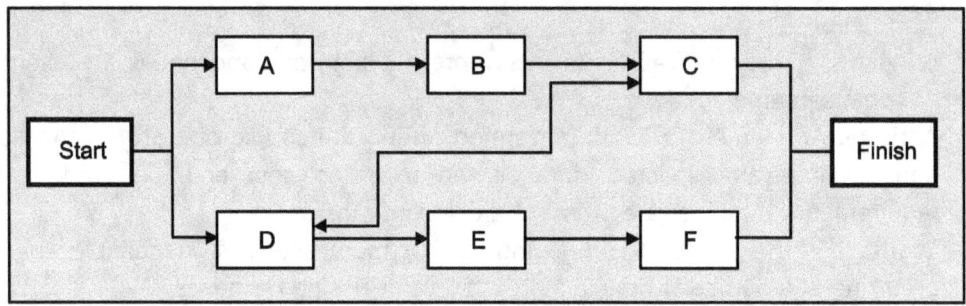

Fig. 4.3: Precedence Diagram Method (Activity On Node - AON)

When there are multiple activities with no predecessors, it is usual to show them all emanating from a single node called "Start". Similarly, when multiple activities have no successors, it is usual to show them connected to a node called "End". In the preceding examples, rectangles (nodes) represent the activities; hence it is called an activity –on- node (AON network).

Some network diagrams are also represented as Activity by Arrow.

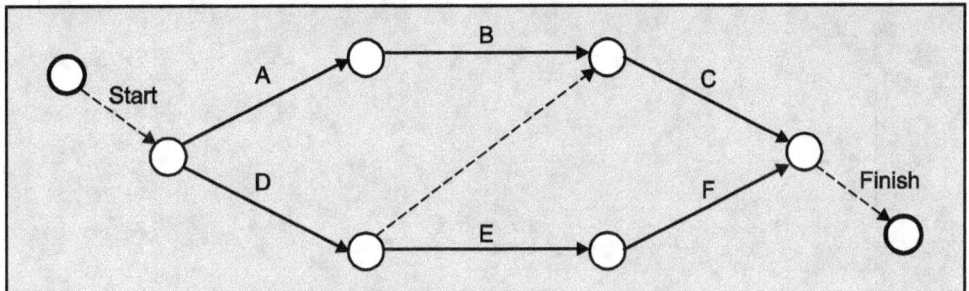

Fig. 4.4: Arrow Diagram Method or Activity by Arrow

Arrow Diagramming Method (ADM): A network diagramming technique in which activities are represented by arrows. The tail of the arrow represents the start and head represents the finish of the activity. (The length of the arrow does not represent the expected duration of the activity). Activities are connected at points called nodes (usually drawn as small circles) to illustrate the sequence in which the activities are expected to be performed.

There are four categories of dependencies or precedence relationships:

- Finish – to – start: "From" activity must finish before the "to" activity can start.
- Finish – to – finish "From" activity must finish before the "to" activity can finish.
- Start to start – "From" activity must start before the "to" activity can start
- Start to finish – "From" activity must start before the "to" activity can finish.

When it was first developed in 1958, CPM used a AON notation and included a way of relating the project schedule to the level of physical resources allocated to the project. This allowed the project manager to trade time for cost, or vice versa. In CPM, two activity times and two costs often specified each activity. The first time/cost combination was called normal and the second set was referred to as crash.

Duration compression is a special case of mathematical analysis that looks for ways to shorten the project schedule without changing the project scope (e.g. to meet imposed dates or other schedule objectives). Duration compression includes techniques such as:

4.3.3 Crashing a Project

Crashing is something in which cost and schedule trade off are analysed to determine how to obtain the greatest amount of compression for the least incremental cost. Crashing does not always produce viable alternative and often results in increased cost. In other words, crashing a project is taking action to decrease the total project duration after analysing a number of alternatives to determine how to get the maximum duration compression for the least cost.

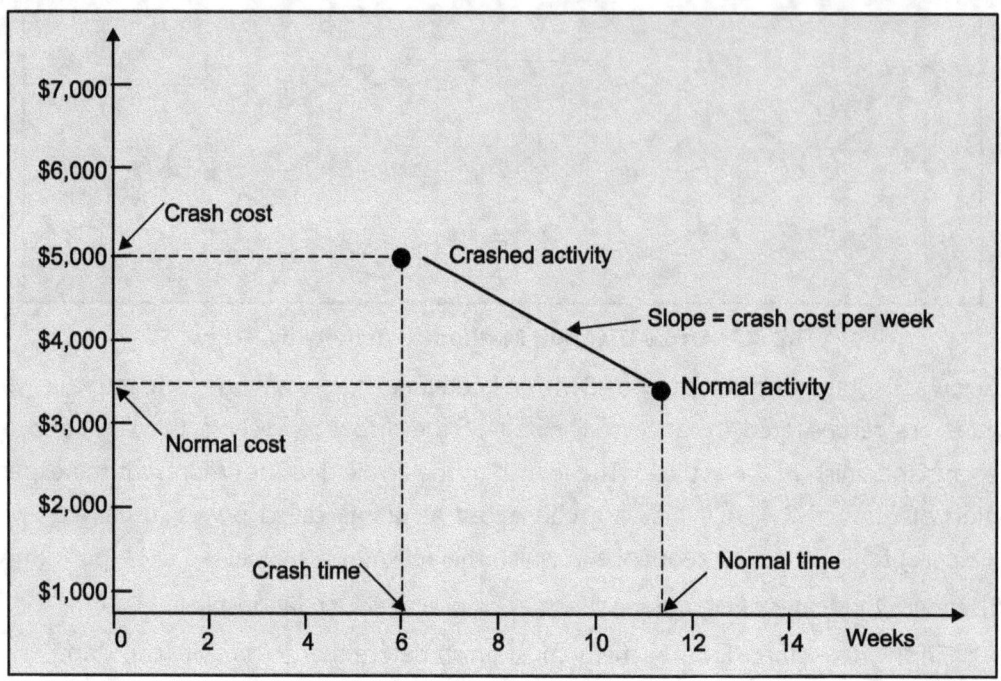

Fig. 4.5 Project Crashing

To compute a cost/time slope for each activity that can be expedited (crashed) slope is defined as follows:

$$\text{Slope} = \frac{\text{Crash cost} - \text{Normal cost}}{\text{Crash time} - \text{Normal time}}$$

i.e. the cost per duration of crashing a project. The slope is negative, indicating that as the time required for a project or task is decreased, the cost is increased.

Time-Cost Relationship

- Crashing costs increase as project duration decreases.
- Indirect costs increase as project duration increases.
- Reduce project length as long as crashing costs are less than indirect costs.

Duration Compression:

It looks for ways to shorten the project Schedule without changing the project scope

Crashing: Reducing project time by expending additional resources.

Crash time: An amount of time an activity is reduced.

Crash cost: Cost of reducing activity time.

Goals reduce project duration at minimum cost.

4.3.4 Resource Allocation Problem

A limitation of the scheduling procedures is that they do not address the issues of resource utilisation and availability. The focus is on time rather than physical resources. Also, in the discussion that follows it will not be enough to refer to resource usage simply as cost. Instead, we should refer to individual types of labour, specific facilities, kinds of materials, individual pieces of equipment and other discrete inputs that are applicable to an individual project but are restricted in availability. Time itself is a critical resource in project management, one that is unique as it cannot be renewed.

Schedules must be assessed not just in terms of meeting the project milestones, but also in terms of the timing and use of scarce resources. A fundamental measure of the project manager's success in the project management is the continuous process of cost benefit analysis.

Seldom, it is possible that some additional (useful) resources can be added at little or no cost to the project throughout a crisis period. At other times, some resources in abundant supply may be traded for scarce resources. However, many times this trade involves additional costs to the organisation, so a primary responsibility for the project manager is to make do with what is available.

The extreme points of the relationship between time used and resource used are:

Time Limited: The project must be finished by a certain time, using as few resources as possible. But it is time, not resource usage that is critical.

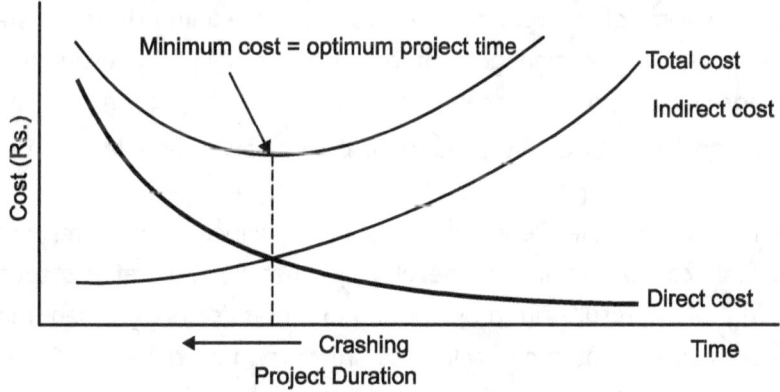

Fig. 4.6 Time-Cost Trade off

4.3.5 Resource Loading

Resource loading describes the amounts of individual resources and existing schedule requirements at a specific time periods. Hence, it is irrelevant whether we are considering a single work unit or several projects. The loads (requirements) of each resource type are merely listed as a function of time period. Resource loading gives a general understanding of the demands of a project or set of projects will make on a firm's resources. Despite of the specific techniques used to lessen the demands it is also a first step in attempting to reduce excessive demands on certain resources.

If resources of a project are improved by 10%, the output of the project usually does not improve by 10% and the time required for the project does not decline by same amount. The output and the time may not change at all or may change by an amount seemingly not related to 10%.

Due to disruptions, emergencies, maintenance requirements, personnel issues and easy inefficiency of any resource that is scheduled for full production over an extended time period. Also, illness will surely occur in this long time frame. Furthermore, will the facilities, equipment, materials and the work itself be ready for the engineers when they move to the next task? Will everything show up precisely when it is needed? Will there be no delays in the work preceding what the engineers are expected to do? Will there be no scope changes in the preceding work, thus the delaying the succeeding tasks scheduled for the engineers? As you can see, we expect there to be "unexpected" delays for multiple reasons, hence the admonition to never schedule a resource for more than 85 -90% of its capacity.

4.3.6 Resource Leveling

Resource leveling aims to minimise the period by period differences in resource loading by shifting tasks in their slack allowances. The aim is to create a smoother distribution of resource usage. Any form of network analysis in which scheduling decisions start and finish dates are driven by resource management concerns (e.g. limited resource availability or difficult to manage changes in resource levels).

Mathematical analysis frequently produce a preliminary schedule that demands more resources during certain time periods than that are available or requires changes in resource levels that are not manageable. Requirements such as "allocate scarce resources to critical path activities first" can be applied to develop a schedule that reflects such constraints. Resource leveling often results in project duration that is longer than the preliminary schedule. The technique is at times called as "resource based method" especially when implemented with computerised optimisation. Resource leveling may have a significant influence on the preliminary estimates of resource requirements.

4.3.7 Constrained Resource Allocation

Resource constraint scheduling is a special case of resource leveling where requirements involved are limitations on the quantity of resources available. Thus, resource leveling is creating project schedule based on the resource availability. It is usually applied to the project that has CPM already been applied.

Far too often, PMs are surprised by resource constraints. The cause of this condition is usually the direct result of a failure to include resource availability in risk identification activities. The lack of a resource where and when it is needed can have many causes, but the most common causes are not difficult to identify and mitigate: failure of a supplier to produce and/or deliver the assignment of the resource to another activity, and loss or theft of a resource. PMs often apply risk management techniques to resources known to be scarce, but neglected to consider the more common resources that usually cause the problems.

There are two fundamental approaches to constrained resource allocation problems: heuristics and optimisation models. Heuristic approaches employ rules of thumb that have been found to work reasonably well in similar situations. They neck better solutions. Optimisation approaches seek the best solutions but are far more limited in their ability to handle complex situations and large problems.

Heuristic Methods

Heuristic approaches to constrained resource scheduling problems are in wide, general use for a number of reasons. First, they are the only feasible methods of attacking the large, non-linear, complex problems that tend to occur in the real world of project management. Second, while the schedules that heuristics generate may not be optimal, they are usually quite good - certainly good enough for most purposes. Commercially available, computer programs handle large problems and have had considerable use in industry. Further, modern simulation techniques allow the PM to develop many different schedules quickly and to determine which, if any, are significantly better than current practice. If a reasonable number of simulation runs fail to produce significant improvement, the PM can feel fairly confident that the existing solution is a good one.

Optimising Methods

In the past several years, a wide range of attacks have been made on the problems of resource allocation and scheduling when resources are constrained. Some of these depend on sophisticated mathematical and/or graphical tools and may be quite powerful in what they can do. The methods to find an optimal solution to the constrained resource scheduling problem fall primarily into two categories: mathematical programming (linear programming, LP, for the most part) and enumeration. In the late 1960's and early 1970's, limited enumeration techniques were applied to the constrained resource problem with some success. Advances in linear programming (LP) techniques now allow LP to be used on large constrained resource scheduling problems. Other approaches have combined programming and enumeration methods.

4.4 The Planning Monitoring Controlling Cycle

The purpose of project monitoring and controlling is to provide an understanding of and communicate the project's progress, thus identifying when the projects performance deviates significantly from the plan so that appropriate corrective actions and preventive actions are taken. Project activity monitoring is an aspect of project management that is performed through the project. Controlling is the aspect wherein corrective and preventive actions are taken. It is the project manager who must ensure that the monitor and control process is effectively executive.

The key things to be planned, monitored and controlled are time (Schedule), cost (Budget) and performance (Specifications) these encompass the fundamental objectives of the project.

We could cite some examples:

- A major construction ran over budget by 63% and over scheduled by 48% because the project manager decided that, since "he had managed similar projects several times before, he knew what to do without going into all that details that no one looks at it anyway."

- A large industrial equipment supplier "took a bath" on a project design to develop a new area of business because they applied the same planning and control procedures to the new area that they had used successfully on previous, smaller less complex jobs.

- Computer store won a competitive bid to supply a computer, five terminals and associated software to the ABC office of a national firm. Admittedly insufficient planning made the installation significantly late. Performance of the software was not close to specified levels. This failed job prevented the firm from being invited to bid on more 20 similar installations planned by the client.

The planning (budgeting and scheduling) methods significantly reduce the extent and cost of poor performance and time/cost overruns. It does not guarantee a trouble free project, but merely declines the risk of failure. It is useful to perceive the control process as a closed loop system, with revised plans and schedules (if warranted) following corrective actions. It is also useful to construct this process as an internal part of the organisational structure of the project, not something external and imposed on it or worst, in conflict with it.

Designing Monitoring System

The foremost step in setting up any monitoring system is to discover the key factors to be controlled. Project manager should define precisely which specific characteristics of performance cost and time must be controlled and then set up exact boundaries in which control should be maintained. There may also be other factors of importance worth noting, at least at milestones or review points in the life of a project.

For instance, the number of labour hours used, number or extent of process or output changes, the level of customer satisfaction and similar items may be worthy of note on individual projects. Top sources of items to be monitored are the project action plan and the risk management plan. The action plan explains what is being done, when and the planned level of resource usage for each task, work package and work element in the project. Monitoring the risks found in the risk management plan makes the project manager and project team prepared for specific risks and thus lowers the probability of surprises.

How to collect data:

A large proportion of all data collected takes one of the following forms, each of which is apt for some types of measures:

- **Frequency Counts:** A simple tally of the repetition of an event. This type of measure is frequently used for "complaints", number of times a project report is late, "days without accident", Bugs in a computer program and like items. The data are generally easy to collect and are often reported as events per unit time or events as a percent of a standard number. Even with such easy counts, data may be complex to collect. Items such as errors, complaints often go unreported by individuals or groups not particularly keen to advertise malperformance.
- **Raw Numbers:** Dates, currency, hours, physical amounts of resources used and specification are typically reported in this way. These numbers are reported in a broad variety of ways, but often as direct comparisons with a normal standard number. Also, inconsistency is commonly reported either as the difference among actual and standard or as the ratio of actual to standard. Differences or ratios can also be plotted as a time series to show changes in system performance. While collecting raw project data, it is essential to make sure that all data are collected from sources that function on the same time intervals and with the same rules for data collection.
- **Subjective Numeric Rating:** These numbers are subjective estimates, usually of quality, made by a knowledgeable individuals or groups. They can be reported in most of the same ways that objective raw numbers are; but care must be taken to make sure that the numbers are not controlled in ways only suitable for quantitative measures.
- **Indicators:** When the project manager cannot measure some aspect of system performance directly, it is most likely to find an indirect measure or indicator. The speed with which change orders are processed and changes are included into the project is often a good measure of team efficiency. Response to change may also be an indicator of the quality of communications on the project team. While using indicators to measure performance, the project manager should make sure that the relation between the indicator and the desired performance measure is as direct as possible.

- **Verbal measures:** Measures for such performance characteristics as "quality of team member cooperation", "moral of team members", or "quality of interaction with the client", often take form of verbal characterisations. As long as the set of characterisations is inadequate and the means of the individual teams consistently understood by all, these data serve their purposes logically well.

After data collection has been done, reports on project progress must be generated. These include project status reports, time/cost reports and variance reports among others. Causes and effects should be identified and trends noted. Plans, charts and tables must be updated regularly.

4.4.1 Information Needs and Reporting Process

Everybody related to the project should be suitably tied into the project reporting system. The monitoring system should to be constructed so that it addresses every level of management, but reports need not be of the same depth or at the same frequency for each level. Lower level personnel call for detailed information about individual tasks and the factors affecting such task. Report frequency is generally high. For the senior management levels overview reports describing progress in more aggregated terms with less individual task details except senior management has a special interest in a specific activity or task. Email should be used only for official purpose, not to pass on information or data. The relationship of project reports to the project action plan or WBS is the key to the determination of both report content and frequency. Report must include data that is relevant to the control of specific tasks that are being carried out according to a specific schedule. The nature of the monitoring reports should be consistent with the logic of planning, budgeting and scheduling systems. The primary purpose is to guarantee achievement of the project plan through control.

There are many advantages of the detailed timely reports delivered to the proper people among them are:

- Understanding of goals of the project by all stakeholders.
- Awareness of the progress of the parallel activities, problems and constraints related with coordination among activities.
- Realistic planning for the needs of all groups and individuals working on the project.
- Understanding the relationships of individual task to one another and to the overall project.
- Early warning signals of potential problems and delays in the project.
- Minimising the confusion related with change by reducing delays in communicating the change.
- Faster management action in response to unacceptable or inappropriate work.

- Higher visibility to top management, including attention directed to the immediate needs of the project.
- Keeping the client and other interested outside parties up-to-date on project status, particularly regarding project cost, milestones and deliverables.

Meetings:

- Use meetings for making group decisions or getting input for important problems. Avoid "show and tell" meetings, sometimes called "Status and Review" meetings.
- Have preset starting and stopping times plus written agenda. Stick with both and above all, do not penalise those who show up on time by making them wait for those who are late.
- Make sure homework is done prior to the meeting. Be prepared.
- If you manage the meeting, take your own minutes. The minutes become reality as soon as the meeting is over. It is essential to be left to the most junior person present. Allocate the minutes as soon as possible after the meeting.
- Avoid attributing remarks or view points to individuals in the minutes. Attribution makes people quite cautious of what they say in meetings and hampers creativity as well as controversy. Do not report votes on controversial matters.
- Avoid overly formal rules of procedures. A project meeting is not a parliament though politeness is always in order.

Table 4.1 Meeting Schedules

Sr. No.	Meeting group	Frequency	Attendees
1.	Board meeting		
2.	Engineering		
3.	Marketing		
4.	Sales		
5.	HR/admin/IT		
6.	Accounts/Finance		
7.	Vendors		
8.	Legal Liasoning		
9.	Contractors		
10.	Consultants		
11.	Customers		
12.	Misc.		

Common Reporting problems:

There are three common problems in the design of project reports.

1. Generally, too many details are incorporated, both in the reports and in the input being solicit from workers. Unnecessary details (or too frequent reporting) usually results in the reports not being read. Also, it prevents project team members from finding the information they require. Furthermore, the demand for large quantities of highly detailed input information often results in careless preparation of the data, thereby casting doubt on the validity of reports based on such data.

2. Main problem is the poor interface between the project information system and parent firm's information system. Data are hardly comparable and interaction between the project manager and the organisation's accountants is often stressed.

3. A poor connection between the planning and the monitoring systems. If the monitoring system is not tracking information directly related to the project's plans, control is worthless.

In actual practice issue management log is maintained by the project manager. Example given below:

Not maintaining such records also results in poor project control.

Issue No	Type of issue	Manager Responsible (Functional)	Communication Responsibility	Milestone for corrective action
101	Sales and project team co-ordination	Managing Committee	PMO and sales manager	DD / MM / YYYY
102	Accounts and vendor payments	PMO	Accounts executive	DD / MM / YYYY
103	Vendor delays	PM	PM	DD / MM / YYYY
104	Vendor quality issue	Engineering Team	PM, MIS executive	DD / MM / YYYY
105	Safety issues	PM	All	DD / MM / YYYY
106	People Conflicts	HR	HR manager	DD / MM / YYYY
107	Leaves	HR	HR Manager	ASAP
108	IT/machines	IT	IT	ASAP
109	Legal issues	Advocate/legal advisor	Legal	ASAP

In high value critical business projects change management log is also maintained. Example:

Proposed Change	Approved By	Implementation Responsibility
Budget Items		
Projected increase in project cost	If increase >= 10% of the approved project budget. Management/steering committee	PM
Schedule Items		
Forecast completion dates for key milestones have slipped from the approved baseline.	Less than 15 calendar days – PM Greater than 15 Days up to 60 days Project sponsor Greater than 60 days – Project steering committee	PM
Activity Scope		
New contract or modification to a contract.	All concerned	Changes to the project charter scope by PM
IT Related		
New requirements	All Concerned	Changes to the project charter scope – PM
Contracts		
Changes to definitions of contract	1. PM 2. Vendor	Changes to the project charter scope - PM
Changes in alternatives Identified	PM Project Sponsor	Changes to the project charter scope - PM
ADVICE / ACTION / IMPACT		
Impacts: stage - Analysis / Design / Construction		

4.4.2 Earned Value Analysis

The monitoring of performance for the entire project is critical. Individual task performance must be monitored carefully as the timing and co-ordination between individual tasks is essential. But overall project performance is the root of the matter and should not be overlooked. One way of measuring overall performance is by using an aggregate performance measure called earned value. Earned value analysis, in its various forms is most commonly used method for measuring project performance. It incorporates scope, cost, and schedule measures to assist the project management team and their project performance. It compares the amount of work that was planned with what was actually accomplished to determine if cost and schedule performance is as planned.

Earned value involves calculating three key values for each activity:

The budget, also called the budgeted cost of work scheduled (BCWS), is that portion of the approved cost estimate planned to be spent on the activity during the given period.

- The actual cost, also called the actual cost of work performed (ACWP), is the total of direct and indirect cost incurred in accomplishing work in the activity during a given period.

- The earned value, also called the budgeted cost of work performed (BCWP), is a percentage of the total budget equal to the percentage of the work actually completed. Many earned value implementations use only a few percentages (e.g. 30%, 70%, 90%, 100%) to simplify data collection. Some earned value implementations use only 0% or 100% (done or not done) to help ensure objective measurement of performance.

- These three values are used in combination to provide measures of whether or not work is being accomplished as planned. The most commonly used measures are

  The Cost Variance   (CV = BEWP −ACWP)

  The Schedule Variance   (SV = BCWP − BCWS)

  The Cost of Performance index   (CPI = BCWP/ACWP)

The Cumulative CPI (the sum of all individual BCWPs divided by the sum of all individual ACWPs) is widely used to forecast project at completion. In some application areas the schedule performance index (SPI = BCWP/BCWS) is used to forecast the project completion date.

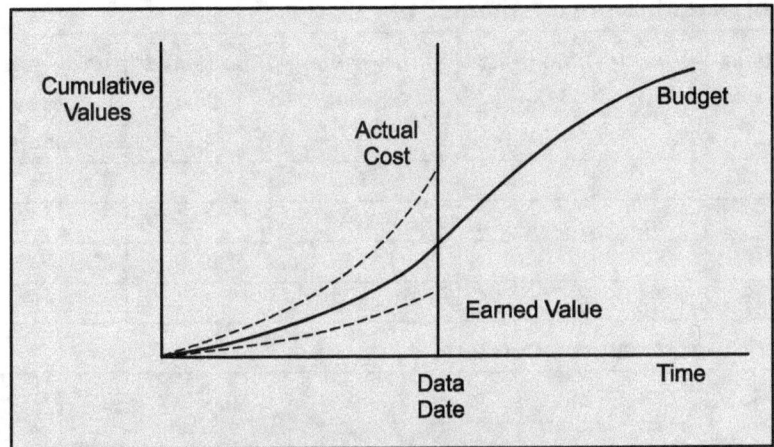

Fig. 4.7 Earned Value Analysis

Reference PMBOK®

4.5 Fundamental Purpose of Control

The two fundamental objectives of control are:

- The regulation of results through the alteration of activities.
- The stewardship of organisational assets.

The project manager should guard the physical assets of the organisation, its human resources and its financial resources. The processes for preserving these three different kinds of assets are different.

Types of Control:

1. Physical Assets Control:

Physical asset control demands control of the use of physical assets. It is concerned with asset maintenance, whether preventive or corrective. If the project uses a huge amount of physical equipments, the project manager also has the problem of setting up maintenance schedules in a way to keep the equipment in operating condition while minimizing intervention with ongoing work. It is essential to achieve preventive maintenance prior to the start of that final section of the project life cycle known as the "Last Minute Panic". Physical inventory, whether equipment or material must also be controlled. It must be received, inspected, and possibly stored prior to use. Records of all incoming shipments must be carefully authorized. Details such as project library, project coffee maker, project office furniture and all the other minor bits and pieces must be counted, maintained and conserved.

Templates used in industry for controlling procurement.

(a) Summary of materials procurement list.

Activity ID	Material	Vendor ID	Contract Terms	Procurement Schedule	Budgeted Cost	Projected Cost by Vendors	Difference

(b) Amendment report on procurement

Activity ID	Materials	Vendor	Risk			Risk Impact			Alternative Identification	Contract Terms Based on Alternatives	Total Time Change	Total Cost Impact
			H	M	Low	H	M	Low				

2. **Human Resource Control:**

Stewardship of human resources requires controlling and maintaining the growth and development of people. Projects provide particularly fertile ground for cultivating people, because projects are unique, differing one from another in many ways, it is possible for people working on projects to gain wide range of experience in a reasonably short time. Devices as employee appraisals, personnel performance indices, and screening methods for appointment, promotion, and retention are not particularly satisfactory devices for ensuring that the conservation function is being properly handled.

3. **Financial resource control:**

(a) It is difficult to separate the control mechanism aimed at conservation of financial resources from those focused on regulating resource use. Capital investment controls work to conserve the organisation's assets by insisting that certain conditions be met before capital can be expended and those same conditions usually regulate the use of capital to achieve the organisation goals of high return on investments. The techniques of financial control, both conservation and regulation, are well known. They include current asset controls, project budgets as well as capital investment controls. These controls are exercised through a series of analysis and audits conducted by the accounting/controller function for the most part.

(b) The project manager is responsible for the conservation and proper use of resources owned by the client or owned by the parent and charged to the client.

4.5.1 Three Types of Control Process

Process of controlling a project is far more complex than simply waiting for something to go wrong and then, if possible, fixing it. We must decide at what milestones in the project we will try to exert control, what needs to be controlled, what shall be the parameters of measurement, how much percentage of fluctuation can be accepted and what kind of interventions should be used and how to spot and correct potential fluctuations before they occur. In a project, it is very simple to lose sight of the actual objectives. Large projects acquire a life of their own and, if left to them, can spin out of control.

There have to be mechanisms to control the project and to make sure that the project is taking place as planned. Mostly, the control over a project focuses on the following three elements of the project:

(i) Performance

(ii) Cost

(iii) Time

The main purpose of having controls is to find out if there is a problem and then to modify course by taking corrective measures. Project control is chiefly to have systems to identify problems before they manifest themselves. There are three basic types of control mechanisms- cybernetic, go/no-go, and post-performance.

1. Cybernetic Control:

This is the most universal kind of control mechanism. A project has inputs and outputs. The outputs can be in the form of milestones that have to be met. Cybernetic controls focus on the outputs. If these milestones or outputs do not match with the set standards, then the situation is investigated to see if there is enough cause to change patterns of activity.

For example, a project to get a showroom ready for opening would target certain dates for completion of electric wiring, plastering, and painting. If the date of completion of wiring gets delayed, the schedule of activities has to be modified and the pace has to be stepped up to meet the scheduled opening day.

The main aim is to reduce deviations from a standard. The more the deviation, more is the attention the situation warrants.

2. Go/No-go Control:

Go/no-go control takes the form of testing to certify certain preconditions before a task is undertaken. This type of control can be used for a specific part of the project too.

Let us take the same example of a showroom. The plastering will begin only after the wiring and plumbing are done. So, if the plastering does not start off in time, then clearly there have been some delays in the preceding tasks.

Go/no-go controls are linked to the actual plans and are not separately set on a calendar.

3. **Post-performance Control:**

Post-performance controls are applied after the achievement of the project or the task. The focus here is not on changing what has already happened but in making sure that good and bad practices are recorded for being of some help in future projects.

For example, if in the showroom project, an analysis of delays reveals that it is very difficult to manage the availability of electricians and masons, this knowledge will be of help while planning and implementing the next showroom inauguration.

The post-performance controls include a set of recommendations on how to enhance future projects.

4.5.2 Comments on the Design of Control Systems

"Systems that evaluate, monitor, and control different aspects and departments of an organisation. Their purpose is to effectively and efficiently use resources in reaching the organisations objectives."   *– (Prakash, Ravish)*

Well designed and implemented project control systems offer an efficient and effective way of working. It is specifically because project control systems are implemented after detailed design, which comprises alignment with corporate internal controls that add to the internal controls of the organisation.

Schedule, cost, change, and document control are the four main areas for project controls systems.

- **Schedule control:** The management of the project plan and the control of the milestones, activities and deliverables in the agreed constraints. By using a single system there is a single source of project data.
- **Cost control:** The management of the project's budget, actual cost reporting and forecasting. As cost control systems are generally tightly integrated with the corporate ERP systems, there is no issue with Delegation of Authority (DoA) levels, segregation of duties controls, nor is time wasted merging various systems. The reporting requirements can be set and defined at the program level for multiple projects to compare for effective benchmarking. Cost control systems are transaction based for changes to forecasts to be audited. Integration with the schedule control system will make sure that there are accurate and up-to-date forecasts accessible.
- **Change control:** By defining the Delegation of Authority levels and expert review pathways a change control workflow may be designed so that any proposed change to the project is reconsidered by the right person at the right time. By incorporating this with the cost, schedule and document control systems it will guarantee approved changes reflected in the schedule, forecast and design documents.
- **Document control:** While working on difficult projects it is very important to ensure that the most current documents are available to all the staff. These may be design

documents, control procedures or the latest forecasts and budgets people are working toward achieving. Document control is vital in the implementation of Building Information Modelling.

Some control strategies for maximising effectiveness

- Rules detailing procedures for tasks, systems and processes. These instructions allow for detailed notes on results, greater flow in improvement and better-managed time and materials.
- Creating set guidelines for Quality Assurance
- Present to professionals improved, comprehensive written and structured guidelines.
- Making materials digitally accessible saves money and time in paperwork and improvements, as information is more readily available. In other words using on-line platforms to order materials monitor and process request will enable better control over the project. Also, real time data eases the material handling process within the project

Effective controls should be

- Strategic and results oriented
- Understandable
- Encourage self-control
- Timely and exception oriented
- Positive in nature
- Fair and objective
- Flexible

Management and control systems are valuable when their functions are carried out accurately and people implementing their functions are aware of their limitations. In short, the role of project controls is to present a 'True and Fair' view on the position of a capital project. This allows management to report externally with confidence, and to put into place mitigation if a project is neither performing as expected nor as required. Additionally, well designed and implemented project control systems provide an efficient and effective way of working. Less time is spent 'managing the systems and processes' so that the people working on the project can focus on their 'Value Adding Activities' and can convey the capital project that the business needs, on time and on budget

4.5.3 Control as a Function of Management

Controlling consists of verifying whether everything occurs in conformities to the plans adopted, instructions issued and principles established. Controlling ensures that there is effective and effluent utilisation of organisational resources so as to achieve the planned goals. Controlling measures the deviation of actual performance from the standard performance, discovers the causes of such deviations and helps in taking corrective actions.

According to Brech, "Controlling is a systematic exercise which is called as a process of checking actual performance against the standards or plans with a view to ensure adequate progress and also recording such experience as is gained as a contribution to possible future needs.'

According to Donnell, "Just as a navigator continually takes reading to ensure whether he is relative to a planned action, so should a business manager continually take reading to assure himself that his enterprise is on fight course."

Controlling has got two basic purposes:

1. It facilitates co-ordination
2. It helps in planning

Features of controlling

Following are the characteristics of controlling function of management:

1. **Controlling is an end function:** A function which comes once the performances are made in conformities with plans.
2. **Controlling is a pervasive function:** It is performed by managers at all levels and in all type of concerns,
3. **Controlling is forward looking:** Because effective control is not possible without past being controlled. Controlling always looks at the future so that follow-up can be made whenever required.
4. **Controlling is a dynamic process:** Since controlling requires taking reviewable methods, changes have to be made wherever possible.
5. **Controlling is related with planning:** Planning and Controlling are two inseparable functions of management. Without planning, controlling is a meaningless exercise and without controlling, planning is useless. Planning presupposes controlling and controlling succeeds 'planning'.

Process of controlling

Controlling as a management function involves following steps:

1. **Establishment of standards:** Standards are the plans or the targets which have to be achieved in the course of business function. They can also be called as the criterions for judging the performance- Standards generally are classified into two:
    *   **Measurable or tangible:** Those standards which can be measured and expressed are called as measurable standards. They can be in form of cost, output, expenditure, time, profit, etc.
    *   **Non-measurable or intangible:** There are standards which cannot be measured monetarily. For example- performance of a manager, deviation of workers, their attitudes towards a concern. These are called as intangible standards.

    Controlling becomes easy through establishment of these standards because controlling is exercised on the basis of these standards.

2. **Measurement of performance:** The second major step in controlling is to measure the performance. Finding out deviations becomes easy through measuring the actual performance. Performance levels are sometimes easy to measure and sometimes difficult. Measurement of tangible standards is easy as it can be expressed in units, cost, money terms, etc. Quantitative measurement becomes difficult when performance of manager has to be measured. Performance of a manager cannot be measured in quantities, it can be measured only by:

    *   Attitude of the workers,
    *   Their morale to work,
    *   The development in the attitudes regarding the physical environment, and
    *   Their communication with the superiors.

    It is also sometimes done through various reports like weekly, monthly, quarterly, yearly reports.

3. **Comparison of actual and standard performance:** Comparison of actual performance with the planned targets is very important. Deviation can be defined as the gap between actual performance and the planned targets. The manager has to find out two things here - extent of deviation and cause of deviation. Extent of deviation means that the manager has to find out whether the deviation is positive or negative or whether the actual performance is in conformity with the planned performance. The managers have to exercise control by exception. He has to find out those deviations which are ethical and important for business. Minor deviations have to be ignored. Major deviations like replacement of machine appointment of workers, quality of raw material, rate of profits, etc. should he looked upon consciously. Therefore it is said, "if a manager controls everything, he ends up controlling nothing." For example, if stationery charges increase by a minor 5 to 10%, it can be called as a minor deviation. On the other hand, if monthly production decreases continuously, it is called as major deviation.

    Once the deviation is identified, a manager has to think about various causes which have led to deviation. The causes can be:

    *   Erroneous planning,
    *   Co-ordination loosens,
    *   Implementation of plans is defective, and
    *   Supervision and communication is ineffective, etc.

4. **Taking remedial actions:** Once the causes and extent of deviations are known, the manager has to detect those errors and take remedial measures for it. There are two alternatives here:
    - Taking corrective measures for deviations which have occurred; and
    - After taking the corrective measures, if the actual performance is not in conformity with plans, the manager can revise the targets. It is here the controlling process comes to an end. Follow up is an important step because it is only through taking corrective measures, a manager can exercise controlling.

Types of Management controls:

- **Management by Exception**: Focuses attention on substantial differences between desired and actual performance. It can save the managers time, energy, and other resources, and concentrates efforts on areas showing the greatest need.
- **Types of exceptions:**
    - Problem situation - below standard
    - Opportunity situation – above standard
- **Feed forward Controls:** Ensure the right directions are set and the right resource inputs are available:
    - Employed before a work activity begins.
    - Ensures that:
    - Objectives are clear.
    - Proper directions are established.
    - Right resources are available.
    - Focuses on quality of resources.
    - Prevents "anticipated" problems
    - Built in at the start (or before)
- **Concurrent Controls**: Ensure the right things are being done as part of work-flow operations:
    - Focus on what happens during work process.
    - Monitor ongoing operations to make sure they are being done according to plan.
    - Can reduce waste in unacceptable finished products or services.
    - Occurs while activity in progress
    - Ensures standards being met; Correct before they become too costly
    - Often built into new technology
- **Feedback Controls:** Ensure that final results are up to desired standards:
    - Take place after work is completed i.e. Control after action has occurred
    - Focus on quality of end results.
    - Provide useful information for improving future operations. Good feedback on effectiveness of planning

- **Management by objective:** A process of joint objective setting between superior and subordinate.
  - A structured process of regular communication.
  - Supervisor/team leader and workers jointly set performance objectives, establish standards, and choose actions.
  - Workers act individually to perform tasks; supervisors act individually to provide necessary support.
  - Supervisor and workers jointly review results, discuss implications, and renew the cycle.
- **Example of measured performance to standards**
  - Profitability
  - Market position
  - Productivity
  - Product leadership
  - Personnel development
  - Employee attitudes
  - Social responsibility
  - Reflecting the relative balance between short- and long-range goals
  - Workers' performance objectives for a specific time period.
  - Plans through which performance objectives will be accomplished.
  - Standards for measuring accomplishment of performance objectives.
  - Procedures for reviewing performance results.

Points to Remember

- PERT is a management process of controlling and analysing a system or program using periodic time and money reports, often computer generated, to determine money and labour status at any given time.
- PERT forces managers to plan their projects critically and analyse all factors affecting the development of the plan. The process of the network analysis demands that the project planning be performed on considerable detail from start to finish.
- CPM is a network analysis technique used to calculate project duration by analysing the sequence of activities (on which path) having the least amount of scheduling flexibility (the least amount of float).
- Monte Carlo Analysis is a scheduled risk assessment technique that performs a project simulation several times in order to calculate a distribution of likely results.

- Following are the steps in CPM and PERT Project Planning:
  - (a) Specify the individual activities.
  - (b) Determine the sequence of those activities.
  - (c) Draw a network diagram.
  - (d) Estimate the completion time for each activity.
  - (e) Identify the critical path (longest path through the network)
  - (f) Update the CPM diagram as the project progresses.
- Crashing a project is taking action to decrease the total project duration after analysing a number of alternatives to determine how to get the maximum duration compression for the least cost.
- Resource loading describes the amounts of individual resources and existing schedule requirements at a specific time periods.
- Resource levelling aims to minimise the period by period differences in resource loading by shifting tasks in their slack allowances. The aim is to create a smoother distribution of resource usage.
- Resource constraint scheduling is a special case of resource levelling where requirements involved are limitations on the quantity of resources available. Thus, resource levelling is creating project schedule based on the resource availability.
- The purpose of project monitoring and controlling is to provide with an understanding of and communicate the project's progress, thus identifying when the projects performance deviates significantly from the plan so that appropriate corrective actions and preventive actions are taken.
- Earned value analysis, in its various forms is most commonly used method for measuring project performance. It incorporates scope, cost, and schedule measures to assist the project management team and their project performance.
- Controlling consists of verifying whether everything occurs in conformities the plans adopted, instructions issued and principles established. Controlling ensures that there is effective and effluent utilisation of organisational resources so as to achieve the planned goals.
- The three types of control processes are:
  - (a) Cybernetic Control
  - (b) Go/No-go Control
  - (c) Post-performance Control

Questions for Discussion

1. What are the types of control processes?
2. Describe PERT and CPM.
3. Explain risk analysis using simulation with crystal ball 2000.
4. Define critical path method.
5. Discuss the planning - monitoring - controlling cycle.
6. Summarise earned value analysis.
7. What are the fundamental purposes of control?
8. Elaborate control as a function of management.

■■■

Chapter 5...

Purposes of Evaluation

Contents ...

Learning Objectives ...

- To understand the purposes of evaluation - goals of the system
- To describe the project audit
- To know the construction and use of the audit report
- To discuss the project audit life cycle
- To explain some essentials of an audit/evaluation
- To define the varieties of project termination
- To understand when to terminate a project
- To summarise the process of project termination

5.1 Project Evaluation

5.1.1 Introduction

A project is an investment activity where we use capital resources to create a producing asset from which we can expect to realise benefits over an extended period of time. Or a project is an activity on which we will spend money in expectation of returns and which logically seems to lend itself to planning, financing and implementation as a unit. A project should have the following characteristics:

1. It should have a specific starting point and specific ending point.
2. Its major costs and returns should be measurable.
3. It should have a specific geographic location.
4. It should have a specific clientele group.
5. It should have a well-defined time sequence of investment and production activities.

5.1.2 Levels of Project Evaluation

Project evaluation is required to be done at three levels. Once the initial planning is completed, it is essential to re-check for the gaps or re-plan for certain aspects that have evolved during the planning process. Redefining of milestones, risk list and corrective planned actions are some of the outcomes of evaluation during planning stage.

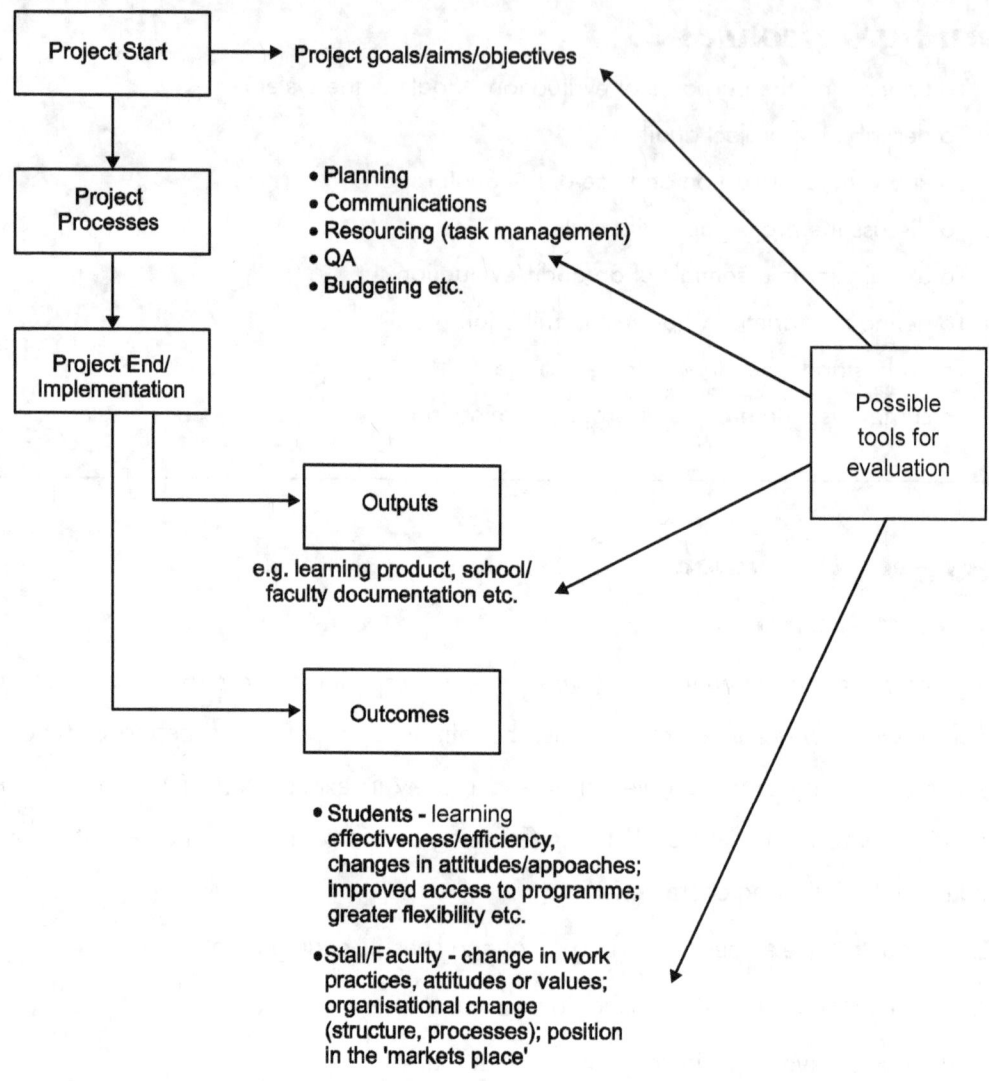

Fig. 5.1

During execution, step-by-step process of collecting, recording and organising information about project results, including short-term outputs (immediate results of activities, or project deliverables), is required to be noted. This information is useful for the next similar projects. This information is also called as project's historical information.

The final deliverables of the project needs to be checked with reference to the customer requirements or promised outcomes. They are to be evaluated on major aspects such as:

- Quality of the final product or service.
- Product delivery schedule including time variance, cost variance.
- Product performance.

Project evaluation is not limited to after the fact analysis. It is conducted several times during project life cycle. This is done through a process called project audit. Project audit is a means for checking the progress and performance of the project or compare it with other similar project.

5.1.3 Goals of the System/ Purpose of Project Evaluation

Purpose of evaluation is to help the organisation to achieve project's goals corresponding to organisation goals. The evaluation is done to – understand outcomes from each process or the total process. This will improve the project's performance. Certainly the major element in the evaluation of a project is its success. They can be classified into four main points:

1. The project's efficiency is meeting both the budget and the schedule. This has been the primary focus for achieving time, cost and performance objectives.

2. An important dimension is the customer impact and satisfaction. This includes meeting the project's technical, qualitative and operational requirements, including factors relating to royalty and repurchase, fulfilling the customer's actual requirement, solving major operational problems of the customer.

3. Business or direct success is level of commercial success and market share. For internal projects, however, the factors might be those such as yield, cycle times, processing steps, quality etc.

4. Future potential, this includes a new market, developing a new line of products or services, or in case of internal project developing a new technology, skills, or competencies.

Thus evaluation of the project helps:

1. Improve understanding of the ways in which projects may be of value to the organisation.

2. Improve the processes for organising and managing projects.

3. Provide an environment in which project team members can work creatively together.

4. Identify organisational strengths and weakness in project-related personnel, management and decision-making techniques and systems.

5. Identify and improve the response to risk factors in the firm's use of projects.

6. Allow access to project policy decision-making by external stakeholders.

7. Improve the way projects contribute to the professional growth of project team members.

8. Identify project personnel who have high potential for managerial leadership.

9. Identification of problems and risks involved and preparation of contingency plans.

10. Clarify performance. Mapping the cost and time relationships and benchmarking the expected chance and result in reduction in cost.
11. Locate opportunities for future technological advances.
12. Evaluate the quality of project and project management.
13. Identify mistakes, find solutions and create strategies to avoid them in the future.
14. Provide information to the client.
15. Reconfirm the organisation's interest and commitment to the project.

5.2 The Project Audit

5.2.1 Introduction

A project audit basically offers an opportunity to uncover the issues, concerns and challenges encountered during the execution of a project. It affords the project manager, project sponsor, and project team a temporary view of what has gone well and what needs to be improved with the project to accomplish it productively. A project audit can also be used to develop success criteria for future projects. This review provides an opportunity to discover what elements of the project were successfully managed and which ones presented challenges. This will help the organisation make out what it needs to do so that blunders are not repeated on upcoming projects.

A project audit is a systematic and detailed evaluation of the management of a project, its methodology and procedures, its records, its properties, its budgets and expenditures, its degree of completion, its feasibility, and influence on the organisation. It can deal with the project as a whole or only partly. The audit directly looks at the systems and its use. The project audit also studies the financial, managerial, and technical aspects of the project as an incorporated set applied to a specific project in a specific organisational environment.

What is an audit? "Audit is an evaluation of a person, organisation, system, process, project or product. Audits are performed to ascertain the validity and reliability of information, and also provide an assessment of a system's internal control."- (ask define)

- Why Audits are done:
  - o Verify Data of processes or operations.
  - o Judge effectiveness of the current processes.
  - o Judge effectiveness of meeting standard requirements.
  - o Provide information about problem areas
- Financial:
  - o Examine the accuracy of financial statements
  - o Ensure accounts/statements meet organisations standards and policy requirements of how there conducted.

- Internal
  - Is done within an organisation to examine and evaluate their activities and records.
- Project Management
  - Health of the project to see if it's on track and meeting demand.
  - To see if the project can be enhanced
- Quality
  - Ensure that procedural activities are met
  - Current (QMS) meets national or organisational standards
  - Regulatory requirement (ex: FDA or higher education)

The project audit should at least contain the following:

Status:
- Confirm status on the basis of completion of tasks as planned in the project.
- Present status of the project. It has to check the completed work and match it with the planned level of completion.

Predictions:
- **Future status**: It needs to identify significant schedule changes and indicate the nature of the changes.
- **Status of critical tasks**: The actions performed on the critical task that determines the success or failure of the project.

Measurement:
- Financial terms plus schedule, progress, resource usage, status of milestones identified during project planning.
- **Risk assessment:** Identification of the potential for the project failure or monitory loss.

Record Keeping System:
- No standard system is available; it uses any desired formats by individual organisation or dictated by contract or sometimes governed by quality control processes such as ISO.

Project History:
- Creating the project assets for future that is, information that may be pertinent to other similar projects.
- Sometimes formats for storing data are not available, in such cases, data structure and database must be designed and used to start audit.

Recommendations:
- Often required and may cover any aspect of the project or its management.

Qualifications:

- It focuses on shortcomings of audit forces. For example, lack of technical expertise, lack of funds or time.
- This also indicates the limitations of the audit. It also forms identification of assumptions or limitations that affect the data in the audit.

Note that the project audit is not the financial audit. The project audit is far broader in scope and may deal with the project as a whole or any component or set of components of the project. It is meant to ensure that the project is being appropriately managed.

5.2.2 Project Audit Venting

Regardless of whether the project audit is conducted mid-term on a project or at its conclusion, the process is similar. It is generally recommended that an outside facilitator conduct the project audit. This ensures confidentiality, but also allows the team members and other stakeholders to be candid. They know that their input will be valued and the final report will not identify individual names, but only facts will be represented. Often, individuals involved in a poorly managed project will find that speaking with an outside facilitator during a project audit allows them to openly express their emotions and feelings about their involvement in the project and/or the impact the project has had on them. This "venting" is an important part of the overall audit.

5.2.3 Phases of Project Audit

A project audit consists of three phases:

- **Phase 1:** Defining the criteria's for the project's success and develop list of questionnaire
- **Phase 2:** In depth Research
- **Phase 3:** Generate reports

Phase 1: Defining criteria's and preparation of questionnaire

- **Success Criteria Development**

  Discuss with the stakeholders, project owner and customers and identify the "success criteria" for the project audit. This ensures that their individual and collective needs are met.

- **Prepare list of Questionnaire**

  Develop a questionnaire to be sent to each member of the core project team and selected stakeholders. It is observed that people often complete the questionnaire in advance to the discussion meetings. It helps them to focus their thoughts. The actual one on one meeting provides the project manager with the opportunity to gain deeper insights into the comments. The questionnaires help project manager to reflect on the project's successes, failures, challenges and missed opportunities.

- **Type of Audit Questions**

  There are many questions that can be asked. It is easiest to develop open-ended questions. Develop the questions so that they will help to identify the major project successes; the major project issues, concerns and challenges; how the team worked together; conflict areas within team, how vendors were managed; how reporting and meetings were handled; how risk and change was managed, etc.

Phase 2: In depth Research

- Schedule and conduct meetings with the project sponsor, project manager and project team members in order to identify the past, current and future issues, concerns, challenges and opportunities.
- It is essential to discuss with stakeholders including vendors, suppliers, contractors, other project internal and external resources and selected customers. This also enables the smooth transactions as well as gives insight to the project manager for defining the contract terms in the future projects.
- Develop questionnaire that probes deeply into the issues, challenges and concerns to get to the root causes of the problems.
- Review all historical and current documentation related to this project including:
  o Team structure
  o Scope statement
  o Business requirements
  o Project plan
  o Milestone report
  o Meeting minutes
  o Action items
  o Risk logs
  o Issue logs
  o Change logs
- Review the project plan and determine how the "Vendor Plan" has been incorporated into the overall project plan.
- Interview selected Stakeholders to identify and determine what their expectations of the project had been and to identify to what extent their expectations have been met.
- Review the project quality management plan and identify the issues, concerns and challenges in the overall management of the project and to identify the opportunities that can improve product quality/service. This also helps the organisation to develop maturity in process followed.
- Document the lessons learned that can improve the performance of other future projects within the organisation.

Phase 3: Generate Reports
- Compile the information collected from discussion and meetings with all stakeholders.
- Compile the information collected from individuals who only completed the questionnaire.
- Consolidate the findings from the project documentation review.
- Specify the identified issues, concerns and challenges presented through the review of the project quality management and isolate the opportunities you believe that may be realised.
- Note the identified project's issues, concerns and challenges.
- Specific recommendations that state the project's opportunities that can be achieved.
- Identify the lessons learned that can improve the performance of future projects within the organisation.
- Finalise the creation of the report and recommendations on the basis of the findings and present this detailed report and recommendations including the road map to get future projects to the "next level" of performance.
- Project auditors believe that a project quality audit should achieve three goals:
  - It should identify existing problems on the project.
  - Understand the impact on the project where problems would have occurred if changes are not made.
  - State recommendations where changes should be made.

5.2.4 Depth of Audit

Time and money are the two most common criteria for the depth of investigation and level of details presented in the audit report. While an audit can be performed at any level, three distinct levels are recognised and widely used:

1. **The General Audit:** It gives overview of projects performance. It does not describe details of the internal project shortcomings or actions taken thereupon
2. **The Detailed Audit:** It usually covers the entire project performance in depth.
3. **The Technical Audit:** It focuses on the complexities or problem areas that were handled within process to control the outcome

5.2.5 Timing of the Audit

Audits are performed based on all significant size or importance of project. The first audits are usually done early in the project's life, since it is easier to deal with it. Early audits focus on the technical issues in order to make sure that the key technical problems have been resolved or have a mitigation plan ready. Audits that are done in latter stages in the project life cycle are of less immediate value to the project, but are of more value to the parent organisation. The post project audit is often a legal necessity because the client specifies such an audit report in the contract. Post project report also serves as managerial feedback to the parent firm. It is essential to account for all project property and expenditures.

5.2.6 Construction and Use of Audit Report

It is useful to establish a general format to which all audit reports must confirm. This makes it possible for project managers, auditors, and organisational management to have the same understanding of, and expectations for the audit report as a communication device.

Negative comments about individuals or groups associated with the project should be avoided. The following items cover the minimum information that should be contained in the audit report.

1. **Introduction:** This section contains the description of the project that gives basic information of the project contents. Project objectives must be clearly defined. In case of complex projects, explanatory points can be incorporated.

2. **Current Status:** Present status of the project. It usually consists of:

   o **Cost:** Here the actual cost is compared with that of the projected or budgeted cost. The frequency for such audit is clearly defined.

   o **Schedule:** Performance in terms of planned events or milestones is reported. It should clearly indicate the completed portion of the project and percentage of completion of all unfinished task for which estimates are required.

   o **Progress:** It compares work completed with resources used. Earn value charts or tables may be used for this purpose. The information is collected to identify problems with specific tasks or sets of tasks such as amount of time consumed with respect to projections regarding the remaining time and the amount of remaining planned expenditures.

   o **Quality:** Quality is measure of the degree to which the output of a system confirms to pre-specified characteristics. If there is detailed quality specification associated with the project, this section of the report may have to include full review of the quality control procedures, along with full disclosure of the results of the quality tests conducted to date.

   o **Resource Usage:** It also gives a clear picture of the resources utilised and future resource requirements including the skill levels and associated costs for procuring the resources.

   o **Future Project Status:** Conclusions regarding progress together with recommendations for any changes in technical approach, schedule or budget that should be made in the remaining task. No assumptions should be made about technical problems that are still under investigation at the time of the audit. Project audit/evaluation reports are not appropriate documents for rewriting project proposals.

   o **Critical Decision Issues:** All issues that require close monitoring by senior management should be included along with brief explanation of the relationships between these issues and the objectives of the project. A brief discussion of time, cost, performance, trade-offs will give senior management useful input information for decisions about the future of the project.

o **Risk Management:** Verification of contingency plans and their deviation from the planned project estimates are prepared. They also may consider the reasons for some major deviations that affected the success or failure of the project.

o **Limitations and Assumptions**: Auditor should specifically include the statement in the report covering any assumptions, limitations on the accuracy or validity of the report.

Structure of report: The standard structure of a report should contain the following

- Title
- Executive summary
- Introduction
- Materials and methods
- Results and discussions
- Conclusions
- Recommendations
- Typography
- Rule of thumb: no more than two fonts
- Simple and clear fonts are best for reading comprehension except on the web
- Effective: if you use sans-serif for your headlines, use a serif for your body text and vice-versa.

5.2.7 Uses and Benefits of Audits

The benefits of a project audit are that it exposes and reveals all the problems that the project is facing, and also suggests solutions. A project audit can instantly raise a red flag when a project that was apparently progressing normally and was considered to be good enough is not doing well in reality. In such case, the firm can take a quick decision either to terminate the project, to change the project manager, or to increase the funds. Project audits can also help identify when a project is about to go off-track. If the project goes off-track, with missed milestones or a ballooning budget, many businesses choose to conduct a project audit. Project audits gauge the current progress of the project and plan to overcome underlying weaknesses in management or methodologies, typically through a structured series of questions. Additionally, a project audit can provide the following benefits:

1. Show possible areas for improvement.
2. Show possible methods and processes that are outdated and need to be revised.
3. Increase reaction time to address problems or possible problems.

4. Gives the organisation a sense of what's "really" going on and where the organisation stands.
5. Improve project performance.
6. Boost customer and stakeholder satisfaction.
7. Save expenses.
8. Offer early problem diagnostics.
9. Clarify performance/expenditure/plan relationships.
10. Identify future opportunities for improvement.
11. Assess performance of the project team.
12. Notify client of project status/prospects.
13. Reconfirm possibility of/commitment to project.

5.2.8 Responsibilities of Project Auditor/Evaluator

The auditor/evaluator must maintain political and technical independence during the audit and treat all information gathered as confidential until the audit is completed.

Following are the steps for carrying out an audit:
1. Create a small team of experienced experts.
2. Familiarise the team with the requirements of the project.
3. On completion, debrief the project's status to the management.
4. Prepare a written report in a prescribed format.
5. Distribute the report to the project manager and the project team for their response.
6. Follow-up to see if the recommendations have been implemented.

5.2.9 The Project Audit Life Cycle

Like the project life cycle, the audit has a life cycle composed of systematic steps:

1. **Project Audit Initiation:** It indicates start of the audit process. It defines the purpose and scope of the audit. It includes steps involved in collecting sufficient information to determine the proper audit methodology.

2. **Project Baseline:** This phase normally consists of identifying the performance area to be evaluated and determining benchmark standards for each area or some other process. This helps in ascertaining management performance expectations for each area, and developing a program to measure and assemble the available information.

3. **Establishing an Audit Database:** Once the baseline standards are established, execution of the audit begins. The next step is to create a database for use by the audit team. Depending on the purpose and scope of the audit, the database might include information needed for assessment of project organisation, management and control, past and current project status, scheduled performance, cost performance

and output quality as well as plans for the future of the project. The information may vary from a highly technical description of performance to behaviour-based description of the interaction of the project team members.

4. **Basic Analysis of the Project:** The purpose of the audit is to improve the project being audited as well as to improve the entire process of managing projects.

5. **Audit Report:** Includes the preparation of the audit reports, arranged in specific formats. A set of recommendations, together with a plan for implementing them, is also a part of the audit report.

6. **Audit Termination:** After the audit is complete, the audit process needs to be terminated. On termination the final report and recommendations are released, a review of the audit process is conducted; it is done to improve the methods for conducting the audits in future. On completion of review process, the audit is truly complete and the audit team is formally disbanded.

5.2.10 Some Essentials of the Audit /Evaluation Team

The choice of the audit/evaluation team is critical to the success of the entire process. It may seem unnecessary to note that the team members should be selected because of their ability to contribute to audit/evaluation procedure. The size of the team will generally be a function of the size and complexity of the project.

1. **Access to Records:** In order for the audit/evaluation team to be effective, it must have free access to all information relevant to the project.

2. **Access to Project Human Resources:** The auditor/evaluator must protect the sources of confidential information and must not become a means for leaking such information.

3. **Project Termination:** All projects have finite start and end date. There are several reasons for project termination however, project history forms the integral part of project termination.

4. **Purpose:** The auditor/evaluator is well aware of the fact why the team exists. They consciously invest in achieving its mission and goals.

5. **Priorities:** The auditor knows what needs to be prepared next, by whom and by when to attain team goals.

6. **Roles:** The auditor/evaluator knows their roles in getting tasks done and when to permit a more skilful member to do a specific task.

7. **Decisions:** Authority and decision-making lines are clearly understood.

8. **Conflict:** Conflict is dealt openly and is considered important to decision-making and personal growth.

9. **Personal Traits:** The auditor/evaluator make sure their unique personalities are appreciated and well utilised.
10. **Norms:** Group norms for working together are set by them fairly and seen as standards for everyone in the groups.
11. **Effectiveness:** The auditor/evaluator find team meetings efficient and productive.
12. **Success:** The auditor/evaluator knows clearly when the team has met with success and shares this equally and proudly.
13. **Training:** Opportunities for feedback and updating skills are provided by the auditor/evaluator and taken advantage of by team members.

5.3 Project Termination

Termination of a project is inevitable. It may be due to completion or risks that were beyond mitigation levels or unmanageable issues that resulted in financial loss in the project. How and when it is terminated may have a long lasting impact on the organisation and its employees. The success of future projects may also depend on not only the success of past ones, but also on how the learning's from the unsuccessful projects were handled by the organisation and its stakeholders.

It has been observed that external and internal factors influence the success or failure of projects. Organising a project's termination process is especially important when it has failed, because of the lasting impact on future projects as well as the organisation's image. Including project team members in the termination process will increase their loyalty and commitment, not only to the organisation but also to the success of future projects. At the end of a project a post-audit report will be prepared that summarises the project and provides recommendations for similar projects in the future. Lastly, as a project is closed down or completed, it is important that senior management recognise the contributions of the project team.

When the project teams accept the termination of the project it is said to be termination by inclusion. In such case, the complete project team and its equipment are transferred to a new division. This encounters significant changes in daily routine procedures and results into high stress and frustrations within team members. Project managers need to put extra effort to keep team motivated for next projects.

The highest challenge faced by the organisation is to integrate the project's resources, personnel, and functions are absorbed as a part of the original organisation post termination. This is also known as termination by integration. The major problem associated with this termination process is the ability of the organisation to merge the technological differences between the project and the organisation.

5.3.1 When to Terminate a Project

The factors considered for termination of a project depend on some of the following

(a) When the project scope exceeds the budget. When the customer or a project owner's requirements exceeds that of the earlier estimated project budgets, the project may be considered for termination.

(b) When the demand for the product or service is nullified.

(c) When the risk is unavoidable and its impact cannot be mitigated.

(d) When key resources or personnel or their replacement are not available.

(e) When desired quality standards are not achievable.

For project termination multiple factors need to be considered. "A project that has very little salvage value and high closing costs, which may include payments to terminate employees, penalties for breached contracts, and losses from the closing of facilities, will be much more difficult to abandon than a project in which expenditures are recoverable and exit is easy" (**Staw & Ross, 1987**). For example, construction project if terminated usually incurs high cost overruns. Such projects need additional funding or need to be permanently discarded.

Standard practice of monitoring projects is by setting milestones. Keeping track of project's progress based on milestones gives a comprehensive control on the project. In addition, risks avoidance and mitigation strategies if implemented as per plan can prevent project termination.

Many mathematical models can be used to evaluate whether or not to continue a project. The common way is to rely on financial techniques such as payback or net present value. However, any final decision is to be taken in account of other important strategic factors such as organisation brand or at times organisations future survival needs to be considered.

Other techniques used to monitor the projects throughout their life cycle are:

(a) **Cybernetic Control Processes:** In this process the outcomes from the project are constantly monitored and compared with the project plan especially the schedules. All the stakeholders are then aware of the changes in the schedule and the corrective action to be taken. This model is generally used for monitoring performance, time, and cost of the project so that it is not terminated prematurely because of poor planning or control.

(b) **Go/No-Go Control Processes:** In this process the monitoring is done at specific intervals. For example, project manager set milestones and value how the progress happens against the completion of milestone. This process is also used for quantifying risks that might occur. Here the values are given specific weight and compared against the benchmark or project plans.

5.3.2 The Project Termination Process

A plan must be developed to terminate, despite the fact that a successful project is completed by inclusion, integration, or extinction. A project-oriented organisation may have a "termination manager" whose main task is to effectively and efficiently end projects. There is a systematic process followed by organisations for termination or untimely closure of the project. It essentially requires to

- Check that the project is complete and documented.
- Determine what records (manuals, reports, and other paperwork) are to be kept and place them in storage.
- Ensure delivery and client acceptance.
- Ensure that all bills have been paid and that the final invoice has been sent to the client.
- Redistribute materials, team members, equipments and any other resources to the other projects.
- Manage responsibility for product support or after sales support, if necessary.

Senior management and the team leader must recognise and reward the accomplishments of the project team even if the project has been terminated. This creates success and the motivation to do well for the next projects. Acknowledging the dedication and achievements of the project team will enable team members to proceed to their next assignment with a more loyal and positive attitude.

5.3.3 Impact of Project Termination

A project may be cancelled for a variety of reasons, including lack of funding, technologically becoming absolute, change in consumer demands, loss of the project manager or financial losses incurred in the project. Project cancellation can affect organisation's brand name, employee performance and most importantly the trust. It is very important that the transparency in communication with the team as to why the project has to be terminated needs to be established by the project manager.

Factors that influenced employee performance due to cancellation of a project:

1. Communication between management and the project team for the reasons for cancellation.
2. Detailed due diligence to be carried out before announcing the cancellation of the project.
3. Effective planning and leadership of the project.
4. Prompt and comparable reassignment of project personnel.
5. Acknowledgment of the efforts of the project team.
6. Participation of the project team in the cancellation decision-making process.

The impact of project termination on organisation's market value or brand value has to be considered before termination. The documentation for project termination is valuable source to help future project managers. It not only includes what worked, but also what did not, and recommendations for similar projects in the future.

The documentation should necessarily include project culture, how well the organisation's structure helped or hindered the project and individual attitudes and behaviours observed during their performance since all these factors impact very strongly and may result into project termination. For monitoring and controlling the project's accurate forecasting, planning, budgeting, scheduling, allocating specific resources used during the project will help improve the future projects.

5.3.4 Reasons for Project Termination

1. Project is completed ahead of schedule and handed over to the sponsors/ users.
2. Premature abandonment due to technical grounds that impede achievement of core goals.
3. It is suddenly found that another group publishes results in same core area of interest.
4. The principal investigator or an equivalent person suddenly quits and the project cannot continue as planned and the project has to be terminated, as putting on hold will be counter-productive.
5. Unanticipated loss of human, funding and other valuable resources.
6. A variety of insurmountable problems may force termination of the project.
7. An interim review suggests the project will not help achieve the desired objectives.

5.3.5 The Varieties of Project Termination

A project can be said to be terminated when work on the matter of the project has ceased or slowed to the point that further progress on the project is no longer possible, when the project has been indefinitely delayed, when its resources have been deployed to other projects. There are four fundamentally different ways to close out a project.

- Extinction
- Addition
- Integration
- Starvation

1. Termination by Extinction

The project is closed because it has been successful and achieved its objectives or goals. The Final product developed is handed over to the client. The project may also be stopped in case it is unsuccessful or has been outdated. For example, if the new drug failed its efficacy tests; there are better, faster, cheaper alternatives available, or it may not be cost effective or take too long to produce desired results. When a decision is made to terminate the project by extinction, most noticeable thing is that all activities of the project matter are ceased.

2. Termination by Addition

Most projects are in-house that is, carried out by project team for use in the parent organisation. If the project is a major success, it may be terminated by converting into a subsidiary unit. If this subsidiary unit achieves economic stability it is then converted into a depended unit.

3. Termination by Integration

In Information technology projects, several parts of the project are independently developed and tested. To fulfill the customer requirement a single product needs to be delivered, hence the independent parts are then put together to form a single product. This is called as project integration. On completion of integration process, the final product is then dispatched to the customer and project assets are generated and recorded. This forms the last stage of project life cycle of such projects. This is called as termination by integration.

4. Termination by Starvation

Slow starvation by budget decrement. Almost anyone who is involved with projects over a sufficient period of time to have covered a business recession has had to cope with budget cuts. Budgets cuts, decrements, are not rare. Since they are common they are sometimes used to mask a project termination. In such a case, the project budget might receive a deep cut or series of small cuts, large enough to prevent further progress on the project and to force the reassignment of many project team members.

Conclusion

Projects have a life cycle. They are born from an idea, developed into a finished product or service, and then terminated. As a project moves through this process, the project manager and senior management should continually monitor the project's critical success factors to ensure it is still viable. Although terminating a project is inevitable, the timing and planning of this termination can affect future projects and possibly the entire organisation. Just as successful projects can have a positive impact on the organisation, unsuccessful projects can have the opposite effect. To minimise this unfortunate side effect, management must be especially sensitive to the needs of its employees during the termination process. Cancellation, in particular, can have a profound and lasting affect on the organisation and its employees. Lastly, the final report is the opportunity to reflect on the project - to document its successes and shortcomings and make recommendations for the future.

Points to Remember

- A project is an investment activity where we use capital resources to create a producing asset from which we can expect to realise benefits over an extended period of time.

- Project evaluation is required to be done at three levels. Once the initial planning is completed, it is essential to re-check for the gaps or re-plan for certain aspects that have evolved during the planning process.

- Purpose of evaluation is to help organisation to achieve project's goals corresponding to organisation goals. The evaluation is done to understand outcomes from each process or the total process.

- A project audit basically offers an opportunity to uncover the issues, concerns and challenges encountered during the execution of a project. It affords the project manager, project sponsor, and project team a temporary view of what has gone well and what needs to be improved with the project to accomplish it productively.

- Audit is an evaluation of a person, organisation, system, process, project or product. Audits are performed to ascertain the validity and reliability of information, and also provide an assessment of a system's internal control.

- Audits are performed based on all significant size or importance of project. The first audits are usually done early in the project's life, since it is easier to deal with it.

- A project audit can instantly raise a red flag when a project that was apparently progressing normally and was considered to be good enough is not doing well in reality.

- Project cancellation can affect organisation's brand name, employee performance and most importantly the trust. It is very important that the transparency in communication with the team as to why the project has to be terminated needs to be established by the project manager.

- Termination of a project is inevitable. It may be due to completion or risks that were beyond mitigation levels or unmanageable issues that resulted in financial loss in the project.

- A plan must be developed to terminate, despite the fact that a successful project is completed by inclusion, integration, or extinction. A project-oriented organisation may have a "termination manager" whose main task is to effectively and efficiently end projects.

Questions for Discussion

1. What do you understand by a project audit?

2. What are the steps for auditing a project?

3. What should be the structure of the project report?

4. What are the essentials of the project evaluation team?

5. What do you understand by project termination?

■■■

APPENDIX

The Project Knowledge Areas

- Project Integration Management
- Project Scope Management
- Project Time Management
- Project Cost Management
- Project Quality Management
- Project Human Resource Management
- Project Communications Management
- Project Risk Management
- Project Procurement Management
- Knowledge Areas
- A Guide to the Project Management Body of Knowledge

Project Integration Management

Project Integration Management includes the processes required to ensure that the various elements of the project are properly co-ordinated. It involves making trade-offs among competing objectives and alternatives in order to meet or exceed stake-holder needs and expectations. While all project management processes are integrative to some extent, the processes described in this appendix are primarily integrative.

- **Project Plan Development** - taking the results of other planning processes and putting them into a consistent, coherent document.
- **Project Plan Execution** - carrying out the project plan by performing the activities included therein.
- **Overall Change Control** - coordinating changes across the entire project.

These processes interact with each other and with the processes in the other knowledge areas as well. Each process may involve effort from one or more individuals or groups of individuals based on the needs of the project. Each process generally occurs at least once in every project phase.

Although the processes are presented here as discrete elements with well-defined interfaces, in practice they may overlap and interact in ways not detailed here.

The processes, tools, and techniques used to integrate project management processes are the focus here. For example, project integration management comes into play when a cost estimate is needed for a contingency plan or when risks associated with various staffing alternatives must be identified. However, for a project to be completed successfully, integration must also occur in a number of other areas as well.

For example:

- The work of the project must be integrated with the ongoing operations of the performing organisation.
- Product scope and project scope must be integrated.
- Deliverables from different functional specialties (such as civil, electrical, and mechanical drawings for an engineering design project) must be integrated.

✪ ✪ ✪

Project Scope Management

Project Scope Management includes the processes required to ensure that the project includes all the work required, and only the work required, to complete the project successfully. It is primarily concerned with defining and controlling what is or is not included in the project.

- **Initiation:** Committing the organisation to begin the next phase of the project.
- **Scope Planning:** Developing a written scope statement as the basis for future project decisions.
- **Scope Definition:** Subdividing the major project deliverables into smaller, more manageable components.
- **Scope Verification:** Formalising acceptance of the project scope.
- **Scope Change Control:** Controlling changes to project scope.

These processes interact with each other and with the processes in the other knowledge areas as well. Each process may involve effort from one or more individuals or groups of individuals based on the needs of the project. Each process generally occurs at least once in every project phase.

Although the processes are presented here as discrete elements with well-defined interfaces, in practice they may overlap and interact in ways not detailed here.

In the project context, the term "scope" may refer to:

- Product scope: The features and functions that are to be included in a product or service.
- Project scope: The work that must be done in order to deliver a product with the specified features and functions.

The processes, tools and techniques used to manage project scope are the focus here. The processes, tools, and techniques used to manage product scope vary by application area and are usually defined as part of the project life cycle.

A project consists of a single product, but that product may include subsidiary elements, each with their own separate but interdependent product scopes. For example, a new telephone system would generally include four subsidiary elements — hardware, software, training, and implementation.

Completion of the product scope is measured against the requirements while completion of the project scope is measured against the plan. Both types of scope management must be well integrated to ensure that the work of the project will result in delivery of the specified product.

✪ ✪ ✪

Project Time Management

Project Time Management includes the processes required to ensure timely completion of the project.

- **Activity Definition:** Identifying the specific activities that must be performed to produce the various project deliverables.
- **Activity Sequencing:** Identifying and documenting interactivity dependencies.
- **Activity Duration Estimating:** Estimating the number of work periods which will be needed to complete individual activities.
- **Schedule Development:** Analyzing activity sequences, activity durations, and resource requirements to create the project schedule.
- **Schedule Control:** Controlling changes to the project schedule.

These processes interact with each other and with the processes in the other knowledge areas as well. Each process may involve effort from one or more individuals or groups of individuals based on the needs of the project. Each process generally occurs at least once in every project phase.

Although the processes are presented here as discrete elements with well defined interfaces, in practice they may overlap and interact in ways not detailed here.

On some projects, especially smaller ones, activity sequencing, activity duration estimating, and schedule development are so tightly linked that they are viewed as a single process (e.g., they may be performed by a single individual over a relatively short period of time). They are presented here as distinct processes because the tools and techniques for each are different.

At present, there is no consensus within the project management profession about the relationship between activities and tasks:

- In many application areas, activities are seen as being composed of tasks. This is the most common usage and also the preferred usage.
- In others, tasks are seen as being composed of activities.

However, the important consideration is not the term used, but whether or not the work to be done is described accurately and understood by those who must do the work.

❂ ❂ ❂

Project Cost Management

Project Cost Management includes the processes required to ensure that the project is completed within the approved budget.

- **Resource Planning:** Determining what resources (people, equipment, materials) and what quantities of each should be used to perform project activities.
- **Cost Estimating:** Developing an approximation (estimate) of the costs of the resources needed to complete project activities.
- **Cost Budgeting:** Allocating the overall cost estimate to individual work items.
- **Cost Control:** Controlling changes to the project budget.

These processes interact with each other and with the processes in the other knowledge areas as well. Each process may involve effort from one or more individuals or groups of individuals based on the needs of the project. Each process generally occurs at least once in every project phase.

Although the processes are presented here as discrete elements with well-defined interfaces, in practice they may overlap and interact in ways not detailed here. Project cost management is primarily concerned with the cost of the resources needed to complete project activities. However, project cost management should also consider the effect of project decisions on the cost of using the project product. For example, limiting the number of design reviews may reduce the cost of the project at the expense of an increase in the customer's operating costs. This broader view of project cost management is often called life-cycle costing.

In many application areas predicting and analysing the prospective financial performance of the project product is done outside the project. In others (e.g., capital facilities projects), project cost management also includes this work. When such predictions and analysis are included, project cost management will include additional processes and numerous general management techniques such as return on investment, discounted cash flow, payback analysis, and others.

Project cost management should consider the information needs of the project stakeholders—different stakeholders may measure project costs in different ways and at different times. For example, the cost of a procurement item may be measured when committed, ordered, delivered, incurred, or recorded for accounting purposes.

When project costs are used as a component of a reward and recognition system, controllable and uncontrollable costs should be estimated and budgeted separately to ensure that rewards reflect actual performance.

❂ ❂ ❂

Project Quality Management

Project Quality Management includes the processes required to ensure that the project will satisfy the needs for which it was undertaken. It includes "all activities of the overall management function that determine the quality policy, objectives, and responsibilities and implements them by means such as quality planning, quality control, quality assurance, and quality improvement, within the quality system".

- **Quality Planning:** Identifying which quality standards are relevant to the project and determining how to satisfy them.
- **Quality Assurance:** Evaluating overall project performance on a regular basis to provide confidence that the project will satisfy the relevant quality standards.
- **Quality Control:** Monitoring specific project results to determine if they comply with relevant quality standards and identifying ways to eliminate causes of unsatisfactory performance.

These processes interact with each other and with the processes in the other knowledge areas as well. Each process may involve effort from one or more individuals or groups of individuals based on the needs of the project. Each process generally occurs at least once in every project phase.

Although the processes are presented here as discrete elements with well-defined interfaces, in practice they may overlap and interact in ways not detailed here.

The basic approach to quality management described in this section is intended to be compatible with that of the International Organisation for Standardisation (ISO) as detailed in the ISO 9000 and 10000 series of standards and guidelines. This generalised approach should also be compatible with (a) proprietary approaches to quality management such as those recommended by Deming, Juran, Crosby, and others, and (b) non-proprietary approaches such as Total Quality Management (TQM), Continuous Improvement, and others.

Project quality management must address both the management of the project and the product of the project. Failure to meet quality requirements in either dimension can have serious negative consequences for any or all of the project stakeholders. For example:

- Meeting customer requirements by overworking the project team may produce negative consequences in the form of increased employee turnover.
- Meeting project schedule objectives by rushing planned quality inspections may produce negative consequences when errors go undetected.

❂ ❂ ❂

Project Human Resource Management

Project Human Resource Management includes the processes required to make the most effective use of the people involved with the project. It includes project stakeholders—sponsors, customers, individual contributors, and others.

- **Organisational Planning:** Identifying, documenting, and assigning project roles, responsibilities, and reporting relationships.
- **Staff Acquisition:** Getting the human resources needed assigned to and working on the project.
- **Team Development:** Developing individual and group skills to enhance project performance.

These processes interact with each other and with the processes in the other knowledge areas as well. Each process may involve effort from one or more individuals or groups of individuals based on the needs of the project. Although the processes are presented here as discrete elements with well-defined interfaces, in practice they may overlap and interact in ways not detailed here.

There is a substantial body of literature about dealing with people in an operational, ongoing context. Some of the many topics include:

- Leading, communicating, negotiating, and others Key General Management Skills.
- Delegating, motivating, coaching, mentoring, and other subjects related to dealing with individuals.

- Team building, dealing with conflict, and other subjects related to dealing with groups.
- Performance appraisal, recruitment, retention, labour relations, health and safety regulations, and other subjects related to administering the human resource function.

Most of this material is directly applicable to leading and managing people on projects, and the project manager and project management team should be familiar with it. However, they must also be sensitive as to how this knowledge is applied on the project. For example:

- The temporary nature of projects means that the personal and organisational relationships will generally be both temporary and new. The project management team must take care to select techniques that are appropriate for such transient relationships.

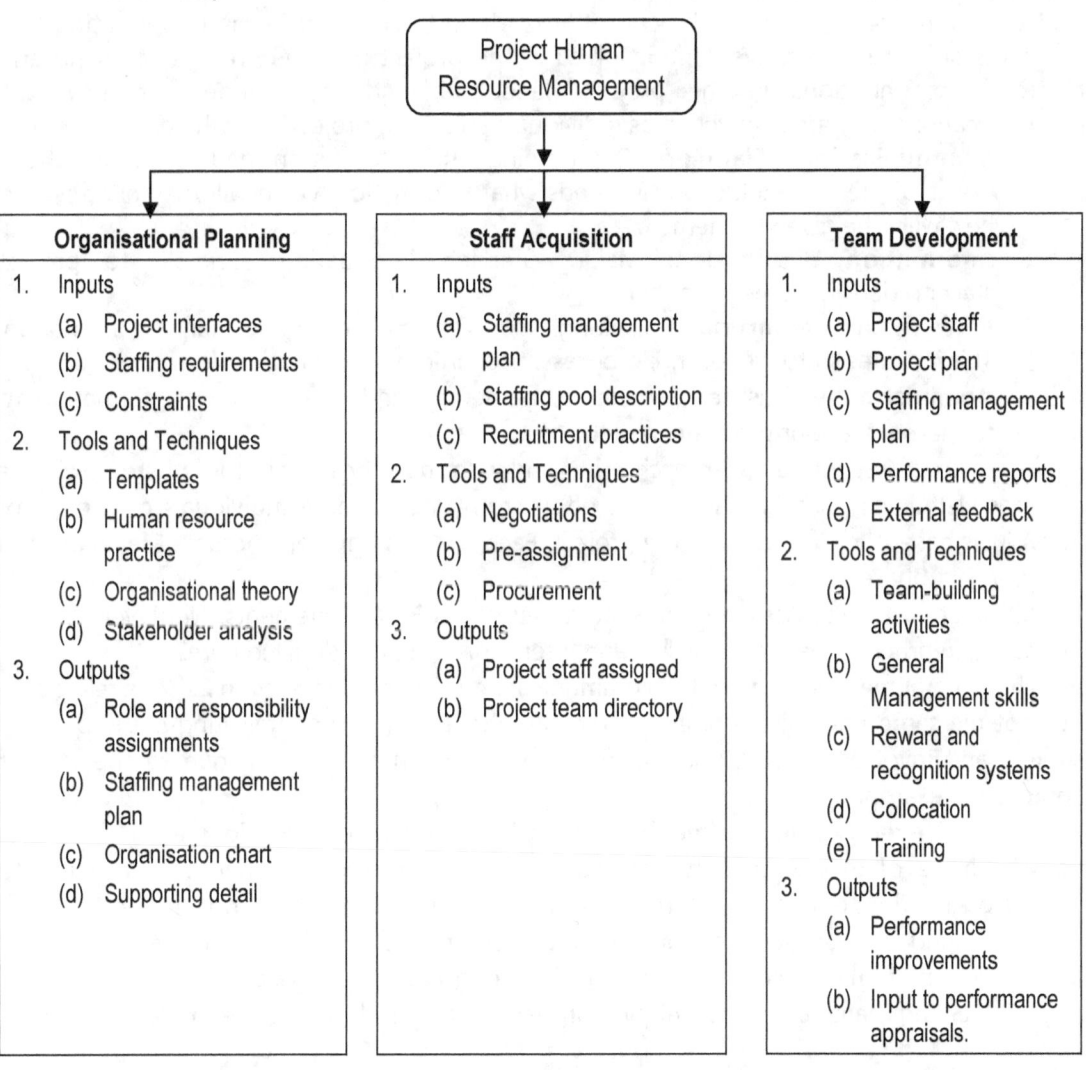

Project Human Resource Management

Organisational Planning

1. Inputs
   (a) Project interfaces
   (b) Staffing requirements
   (c) Constraints
2. Tools and Techniques
   (a) Templates
   (b) Human resource practice
   (c) Organisational theory
   (d) Stakeholder analysis
3. Outputs
   (a) Role and responsibility assignments
   (b) Staffing management plan
   (c) Organisation chart
   (d) Supporting detail

Staff Acquisition

1. Inputs
   (a) Staffing management plan
   (b) Staffing pool description
   (c) Recruitment practices
2. Tools and Techniques
   (a) Negotiations
   (b) Pre-assignment
   (c) Procurement
3. Outputs
   (a) Project staff assigned
   (b) Project team directory

Team Development

1. Inputs
   (a) Project staff
   (b) Project plan
   (c) Staffing management plan
   (d) Performance reports
   (e) External feedback
2. Tools and Techniques
   (a) Team-building activities
   (b) General Management skills
   (c) Reward and recognition systems
   (d) Collocation
   (e) Training
3. Outputs
   (a) Performance improvements
   (b) Input to performance appraisals.

The nature and number of project stakeholders will often change as the project moves from phase to phase of its life cycle. As a result, techniques that are effective in one phase may not be effective in another. The project management team must take care to use techniques that are appropriate to the current needs of the project.

Human resource administrative activities are seldom a direct responsibility of the project management team. However, the team must be sufficiently aware of administrative requirements to ensure compliance.

✿ ✿ ✿

Project Communications Management

Project Communications Management includes the processes required to ensure timely and appropriate generation, collection, dissemination, storage, and ultimate disposition of project information. It provides the critical links among people, ideas, and information that are necessary for success. Everyone involved in the project must be prepared to send and receive communications in the project "language" and must understand how the communications they are involved in as individuals affect the project as a whole.

1. **Communications Planning:** Determining the information and communications needs of the stakeholders: who needs what information, when will they need it, and how will it be given to them.
2. **Information Distribution:** Making needed information available to project stakeholders in a timely manner.
3. **Performance Reporting:** Collecting and disseminating performance information. This includes status reporting, progress measurement, and forecasting.
4. **Administrative Closure:** Generating, gathering, and disseminating information to formalise phase or project completion.

These processes interact with each other and with the processes in the other knowledge areas as well. Each process may involve effort from one or more individuals or groups of individuals based on the needs of the project. Each process generally occurs at least once in every project phase.

Although the processes are presented here as discrete elements with well-defined interfaces, in practice they may overlap and interact in ways not detailed here.

The general management skill of communicating (discussed in Section 2.4.2) is related to, but not the same as, project communications management. Communicating is the broader subject and involves a substantial body of knowledge that is not unique to the project context. For example:

- Sender-receiver models: feedback loops, barriers to communications, etc.
- Choice of media when to communicate in writing versus when to communicate orally, when to write an informal memo versus when to write a formal report, etc.
- Writing style: active versus passive voice, sentence structure, word choice, etc.
- Presentation techniques: body language, design of visual aids, etc.
- Meeting management techniques: preparing an agenda, dealing with conflict, etc.

✿ ✿ ✿

Project Risk Management

Project Risk Management includes the processes concerned with identifying, analysing, and responding to project risk. It includes maximising the results of positive events and minimising the consequences of adverse events.

1. **Risk Identification:** Determining which risks are likely to affect the project and documenting the characteristics of each.

2. **Risk Quantification:** Evaluating risks and risk interactions to assess the range of possible project outcomes.

3. **Risk Response Development:** Defining enhancement steps for opportunities and responses to threats.

4. **Risk Response Control:** Responding to changes in risk over the course of the project.

These processes interact with each other and with the processes in the other knowledge areas as well. Each process may involve effort from one or more individuals or groups of individuals based on the needs of the project. Each process generally occurs at least once in every project phase.

Although the processes are presented here as discrete elements with well-defined interfaces in practice they may overlap and interact in ways not detailed here.

Different application areas often use different names for the processes described here. For example:

- Risk identification and risk quantification are sometimes treated as a single process, and the combined process may be called risk analysis or risk assessment.
- Risk response development is sometimes called response planning or risk mitigation.
- Risk response development and risk response control are sometimes treated as a single process, and the combined process may be called risk management.

✪ ✪ ✪

Project Procurement Management

Project Procurement Management includes the processes required to acquire goods and services from outside the performing organisation. For simplicity, goods and services, whether one or many, will generally be referred to as a "product".

1. **Procurement Planning:** Determining what to procure and when.

2. **Solicitation Planning:** Documenting product requirements and identifying potential sources.

3. **Solicitation:** Obtaining quotations, bids, offers, or proposals as appropriate.

4. **Source Selection:** Choosing from among potential sellers.

5. **Contract Administration:** Managing the relationship with the seller.

6. **Contract Close-out:** Completion and settlement of the contract, including resolution of any open items.

These processes interact with each other and with the processes in the other knowledge areas as well. Each process may involve effort from one or more individuals or groups of individuals based on the needs of the project. Although the processes are presented here as discrete elements with well-defined interfaces, in practice they may overlap and interact in ways not detailed here.

Project Procurement Management is discussed from the perspective of the buyer in the buyer-seller relationship. The buyer-seller relationship can exist at many levels on one project. Depending on the application area, the seller may be called a con-tractor, a vendor, or a supplier.

The seller will typically manage their work as a project. In such cases:

- The buyer becomes the customer and is thus a key stakeholder for the seller.
- The seller's project management team must be concerned with all the processes of project management, not just with those of this knowledge area.
- The terms and conditions of the contract become a key input to many of the seller's processes. The contract may actually contain the input (e.g., major deliverables, key milestones, cost objectives) or it may limit the project team's options (e.g., buyer approval of staffing decisions is often required on design projects).

This chapter assumes that the seller is external to the performing organisation. Most of the discussion, however, is equally applicable to formal agreements entered into with other units of the performing organisation. When informal agreements are involved, the processes described in Project Human Resource Management and Project Communications Management is more likely to apply.

❂ ❂ ❂

Knowledge Areas

Project Integration Management

A subset of project management that includes the processes required to ensure that the various elements of the project are properly coordinated. It consists of:

- **Project plan development:** Taking the results of other planning processes and putting them into a consistent, coherent document.
- **Project plan execution:** Carrying out the project plan by performing the activities included therein.
- **Overall chance control:** Co-ordinating changes across the entire project.

Project Scope Management

A subset of project management that includes the processes required to ensure that the project includes all the work required, and only the work required, to complete the project successfully.

It consists of:

- **Initiation:** Committing the organisation to begin the next phase of the project.
- **Scope planning:** Developing a written scope statement as the basis for future project decisions.
- **Scope definition:** Subdividing the major project deliverables into smaller, more manageable components.
- **Scope verification:** Formalising acceptance of the project scope.
- **Scope change control:** Controlling changes to project scope.

Project Time Management

A subset of project management that includes the processes required to ensure timely completion of the project. It consists of:

- **Activity definition:** Identifying the specific activities that must be performed to produce the various project deliverables.
- **Activity sequencing identifying** and documenting interactivity dependencies.
- **Activity duration estimating:** Estimating the number of work periods which will be needed to complete individual activities.
- **Schedule development:** Analysing activity sequences, activity durations, and resource requirements to create the project schedule.
- **Schedule control:** Controlling changes to the project schedule.

Project Cost Management

A subset of project management that includes the processes required to ensure that the project is completed within the approved budget. It consists of:

- **Resource planning:** Determining what resources (people, equipment, materials) and what quantities of each should be used to perform project activities.
- **Cost estimating:** Developing an approximation (estimate) of the costs of the resources needed to complete project activities.
- **Cost budgeting:** Allocating the overall cost estimate to individual work items.
- **Cost control:** Controlling changes to the project budget.

Project Quality Management

A subset of project management that includes the processes required to ensure that the project will satisfy the needs for which it was undertaken. It consists of:

- **Quality planning:** Identifying which quality standards are relevant to the project and determining how to satisfy them.
- **Quality assurance:** Evaluating overall project performance on a regular basis to provide confidence that the project will satisfy the relevant quality standards.

- **Quality control:** Monitoring specific project results to determine if they comply with relevant quality standards and identifying ways to eliminate causes of unsatisfactory performance.

Project Human Resource Management

A subset of project management that includes the processes required to make the most effective use of the people involved with the project. It consists of:

- **Organisational planning:** Identifying, documenting, and assigning project roles, responsibilities, and reporting relationships.
- **Staff acquisition:** Getting the human resources needed assigned to and working on the project.
- **Team development:** Developing individual and group skills to enhance project performance.

Project Communications Management

A subset of project management that includes the processes required to ensure timely and appropriate generation, collection, dissemination, storage, and ultimate disposition of project information. It consists of:

- **Communications planning:** Determining the information and communications needs of the stakeholders: who needs what information, when will they need it, and how will it be given to them.
- **Information distribution:** Making needed information available to project stakeholders in a timely manner.
- **Performance reporting:** Collecting and disseminating performance information. This includes status reporting, progress measurement, and forecasting.
- **Administrative closure:** Generating, gathering, and disseminating information to formalise phase or project completion.

✪ ✪ ✪

A Guide to the Project Management Body of Knowledge

Project Risk Management

A subset of project management that includes the processes concerned with identifying, analysing, and responding to project risk. It consists of:

- **Risk identification:** Determining which risks are likely to affect the project and documenting the characteristics of each.
- **Risk quantification:** Evaluating risks and risk interactions to assess the range of possible project outcomes.

- **Risk response development:** Defining enhancement steps for opportunities and responses to threats.
- **Risk response control:** Responding to changes in risk over the course of the project.

Project Procurement Management

A subset of project management that includes the processes required to acquire goods and services from outside the performing organisation. It consists of:

- **Procurement planning:** Determining what to procure and when.
- **Solicitation planning:** Documenting product requirements and identifying potential sources.
- **Solicitation:** Obtaining quotations, bids, offers, or proposals as appropriate.
- **Source selection:** Choosing from among potential sellers.
- **Contract administration:** Managing the relationship with the seller.
- **Contract closeout:** Completion and settlement of the contract, including resolution of any open items.

■■■

GLOSSARY

1. Inclusions and Exclusions

This glossary includes terms that are:

- Unique or nearly unique to project management (e.g., scope statement, work package, work breakdown structure, critical path method).
- Not unique to project management, but used differently or with a narrower meaning in project management than in general everyday usage (e.g., early start date, activity, task).

This glossary generally does not include:

- Application area-specific terms (e.g., project prospectus as a legal document unique to real estate development).
- Terms whose use in project management do not differ in any material way from everyday use (e.g., contract).
- Compound terms whose meaning is clear from the combined meanings of the component parts.
- Variants when the meaning of the variant is clear from the base term (e.g., exception report is included, exception reporting is not).

As a result of the above inclusions and exclusions, this glossary includes:

- A preponderance of terms related to Project Scope Management and Project Time Management, since many of the terms used in these two knowledge areas are unique or nearly unique to project management.
- Many terms from Project Quality Management, since these terms are used more narrowly than in their everyday usage.
- Relatively few terms related to Project Human Resource Management, Project Risk Management, and Project Communications Management, since most of the terms used in these knowledge areas do not differ significantly from every-day usage.
- Relatively few terms related to Project Cost Management and Project Procurement Management, since many of the terms used in these knowledge areas have narrow meanings that are unique to a particular application area.

2. Common Acronyms

ACWP	Actual Cost of Work Performed
AD	Activity Description
ADM	Arrow Diagramming Method
AF	Actual Finish date
AOA	Activity-On-Arrow
AON	Activity-On-Node
AS	Actual Start date

BAC	Budget At Completion
BCWP	Budgeted Cost of Work Performed
CCB	Change Control Board
CPFF	Cost Plus Fixed Fee
CPIF	Cost Plus Incentive Fee
CPI	Cost Performance Index
CPM	Critical Path Method
CV	Cost Variance
DD	Data Date
DU	Duration
EAC	Estimate At Completion
EF	Early Finish date
ES	Early Start date
ETC	Estimate (or Estimated) To Complete (or Completion)
EV	Earned Value
FF	Free Float or Finish-to-Finish
FFP	Firm Fixed Price
FPIF	Fixed Price Incentive Fee
FS	Finish-to-Start
GERT	Graphical Evaluation and Review Technique
IFB	Invitation For Bid
LF	Late Finish date
LOE	Level Of Effort
LS	Late Start date
MPM	Modem Project Management
OBS	Organisation(a1) Breakdown Structure
PC	Percent Complete
PDM	Precedence Diagramming Method
PERT	Program Evaluation and Review Technique
PF	Planned Finish date
PM	Project Management or Project Manager
PMBOK	Project Management Body of Knowledge
PMP	Project Management Professional
PS	Planned Start date

QA	Quality Assurance
QC	Quality Control
RAM	Responsibility Assignment Matrix
RDU	Remaining Duration
RFP	Request For Proposal
RFQ	Request For Quotation
SF	Scheduled Finish date or Start-to-Finish
SOW	Statement Of Work
SPI	Schedule Performance Index
SS	Scheduled Start date or Start-to-Start
SV	Schedule Variance
TC	Target Completion date
TF	Total Float or Target Finish date
TS	Target Start date
TQM	Total Quality Management
WBS	Work Breakdown Structure

3. Definitions

Many of the words defined here have broader, and in some cases different, dictionary definitions.

The definitions use the following conventions:

- Terms used as part of the definitions, and are defined in the glossary, are shown in italics.

- When synonyms are included, no definition is given and the reader is directed to the preferred term (i.e. see preferred term).

- Related terms that are not synonyms are cross-referenced at the end of the definition (i.e. see also related term).

Accountability Matrix: See responsibility assignment matrix.

Activity: An element of work performed during the course of a project. An activity normally has an expected duration, an expected cost, and expected resource requirements. Activities are often subdivided into tasks.

Activity Definition: Identifying the specific activities that must be performed in order to produce the various project deliverables.

Activity Description (AD): A short phrase or label used in a project network diagram. The activity description normally describes the scope of work of the activity.

Activity Duration Estimating: Estimating the number of work periods which will be needed to complete individual activities.

Activity-On-Arrow (AOA): See arrow diagramming method.

Activity-On-Node (AON): See precedence diagramming method.

Actual Cost of Work Performed (ACWP): Total costs incurred (direct and indirect) in accomplishing work during a given time period. See also earned value.

Actual Finish Date (AF): The point in time that work actually ended on an activity.

(**Note:** In some application areas, the activity is considered "finished" when work is "substantially complete.")

Actual Start Date (AS): The point in time that work actually started on an activity.

Administrative Closure: Generating, gathering, and disseminating information to formalize project completion.

Application Area: A category of projects that have common elements not present in all projects. Application areas are usually defined in terms of either the product of the project (i.e., by similar technologies or industry sectors) or the type of customer (e.g., internal vs. external, government vs. commercial). Application areas often overlap.

Arrow: The graphic presentation of an activity. See also arrow diagramming method.

Arrow Diagramming Method (ADM): A network diagramming technique in which activities are represented by arrows. The tail of the arrow represents the start and the head represents the finish of the activity (the length of the arrow does not represent the expected duration of the activity). Activities are connected at points called nodes (usually drawn as small circles) to illustrate the sequence in which the activities are expected to be performed. See also precedence diagramming method.

As-of Date: See data date.

Backward Pass: The calculation of late finish dates and late start dates for the uncompleted portions of all network activities. Determined by working backwards through the network logic from the project's end date. The end date may be calculated in a forward pass or set by the customer or sponsor. See also network analysis.

Bar Chart: A graphic display of schedule-related information. In the typical bar chart, activities or other project elements are listed down the left side of the chart, dates are shown across the top, and activity durations are shown as date-placed horizontal bars. Also called a Gantt chart.

Baseline: The original plan (for a project, a work package, or an activity), plus or minus approved changes. Usually used with a modifier (e.g., cost baseline, schedule baseline, performance measurement baseline).

Baseline Finish Date: See scheduled finish date. Baseline Start Date. See scheduled start date. Budget At Completion (BAC). The estimated total cost of the project when done. Budget Estimate. See estimate. Budgeted Cost of Work.

Performed (BCWP): The sum of the approved cost estimates (including any overhead allocation) for activities (or portions of activities) completed during a given period (usually project to-date). See also earned value.

Budgeted Cost of Work Scheduled (BCWS): The sum of the approved cost estimates (including any overhead allocation) for activities (or portions of activities) scheduled to be performed during a given period (usually project-to-date). See also earned value.

Calendar Unit: The smallest unit of time used in scheduling the project. Calendar units are generally in hours, days, or weeks, but can also be in shifts or even in minutes. Used primarily in relation to project management software.

Change Control Board (CCB): A formally constituted group of stakeholders responsible for approving or rejecting changes to the project baselines.

Change in Scope: See scope change.

Chart of Accounts: Any numbering system used to monitor project costs by category (e.g., labour, supplies, materials). The project chart of accounts is usually based upon the corporate chart of accounts of the primary performing organisation. See also code of accounts.

Charter: See project charter.

Code of Accounts: Any numbering system used to uniquely identify each element of the work breakdown structure. See also chart of accounts.

Communications Planning: Determining the information and communications needs of the project stakeholders. Concurrent Engineering. An approach to project staffing that, in its most general form, calls for implementors to be involved in the design phase. Sometimes confused with fast tracking.

Contingencies: See reserve and contingency planning.

Contingency Allowance: See reserve.

Contingency Planning: The development of a management plan that identifies alternative strategies to be used to ensure project success if specified risk events occur.

Contingency Reserve: A separately planned quantity used to allow for future situations which may be planned for only in part (sometimes called "known unknowns"). For example, rework is certain, the amount of rework is not. Contingency reserves may involve cost, schedule, or both. Contingency reserves are intended to reduce the impact of missing cost or schedule objectives. Contingency reserves are normally included in the project's cost and schedule baselines.

Contract: A contract is a mutually binding agreement which obligates the seller to provide the specified product and obligates the buyer to pay for it. Contracts generally fall into one of three broad categories:

- Fixed price or lump sum contracts—this category of contract involves a fixed total price for a well-defined product. Fixed price contracts may also include incentives for meeting or exceeding selected project objectives such as schedule targets.

- Cost reimbursable contracts—this category of contract involves payment (reimbursement) to the contractor for its actual costs. Costs are usually classified as direct costs (costs incurred directly by the project, such as wages for members of the project team) and indirect costs (costs allocated to the project by the performing organisation as a cost of doing business, such as salaries for corporate executives). Indirect costs are usually calculated as a percentage of direct costs. Cost reimbursable contracts often include incentives for meeting or exceeding selected project objectives such as schedule targets or total cost.

- Unit price contracts—the contractor is paid a preset amount per unit. of service (e.g., $70 per hour for professional services or $1.08 per cubic yard of earth removed) and the total value of the contract is a function of the quantities needed to complete the work.

- **Crashing:** Taking action to decrease the total project duration after analyzing a number of alternatives to determine how to get the maximum duration compression for the least cost.

- **Critical Activity:** Any activity on a critical path. Most commonly determined by using the critical path method. Although some activities are –critical" in the dictionary sense without being on the critical path, this meaning is seldom used in the project context.

- **Critical Path:** In a project network diagram, the series of activities which determines the earliest completion of the project. The critical path will generally change from time to time as activities are completed ahead of or behind schedule. Although normally calculated for the entire project, the critical path can also be determined for a milestone or subproject. The critical path is usually defined as those activities with float less than or equal to a specified value, often zero. See critical path method.

- **Critical Path Method (CPM):** A network analysis technique -used to predict project duration by analysing which sequence of activities (which path) has the least amount of scheduling flexibility. Early dates are calculated by means of a forward pass using a specified start date. Late dates are calculated by means of a backward pass starting from a specified completion date (usually the forward pass's calculated project early finish date).

- **Current Finish Date:** The current estimate of the point in time when an activity will be completed.

- **Current Start Date:** The current estimate of the point in time when an activity will begin.

- **Data Date (DD):** The point in time that separates actual (historical) data from future (scheduled) data. Also called as-of' date.

- **Definitive Estimate:** See estimate.

- **Deliverable:** Any measurable, tangible, verifiable outcome, result, or item that must be produced to complete a project or part of a project. Often used more narrowly in reference to an external deliverable, which is a deliverable that is subject to approval by the project sponsor or customer.

- **Dependency:** See logical relationship.

- **Dummy Activity:** An activity of zero duration used to show a logical relationship in the arrow diagramming method. Dummy activities are used when logical relationships cannot be completely or correctly described with regular activity arrows. Dummies are shown graphically as a dashed line headed by an arrow.

- **Duration (DU):** The number of work periods (not including holidays or other non-working periods) required to complete an activity or other project element. Usually expressed as workdays or workweeks. Sometimes incorrectly equated with elapsed time. See also effort.

- **Duration Compression:** Shortening the project schedule without reducing the project scope. Duration compression is not always possible and often requires an increase in project cost.

- **Early Finish Date (EF):** In the critical path method, the earliest possible point in time on which the uncompleted portions of an activity (or the project) can finish based on the network logic and any schedule constraints. Early finish dates can change as the project progresses and changes are made to the project plan.

- **Early Start Date (ES):** In the critical path method, the earliest possible point in time on which the uncompleted portions of an activity (or the project) can start, based on the network logic and any schedule constraints. Early start dates can change as the project progresses and changes are made to the project plan.

- **Earned Value (EV):** (1) A method for measuring project performance. It compares the amount of work that was planned with what was actually accomplished to determine if cost and schedule performance is as planned. See also actual cost of work performed, budgeted cost of work scheduled, budgeted cost of work performed, cost variance, cost performance index, schedule variance, and schedule performance index. (2) The budgeted cost of work performed for an activity or group of activities.

- **Earned Value Analysis:** See definition (1) under earned value.

- **Effort:** The number of labour units required to complete an activity or other project element. Usually expressed as staff hours, staff days, or staff weeks. Should not be confused with duration.

- **Estimate:** An assessment of the likely quantitative result. Usually applied to project costs and durations and should always include some indication of accuracy (e.g., ± x percent). Usually used with a modifier (e.g., preliminary, conceptual, feasibility). Some application areas have specific modifiers that imply particular accuracy ranges (e.g., order-of-magnitude estimate, budget estimate, and definitive estimate in engineering and construction projects).

- **Estimate At Completion (EAC):** The expected total cost of an activity, a group of activities, or of the project when the defined scope of work has been completed. Most techniques for forecasting EAC include some adjustment of the original cost estimate based on project performance to date. Also shown as "estimated at completion." Often shown as EAC Actuals-to-date + ETC. See also earned value and estimate to complete:

- **Estimate To Complete (ETC):** The expected additional cost needed to complete an activity, a group of activities, or the project. Most techniques for forecasting ETC include some adjustment to the original estimate based on project performance to date. Also called "estimated to complete." See also earned value and estimate at completion.

- **Event-on-Node:** A network diagramming technique in which events are represented by boxes (or nodes) connected by arrows to show the sequence in which the events are to occur. Used in the original Program Evaluation and Review Technique.

- **Exception Report:** Document that includes only major variations from plan (rather than all variations).

- **Expected Monetary Value:** The product of an event's probability of occurrence and the gain or loss that will result. For example, if there is a 50 percent probability that it will rain, and rain will result in a $100 loss, the expected monetary value of the rain event is $50 (.5 x $100).

- **Fast Tracking:** Compressing the project schedule by overlapping activities that would normally be done in sequence, such as design and construction. Sometimes confused with concurrent engineering

- **Finish Date:** A point in time associated with an activity's completion. Usually qualified by one of the following: actual, planned, estimated, scheduled, early, late, baseline, target or current.

- **Finish-to-Finish (FF):** See logical relationship. Finish-to-Start (FS). See logical relationship.

- **Firm Fixed Price (FFP) Contract:** A type of contract where the buyer pays the seller a set amount (as defined by the contract) regardless of the seller's costs.

- **Fixed Price Contract:** See firm fixed price contract.

- **Fixed Price Incentive Fee (FPIF) Contract:** A type of contract where the buyer pays the seller a set amount (as defined by the contract), and the seller can earn an additional amount if it meets defined performance criteria.

- **Float:** The amount of time that an activity may be delayed from its early start without delaying the project finish date. Float is a mathematical calculation and can change as the project progresses and changes are made to the project plan. Also called slack, total float, and path float. See also free float.

- **Forecast Final Cost:** See estimate at completion. Forward Pass. The calculation of the early start and early finish dates for the uncompleted portions of all network activities. See also network analysis and backward pass.

- **Fragnet:** See subnet.

- **Free Float (FF):** The amount of time an activity can be delayed without delaying the early start of any immediately following activities. See also float.

- **Functional Manager:** A manager responsible for activities in a specialized department or function (e.g., engineering, manufacturing, marketing).

- **Functional Organisation:** An organisation structure in which staff are grouped hierarchically by specialty (e.g., production, marketing, engineering, and accounting at the top level; with engineering, further divided into mechanical, electrical, and others).

- **Gantt Chart:** See bar chart.

- **Grade:** A category or rank used to distinguish items that have the same functional use (e.g., "hammer") but do not share category same requirements for quality (e.g., different hammers may need to withstand different amounts of force).

- **Graphical Evaluation and Review Technique (GERT):** A network analysis technique that allows for conditional and probabilistic treatment of logical relationships (i.e., some activities may not be performed).

- **Hammock:** An aggregate or summary activity (a group of related activities is shown as one and reported at a summary level). A hammock may or may not have an internal sequence. See also subproject and subnet.

- **Hanger:** An unintended break in a network path. Hangers are usually caused by missing activities or missing logical relationships.

- **Information Distribution:** Making needed information available to project stakeholders in a timely manner.
- **Initiation:** Committing the organisation to begin a project phase.
- **Integrated Cost/Schedule Reporting:** See earned value.
- **Invitation for Bid (IFB):** Generally, this term is equivalent to request for proposal. However, in some application areas it may have a narrower or more specific meaning.
- **Key Event Schedule:** See master schedule.
- **Lag:** A modification of a logical relationship which directs a delay in the successor task. For example, in a finish-to-start dependency with a 10-day lag, the successor activity cannot start until 10 (lays after the predecessor has finished. See also lead.
- **Late Finish Date (LIT):** In the critical path method, the latest possible point in time that an activity may be completed without delaying a specified milestone (usually the project finish date).
- **Late Start Date (LS):** In the critical path method, the latest possible point in time that an activity may begin without delaying a specified milestone (usually the project finish date).
- **Lead:** A modification of a logical relationship which allows an acceleration of the successor task. For example, in a finish-to-start dependency with a 10-day lead, the successor activity can start 10 days before the predecessor has finished. See also lag.
- **Level of Effort (LOE):** Support-type activity (e.g., vendor or customer liaison) that does not readily lend itself to measurement of discrete accomplishment. It is generally characterised by a uniform rate of activity over a specific period of time.
- **Levelling:** See resource leveling.
- **Life-cycle Costing:** The concept of including acquisition, operating, and disposal costs when evaluating various alternatives.
- **Line Manager:** (1) The manager of any group that actually makes a product or performs a service. (2) A functional manager.
- **Link:** See logical relationship.
- **Logic:** See network logic.
- **Logic Diagram:** See project network diagram.
- **Logical Relationship:** A dependency between two project activities, or between a project activity and a milestone. See also precedence relationship. The four possible types of logical relationships are:
  Finish-to-start—the "from" activity must finish before the "to" activity can start.
  Finish-to-finish--the "from" activity must finish before the "to" activity can finish.
  Start-to-start—the "from" activity must start before the "to" activity can start.

- Start-to-finish—the "from" activity must start before the "to" activity can finish. **Loop.** A network path that passes the same node twice. Loops cannot be analysed using traditional network analysis techniques such as CPM and PERT. Loops are allowed in GERT. **Management Reserve.** A separately planned quantity used to allow for future situations which are impossible to predict (sometimes called "unknown unknowns"). Management reserves may involve cost or schedule. Management reserves are intended to reduce the risk of missing cost or schedule objectives. Use of management reserve requires a change to the project's cost baseline. **Master Schedule**. A summary-level schedule which identifies the major activities and key milestones. See also milestone schedule.

- **Mathematical Analysis:** See network analysis.

- **Matrix Organisation:** Any organisational structure in which the project manager shares responsibility with the functional managers for assigning priorities and for directing the work of individuals assigned to the project.

- **Milestone:** A significant event in the project, usually completion of a major deliverable.

- **Milestone Schedule:** A summary-level schedule which identifies the major milestones. See also master schedule. **Mitigation.** Taking steps to lessen risk by lowering the probability of a risk event's occurrence or reducing its effect should it occur.

- **Modern Project Management (MPM):** A term used to distinguish the current broad range of project management (scope, cost, time, quality, risk, etc.) from narrower, traditional use that focused on cost and time.

- **Monitoring:** The capture, analysis, and reporting of' project performance, usually as compared to plan. **Monte Carlo Analysis.** A schedule risk assessment technique that performs a project simulation many times in order to calculate a distribution of likely results. Near-Critical Activity. An activity that has low total float. Network. See project network diagram.

- **Network Analysis:** The process of identifying early and late start and finish dates for the uncompleted portions of project activities. See also Critical Path Method, Program Evaluation and Review Technique, and Graphical Evaluation and Review Technique.

- **Network Logic:** The collection of activity dependencies that make up a project network diagram.

- **Network Path:** Any continuous series of connected activities in a project network diagram.

- **Node:** One of the defining points of a network; a junction point joined to some or all of the other dependency lines. See also arrow diagramming method and precedence diagramming method.
- **Order of Magnitude Estimate:** See estimate.
- **Organisational Breakdown Structure (OBS):** A depiction of the project organisation arranged so as to relate work packages to organisational units.
- **Organisational Planning:** Identifying, documenting, and assigning project roles, responsibilities, and reporting relationships.
- **Overall Change Control:** Co-ordinating changes across the entire project.
- **Overlap:** See lead.
- **Parametric Estimating:** An estimating technique that uses a statistical relationship between historical data and other variables (e.g.. square footage in construction, lines of code in software development) to calculate an estimate. Pareto Diagram. A histogram. ordered by frequency of occurrence, that shows how many re-suits were generated by each identified cause.
- **Path:** A set of sequentially connected activities in a project network diagram.
- **Path Convergence:** In mathematical analysis, the tendency of parallel paths of approximately equal duration to delay the completion of the milestone where they meet.
- **Path Float:** See Moat.
- **Percent Complete (PC):** An estimate, expressed as a percent, of the amount of work which has been completed on an activity or group of activities.
- **Performance Reporting:** Collecting and disseminating information about project performance to help ensure project progress.
- **Performing Organisation:** The enterprise whose employees are most directly involved in doing the work of the project.
- **PERT Chart:** A specific type of project network diagram. See Program Evaluation and Review Technique.
- **Phase:** See project phase.
- **Planned Finish Date (PF):** See scheduled finish date.
- **Planned Start Date (PS):** See scheduled start date.
- **Precedence Diagramming Method (PDM):** A network diagramming technique in which activities are represented by boxes (or nodes). Activities are linked by precedence relationships to show the sequence in which the activities are to be performed.

- **Precedence Relationship:** The term used in the precedence diagramming method for a logical relationship. In current usage, however, precedence relationship, logical relationship, and dependency are widely used interchangeably regardless of the diagramming method in use.

- **Predecessor Activity:** (1) In the arrow diagramming method, the activity which enters a node. (2) In the precedence diagramming method, the "from" activity.

- **Procurement Planning:** Determining what to procure and when.

- **Program:** A group of related projects managed in a co-ordinated way. Programs usually include an element of ongoing activity.

- **Program Evaluation and Review Technique (PERT):** An event-oriented network analysis technique used to estimate project duration when there is a high degree of uncertainty with the individual activity duration estimates. PERT applies the critical path method to a weighted average duration estimate. Also given as Program Evaluation and Review Technique.

- **Project:** A temporary endeavour undertaken to create a unique product or service.

- **Project Charter:** A document issued by senior management that provides the project manager with the authority to apply organisational resources to project activities.

- **Project Communications Management:** A subset of project management that includes the processes required to ensure proper collection and dissemination of project information. It consists of communications planning, information distribution, performance reporting, and administrative closure.

- **Project Cost Management:** A subset of project management that includes the processes required to ensure that the project is completed within the approved budget. It consists of resource planning, cost estimating, cost budgeting, and cost control. Project Human Resource Management. A subset of project management that includes the processes required to make the most effective use of the people involved with the project. It consists of organisational planning, staff acquisition, and team development.

- **Project Integration Management:** A subset of project management that includes the processes required to ensure that the various elements of the project are properly coordinated. It consists of project plan development, project plan execution, and overall change control.

- **Project Life Cycle:** A collection of generally sequential project phases whose name and number are determined by the control needs of the organisation or organisations involved in the project.

- **Project Management (PM):** The application of knowledge, skills, tools, and techniques to project activities in order to meet or exceed stakeholder needs and expectations from a project.

- **Project Management Body of Knowledge (PMBOK):** An inclusive term that describes the sum of knowledge within the profession of project management. As with other professions such as law, medicine, and accounting, the body of knowledge rests with the practitioners and academics who apply and advance it. The PMBOK includes proven, traditional practices which are widely applied as well as innovative and advanced ones which have seen more limited use.

- **Project Management Professional (PMP):** An individual certified as such by the Project Management Institute.

- **Project Management Software:** A class of computer applications specifically designed to aid with planning and controlling project costs and schedules.

- **Project Management Team:** The members of the project team who are directly involved in project management activities. On some smaller projects, the project management team may include virtually all of the project team members.

- **Project Manager (PM):** The individual responsible for managing a project, etc.

- **Project Network Diagram:** Any schematic display of the logical relationships of project activities. Always drawn from left to right to reflect project chronology. Often incorrectly referred to as a "PERT chart."

- **Project Phase:** A collection of logically related project activities, usually culminating in the completion of a major deliverable.

- **Project Plan:** A formal, approved document used to guide both project execution and project control. The primary uses of the project plan are to document planning assumptions and decisions, to facilitate communication among stakeholders, and to document approved scope, cost, and schedule baselines. A project plan may be summary or detailed.

- **Project Plan Development:** Taking the results of other planning processes and putting them into a consistent, coherent document.

- **Project Plan Execution:** Carrying out the project plan by performing the activities included therein performing.

- **Project Planning:** The development and maintenance of the project plan.

- **Project Procurement Management:** A subset of project management that includes the processes required to acquire goods and services from outside the performing organisation. It consists of procurement planning, solicitation planning, solicitation, source selection, contract administration, and contract close-out.

- **Project Quality Management:** A subset of project management that includes the processes required to ensure that the .project will satisfy the needs for which it was undertaken. It consists of quality planning, quality assurance, and quality control.

- **Project Risk Management:** A subset of project management that includes the processes concerned with identifying, analysing, and responding to project risk. It consists of risk identification, risk quantification, risk response development, and risk response control.

- **Project Schedule:** The planned dates for performing activities and the planned dates for meeting milestones.

- **Project Scope Management:** A subset of project management that includes the processes required to ensure that the project includes all of the work required, and only the work required, to complete the project successfully. It consists of initiation, scope planning, scope definition, scope verification. and scope change control.

- **Project Team Members:** The people who report either directly or indirectly to the project manager.

- **Project Time Management:** A subset of project management that includes the processes required to ensure timely completion of the project. It consists of activity definition, activity sequencing, activity duration estimating, schedule development, and schedule control.

- **Projectised Organisation:** Any organisational structure in which the project manager has full authority to assign priorities and to direct the work of individuals assigned to the project.

- **Quality Assurance (QA):** (1) The process of evaluating overall project performance on a regular basis to provide confidence that the project will satisfy the relevant quality standards. (2) The organisational unit that is assigned responsibility for quality assurance.

- **Quality Control (QC):** (1) The process of monitoring specific project results to determine if they comply with relevant quality standards and identifying ways to eliminate causes of unsatisfactory performance. (2) The organisational unit that is assigned responsibility for quality control.

- **Quality Planning:** Identifying which quality standards are relevant to the project and determining how to satisfy them. Remaining Duration (RDU). The time needed to complete an activity.

- **Request for Proposal (RFP):** A type of bid document used to solicit proposals from prospective sellers of products or services. In some application areas it may have a narrower or more specific meaning.

- **Request for Quotation (RFQ):** Generally, this term is equivalent to request for proposal. However, in some application areas it may have a narrower or more specific meaning.

- **Reserve:** A provision in the project plan to mitigate cost and/or schedule risk. Often used with a modifier (e.g., Management reserve, contingency reserve) to provide further detail on what types of risk are meant to be mitigated. The specific meaning of the modified term varies by application area.

- **Resource Levelling:** Any form of network analysis in which scheduling decisions (start and finish dates) are driven by resource management concerns (e.g., limited resource availability or difficult-to-manage changes in resource levels).

- **Resource-Limited Schedule:** A project schedule whose start and finish dates reflect expected resource availability. The final project schedule should always be resource-limited.

- **Resource Planning:** Determining what resources (people, equipment, materials) are needed in what quantities to perform project activities.

- **Responsibility Assignment Matrix (RAM):** A structure which relates the project organisation structure to the work, breakdown structure to help ensure that each element of the project's scope of work is assigned to a responsible individual.

- **Responsibility Chart:** See responsibility assignment matrix. Responsibility Matrix. See responsibility assignment matrix.

- **Retainage:** A portion of a contract payment that is held until contract completion in order to ensure full performance of the contract terms.

- **Risk Event:** A discrete occurrence that may affect the project for better or worse. Risk Identification. Determining which risk events are likely to affect the project. Risk Quantification. Evaluating the probability of risk event occurrence and effect. Risk Response Control. Responding to changes in risk over the course of the project.

- **Risk Response Development:** Defining enhancement steps for opportunities and mitigation steps for threats.

- **S-Curve:** Graphic display of cumulative costs, labour hours, or other quantities, plotted against time. The name derives from the S-like shape of the curve (flatter at the beginning and end, steeper in the middle) produced on a project that starts slowly, accelerates, and then tails off.

- **Schedule:** See project schedule. Schedule Analysis. See network analysis.

- **Schedule Compression:** See duration compression.

- **Schedule Control:** Controlling changes to the project schedule.

- **Schedule Development:** Analysing activity sequences, activity durations, and resource requirements to create the project schedule.

- **Schedule Performance Index (SPI):** The ratio of work performed to work scheduled (BCWP/BCWS). See earned value.

- **Schedule Variance (SV):** (1) Any difference between the scheduled completion of an activity and the actual completion of that activity. (2) In earned value, BCWP less BCWS.

- **Scheduled Finish Date (SF):** The point in time work was scheduled to finish on an activity. The scheduled finish date is normally within the range of dates delimited by the early finish date and the late finish date.

- **Scheduled Start Date (SS):** The point in time work was scheduled to start on an activity. The scheduled start date is normally within the range of dates delimited by the early start date and the late start date.

- **Scope:** The sum of the products and services to be provided as a project.

- **Scope Baseline:** See baseline.

- **Scope Change:** Any change to the project scope. A scope change almost always requires an adjustment to the project cost or schedule. Scope Change Control. Controlling changes to project scope.

- **Scope Definition:** Decomposing the major deliverables into smaller, more manageable components to provide better control.

- **Scope Planning:** Developing a written scope statement that includes the project justification, the major deliverables, and the project objectives.

- **Scope Verification:** Ensuring that all identified project deliverables have been completed satisfactorily.

- **Should-Cost Estimates:** An estimate of the cost of a product or service used to provide an assessment of the reasonableness of a prospective contractor's proposed cost.

- **Slack:** Term used in PERT for float.

- **Solicitation:** Obtaining quotations, bids, offers, or proposals as appropriate.

- **Solicitation Planning:** Documenting product requirements and identifying potential sources. Source Selection. Choosing from among potential contractors.

- **Staff Acquisition:** Getting the human resources needed assigned to and working on the project. Stakeholder. Individuals and organisations who are involved in or may be affected by project activities.

- **Start Date:** A point in time associated with an activity's start, usually qualified by one of the following: actual, planned, estimated, scheduled, early, late, target, baseline, or current.

- **Start-to-Finish:** See logical relationship. Start-to-Start. See logical relationship.

- **Statement of Work (SOW):** A narrative description of products or services to be supplied under contract. Subnet. A subdivision of a project network diagram usually representing some form of subproject. Subnetwork. See subnet.

- **Successor Activity:** (1) In the arrow diagrammatically, method, the activity which departs a node. (2) In the precedence diagramming method, the "to" activity.

- **Target Completion Date (TC):** An imposed date which constrains or otherwise modifies the network analysis.

- **Target Schedule:** See baseline. Task. See activity.

- **Team Development:** Developing individual and group skills to enhance project performance.

- **Team Members:** See project team members.

- **Time-Scaled Network Diagram:** Any project network diagram drawn in such a way that the positioning and length of the activity represents its duration. Essentially, it is a bar chart that includes network logic. Target Finish Date (TF). The date work is planned (targeted) to finish on an activity.

- **Target Start Date (TS):** The date work is planned (targeted) to start on an activity.

- **Total Float (TF):** See float.

- **Total Quality Management (TQM):** A common approach to implementing a quality improvement program within an organisation.

- **Workaround:** A response to a negative risk event. Distinguished from contingency plan in that a workaround is not planned in advance of the occurrence of the risk event.

- **Work Breakdown Structure (WBS):** A deliverable-oriented grouping of project elements which organises and defines the total scope of the project. Each descending level represents an increasingly detailed definition of a project component. Project components may be products or services.

- **Work Item:** See activity.

- **Work Package:** A deliverable at the lowest level of the work breakdown structure. A work package may be divided into activities.

■■■

Time : Three Hours   **Maximum Marks : 80**

N.B. : (i) All questions carry equal marks.
      (ii) Solve any *five* questions.

1. Define Planning? Explain its methods and limitations.   **[16]**

2. Which are the key components of the project proposals? Describe the various methods of submission of project proposal.   **[16]**

3. Explain the concept project charter? Explain the role and benefits of project charter.   **[16]**

4. What is Resource Levelling? Explain its advantages.   **[16]**

5. How to construction an Project audit report? What are the responsibilities of project auditor.   **[16]**

6. Write short notes on (any *two*):   **[16]**

    (a) Goals of Project manager.

    (b) Advantages of forecasting

    (c) Need of project management

    (d) Partnering

    (e) Project termination

    (f) Crystal Ball 2000.

■■■